MY
HUSBAND'S
AFFAIR

BOOKS BY RUTH HEALD

The Mother's Mistake

The Woman Upstairs

I Know Your Secret

The Wedding

The New Girl

The Nanny

The Party on Laurel Street

27: Six Friends, One Year

MY
HUSBAND'S
AFFAIR

RUTH HEALD

bookouture

Published by Bookouture in 2024

An imprint of Storyfire Ltd.
Carmelite House
50 Victoria Embankment
London EC4Y 0DZ

www.bookouture.com

ISBN: 978-1-83525-060-0
eBook ISBN: 978-1-83525-059-4

PROLOGUE

I've waited for this moment for a long time. The evening is warm, the perfect temperature; I'm wearing the sleeveless dress he loves so much and my arms don't even feel cold. Everything is just how I imagined: the waves crashing against the bottom of the cliffs beneath me, the slight breeze in the air, the tinkling sound of laughter that drifts over from the wedding marquee at the other side of the headland.

We're all here together at his seaside villa in the Mediterranean. Me. Him. His wife.

We are soulmates, him and I. Meant to be together. It's been obvious since we first met, that intense spark of electricity between us.

But he wants it all. He wants her stability and housekeeping, the patient wife at home. And he craves my passion and youth. He can't deny the way we are drawn to each other, like magnets.

I can't wait any longer. I can't be in the wings anymore. Soon I will see him and he will have to choose.

He'll choose me. I know he will. There's no contest.

I'll be the one swimming in his outdoor swimming pool,

under the French sun. He'll be rubbing suntan lotion into *my* back. We'll be sipping French wine together in little bistros, as we declare our love for each other, and thank god that we've finally had the courage to leap into our future together.

And as for his wife. She'll never come between us again.

ONE

NOW

'You're so lucky, Jen,' Kirsty, one of the school gate mums, said as she peered into Jen's buggy at her sleeping daughter.

Jen smiled back. Ruby looked angelic now, but she had screamed for most of the day, falling asleep for her nap just as they approached the school where she would collect her two older children.

'Thanks,' she said.

'How old is she now?'

'She turned one a few weeks ago.'

'So back to work for you soon, then?'

Jen glanced down at her feet. 'Well, no. I've decided to stay at home, spend the time with Ruby.'

'Oh wow,' Kirsty said. 'That's amazing. You're so lucky to have Rob and to be able to take the time out.'

Jen nodded. She knew Kirsty was right. Staying at home with her kids was a luxury that Rob's well-paying job allowed her. The truth was she'd wanted to go back to work, but when they'd added up the bills for nursery for the youngest and after-school clubs for both the older children, her salary simply wouldn't have covered it.

Her friend Natasha came up behind her and tapped her on the shoulder, rescuing her from Kirsty's questions. 'Staying at home's harder than it looks,' she said, pushing her sleek dark hair behind her ears and smiling warmly.

'It does feel like hard work sometimes,' Jen said. She'd always put her all into everything she did, but since they'd had the kids her focus had changed from her work as an estate agent to being the best wife and mother she could be. She and Rob were a team, and while he excelled at bringing in the money as regional manager of a chain of estate agents, she had made an effort to excel at running their household, making sure he had freshly cooked meals, the kids were looked after and their home was spotless.

Her older children came out of the school, Jack, her middle child, aged five, running out to her and hugging her, while Lottie, her oldest, ambled out, head down. Jen swallowed. She hoped Lottie had had a better day at school today. They'd moved here eight months before, and from the beginning Lottie had struggled to make friends. Jen had been in to see her teacher, who was doing all she could to encourage the other girls to play with her, but Jen didn't think things were improving much.

They walked home with Natasha and her daughter, Matilda, who was in Jack's class. Jen had been pleased to see Natasha at the school gate the first day the kids had started at school. She'd worked with Rob briefly a while back so Jen had known her a little bit already. It had been good to see a familiar face, and they'd quickly become friends.

Jack and Matilda raced each other up and down the street, while Lottie hung back with Jen as she pushed Ruby in the buggy.

'Coming to the playground?' Natasha asked.

'Not today,' Jen said. She had too much to do. Rob liked his home to look perfect when he got back, and Jen remembered the state she'd left it in when she'd rushed out with Ruby. Ruby's toys were all over the floor, Jen was behind on the washing and she hadn't even started to prep the vegetables for dinner. She'd have to set the kids up with a game to keep them busy while she rushed around. Rob had told her he didn't want the kids having so much screen time, and Jen was trying her best to occupy them with more wholesome pursuits like family games and jigsaw puzzles, despite the blistering arguments these seemed to create.

'How was school?' Jen asked Lottie tentatively, after Natasha had said goodbye at the gate to the park. Lottie just shrugged and stared into the distance. Jen hated how withdrawn she had become lately. She would try to talk to her later, at bedtime, when often the worries she'd had in the day came tumbling out.

A suited porter opened the door of the glass-fronted apartment block for her and she pushed the buggy inside. 'Hello, Patrick,' she said. 'How are you?'

'All good, thank you, Jen.'

Jen smiled as she steered the buggy around the large pot plants and sculptures in the lobby. She hadn't quite got used to the level of luxury in the apartment block. The price of the penthouse Rob had bought for them had been eye-watering, but he had negotiated a discount, and now they were living in the best apartment, in the most sought-after new block in the area.

Even after eight months she still felt a bit out of place, as if she didn't quite belong here, but she was pleased to see her friend Amy at the reception desk. She waved at her and then got in the lift up to the penthouse.

Letting herself in and pushing the buggy through the door, she stopped as she always did to admire the view. The apartment overlooked the Thames, and West London beyond.

'I'm hungry,' Jack whined, pulling her out of her thoughts. 'What's for dinner?'

'Chicken casserole.'

'Yuck,' Lottie said.

'Yeah, yuck, don't we have anything else? Like pasta?'

Jen shook her head. She'd spent hours following the recipe for healthy chicken casserole that the book claimed, 'even fussy eaters will love'. She'd made five portions and frozen them. The first time she'd fed it to the kids, they'd all hated it and she'd ended up scraping most of it into the bin.

'No, you can't have pasta every night,' Jen said. 'Try the chicken again. It's good for you.'

'I'm a vegetarian,' Lottie said dryly.

Jen sighed, trying to control her rising irritation.

'Since when are you vegetarian?' she asked, more confrontational than she'd intended.

'Since today. I won't eat chicken casserole.'

'OK, well, you'll have to have the rice with vegetables.'

Lottie sighed. 'Really?'

'Yes, really.'

'Mum – when will it be ready?' Jack asked impatiently.

A scream interrupted them. Ruby. She'd woken up from her nap.

Jen went over to the buggy, lifted her up and saw that her nappy had leaked into the base of the buggy. She'd need to get some spray and clean it thoroughly.

'I'm sooo hungry,' Lottie said again.

Jen snapped and reached for the television control. 'Just watch TV for a few minutes while I sort everything out,' she said, giving in. 'And don't tell your dad.'

Forty-five minutes later, she'd cleaned the base of the buggy, put a load of washing on, reheated the chicken casserole, cooked the rice and vegetables and was ready to serve everything up. She'd only let the children watch ten minutes of TV, before turning it off and getting out a jigsaw puzzle for them to do. Much to her surprise, when she'd checked on them fifteen minutes ago they were all doing it together, Lottie helping Ruby to put one of the pieces in place. Perhaps Rob was right. Maybe it was possible for them to entertain themselves; she didn't need to always be playing with them or else putting them in front of the TV or their iPads.

Jen dished up the dinners, poured the children water and put everything on the table. She called into the living room for the kids to come through.

Lottie and Jack were there quickly, but were soon frowning and complaining about the food. 'What's for pudding?' asked Jack, swirling his fork round his chicken casserole miserably.

'Eat your dinner first,' Jen said. 'Let me go and get your sister.'

Jen went into the living room to get Ruby so she could put her in her highchair at the kitchen table. She glanced around but couldn't see her.

'Ruby?' she called. She had only just started to walk, and she loved exploring. Jen sighed. She could be anywhere. Luckily the penthouse was all on one floor, so there was no danger of her falling down the stairs.

'Ruby? Are you hiding from me?'

She expected to hear her little girl giggling. She always delighted in hiding under tables and chairs, convinced that Jen couldn't see her. Jen glanced in the corners of the living room, then went into the kids' bedrooms to look for her. She wasn't there either.

She must be hiding under the covers of Jen's bed. That was one of her favourite spots. Jen frowned, adding 'remake the bed' to her mental to-do list.

But when she went into her bedroom there was no bump under the covers. No Ruby. Jen picked up her pace, looking in the en suite bathroom, then the kids' bathroom, before making her way back to the kitchen.

'Where's your sister?' she asked Jack and Lottie. 'Is she hiding from me?'

Lottie shrugged and Jack shook his head. 'I don't know.'

'Weren't you doing the jigsaw together?'

'For a bit. But then we all got bored. She wandered off.'

'Where did she go?' Jen asked, her voice getting higher-pitched. She couldn't have gone out the front door. She'd locked it so you needed the key to get out. Jen had left hers on the side, out of reach. At least she thought she had.

As she glanced towards where she'd left her key, the patio doors caught her eye. They were open.

She ran over and went outside, her heart pounding. Lottie or Jack must have opened them. There was no way Ruby could have done it herself. But she must have gone outside.

Her slide. That must have been what she was looking for.

Rob had spent all the last weekend securing a slide to the balcony, as Ruby's first birthday present.

The balcony went round the entire penthouse, encircling the top floor of the building, and Jen ran round the side to where the slide was. But Ruby wasn't there.

She must be somewhere else on the balcony.

'Ruby?' Jen shouted. She tried to steady her breathing. There was no danger here. The glass panels of the balcony were high, far too high for Ruby to climb. But then she thought of the outdoor dining table where they planned to eat outside when the weather got warmer. Ruby could have climbed on a chair and gone straight over.

'Ruby!' Jen shouted again, as she ran round the balcony. She got to the table and chairs, but they were just as she'd left them. None of them had been dragged to the edge.

But why wasn't Ruby answering her? Jen glanced round frantically. She saw the hot tub in the corner with the best views of the river. It was still covered. Ruby couldn't have gone in there. And it was set back from the edge, so Ruby couldn't have used it to climb up.

Where was she?

Jen spun round, looking for her daughter.

Suddenly she heard a small voice. 'Mama?'

'Ruby?'

Her daughter giggled, pleased with her hiding place.

Jen's breath caught in her throat. The sound was coming from the edge of the building.

She walked over to the edge of the balcony, the breathtaking height suddenly terrifying her.

She looked down.

And there was Ruby. On the other side of the glass panels of the balcony. Sitting on a little ledge, a sheer drop behind her.

TWO

Jen fought back her instinct to scream. She couldn't do anything to scare Ruby, or anything that might cause her to shift position on the ledge.

Ruby was sitting sucking her thumb, totally unfazed by the drop below her. Jen could see that she'd squeezed out of a small gap on the corner between the glass panes of the balcony. Jen swallowed as she looked at the gap. She'd never noticed it before, but it was just wide enough for a small child to fit through. Ruby must have gone through and then dropped down a foot onto the ledge below.

'Ruby?' she said softly. She crouched down on the paving stones and reached through the gap, her heart pounding. 'Take Mummy's hand and come back onto the balcony, OK?'

Ruby took her hand and stood up, as if she didn't have a care in the world. Jen could barely breathe. If she stumbled she'd fall straight off the edge.

Keeping hold of one of Ruby's hands, Jen reached down with her other hand to try and circle her arm around Ruby's tiny waist, so she could pull her up. As she touched her hip

Ruby pulled away a bit, giggling. Her hand slipped out of Jen's and for a moment her legs wobbled.

'Ruby!' Jen shouted, stretching out and managing to grab Ruby's hand again before her daughter tumbled over the edge. She gripped Ruby's hand tightly, and Ruby screamed out in anger as Jen dragged her closer to the wall of the building.

As Ruby kept wailing, Jen grabbed her other hand and pulled her upwards, towards the gap in the balcony. But Ruby was flailing her legs angrily and throwing her head back, and Jen couldn't get her through.

'Please,' Jen said, her voice shaky, 'please, Ruby. For once, cooperate with me. It's not safe.'

But Jen knew you couldn't reason with a one-year-old. Ruby kicked out at the balcony glass, pushing her body violently away from the building, and Jen almost lost her grip once more. Now, she pulled Ruby's arms firmly, and Ruby was so surprised at the strength of it that for a moment she stopped writhing. In that moment, Jen managed to get Ruby's head and upper body though the gap. Ruby started screaming again. Reaching out quickly, Jen grabbed her round the waist and twisted her body to pull her legs through, as Ruby kicked.

'Oh my god,' she said, when Ruby was back beside her. Tears ran down Jen's face. 'Oh my god, Ruby.'

She wrapped her arms round her daughter and hugged her tight, as Ruby kept screaming.

'Mama!' her daughter cried, her eyes confused and angry. Jen could tell she felt completely betrayed. Jen had never handled her so roughly. She noticed she had a long scratch on her arm and Jen felt overwhelmed with guilt. Ruby must have caught herself as Jen dragged her through the gap.

'I'm so sorry,' Jen said, as she hugged her inconsolable daughter. 'I'm so sorry.' Ruby was shaking in her arms.

'I love you so much,' Jen said, her voice choked. She lifted her daughter up and took her away from the balcony, carrying her back inside, shutting and locking the patio doors.

Ruby's crying subsided once they were inside, and Jen took her through to the kitchen and put her in her highchair. 'Don't ever do that again,' she said softly to Ruby. 'Don't ever go onto the balcony alone, without Mummy or Daddy.' Jen stroked her soft wispy hair. She was far too young to understand the dangers.

The only thing Jen wanted was for her children to have a safe, happy childhood, where they didn't have to worry about anything. She wanted them to feel secure and loved, the way she'd never felt herself as a child. But today she had failed catastrophically.

'What's for pudding?' Lottie asked, completely unaware of what had just happened.

Jen turned to her older daughter. 'Did you open the patio door?' she asked.

'I did,' Jack said. 'Ruby wanted to go on her slide.'

'She's not allowed to go out on her own,' Jen said. 'You know that.' Her stomach swirled with emotions; a strange mix of anger and love. She was furious with him for letting Ruby out, but so glad that her family were safe and together.

Jack wrinkled his nose. 'Sorry,' he said. He paused for a split second. 'Is there a pudding today?'

Jen glanced at their plates. 'Not until you've eaten everything on your plate.'

Then she went round the flat and removed all the keys to the balconies, put them on the top shelf of the cupboard in her bedroom and rang her friend Amy from reception.

Amy was up at the penthouse within a couple of minutes. She looked as smart and unflustered as always, her thick blonde hair tied back in a neat ponytail.

'That must have been terrifying for you,' she said, after Jen recounted what happened. She wrapped her arms round Jen and held her for a moment, while Jen tried to gather herself and slow her breathing.

Then she turned to Ruby. 'Don't scare your mummy like that,' she said in a sing-song voice, sweeping Ruby up in her arms and into a hug.

As she put her back down, she said hello to the other children, asking them about school and receiving only grunts in reply.

'So can you show me where the gap is?' Amy said. 'I'll take some photos and get someone to come up and do a temporary fix as soon as possible.'

'Sure,' Jen said, quickly going into the bedroom and retrieving the patio door keys. She strapped Ruby into her high-chair before leading Amy outside. She shivered as she went over to the gap in the balcony and looked down. She could hardly process what had just happened, how close Ruby had come to falling.

'Oh wow,' Amy said, shocked. 'That's far too big. It's definitely not right.'

'I know,' Jen said, shakily. She had no idea how she hadn't noticed it before. Then she remembered that she'd rearranged the pot plants at the weekend while Rob was assembling the slide for Ruby. When they'd bought the flat it had come with a huge plant exactly where the gap was. It had taken two of them to lift it and move it next to the hot tub.

'I think there was a plant there before so I didn't notice,' Jen said guiltily, putting her head in her hands. 'I checked everything in the apartment was safe for the kids when I moved in. Looked for any sharp corners, made sure all the furniture was fixed to the wall, checked the height of the balcony. But somehow I missed this.'

'Don't blame yourself,' Amy said, putting her arm around

her. 'At the end of the day, you're all safe, and Ruby is fine. And now you know there's a problem, we can fix it as soon as possible.'

'Thanks,' Jen said gratefully, feeling calmer.

Amy was taking photos of the gap with her mobile phone and using an app to measure its width and length. 'I think they'll need to replace these two glass panels with bigger ones,' she said. 'Someone more qualified than me will come to have a look. I'll schedule it as urgent. In the meantime I'll get someone to board over the gap. It won't look very pretty but it will be safe.'

'You're a lifesaver,' she said to Amy.

'I think it sounds like you were the lifesaver today. Your quick thinking saved Ruby. I think you deserve a glass of wine.'

Jen smiled nervously. She wasn't a hero. She'd put her daughter in danger by not noticing the gap. 'I think I need one,' she said. 'But the kids need my attention first.'

'It never stops, does it?'

'No,' Jen said. 'But I wouldn't have it any other way.'

'When will Rob be back to help?' Amy asked, as they stepped through the patio doors and back inside the penthouse.

'Not for a couple of hours yet. He's working late.' Jen looked anxiously round the flat. She had so much tidying to do before he came home. The jigsaw puzzle she'd given the kids had just added to the mess.

Amy smiled. 'Well, I'd better get back. I wish I could join you for a glass of wine and a catch-up, but I need to get back to work. We can chat properly on Thursday, at the cat shelter.' They both volunteered there.

'See you soon,' Jen said, kissing Amy on the cheek goodbye.

As Amy left, Jen turned back towards her kids to see one portion of casserole all over the kitchen floor.

. . .

By the time Rob came home that evening, Jen was filled with a familiar exhaustion. He kissed her as he came through the door, and she hung up his coat and walked with him over to the dinner table. It was late and they were both starving. All signs of the kids' mess had been cleared away, and the chicken casserole was languishing in the bin. She'd cooked salmon with potatoes and vegetables for herself and Rob, putting it in the oven when he messaged her to say he was on his way home from work.

Now she sat opposite him surrounded by a perfectly tidy home. She'd changed out of her milk-stained jeans and into a summer dress that he'd bought for her a few weeks ago. Amy had worked miracles with the apartment block's maintenance team and there was already a board over the balcony.

'How was your day?' she asked him.

'Busy,' he said. 'Crazy busy. This regional manager job is something else. I was glad of the promotion, but I need to work such long hours. It's not just managing the properties, it's everything else as well. Looking after the staff, making sure they're happy.'

Jen nodded, and swallowed. She couldn't concentrate on what he was saying, images of Ruby on the ledge still flashing through her mind. She felt so guilty. She'd let her daughter down.

'I need to tell you something,' she said.

'What?' he asked, his eyes softening as he saw the expression on her face. 'What's going on?'

'It was just a mistake,' Jen said quickly, the words rushing out of her. 'I feel awful about it... Ruby got out onto the balcony when I wasn't watching. I was busy cooking the kids' dinner. I'd left them to play with a puzzle.'

'What happened, Jen? Is Ruby alright?'

'She's fine... she just... she managed to squeeze though a gap in the balcony panels and onto a ledge below. I pulled her up. She's OK now. She's scratched her arm, but she was so lucky she didn't fall right off. I can't bear to think about it.' Jen put her hands to her temples and pressed hard. She needed something to take the edge off her guilt, something to calm her down. She took a gulp of the wine Rob had brought back with him; her favourite, a surprise midweek treat. But she swallowed it mindlessly, unable to appreciate it. 'The balcony's been boarded up.'

'She was on a ledge?' Rob said, his eyes wide. 'All the way up here? My god.'

'It was horrible.'

'It must have been absolutely terrifying.' He got up and walked round the dining table, crouching beside her and enveloping her in a tight hug.

'It was,' Jen said, shakily. 'I managed to get her... but oh my god, Rob. What if she'd slipped?'

'She didn't slip. You got her.'

'I know. I just don't understand why the panels weren't closer together.'

Rob's eyes darkened. 'There should never have been any gap. How could the building management have allowed that to happen?' He pulled away from her and took out his phone. 'I'll speak to them. Tell them how completely unacceptable this is. Their incompetence put Ruby's life in danger.'

'They'd put a plant in front of it,' Jen said, realisation dawning that the plant must have been placed deliberately so they wouldn't notice the gap when they moved in. 'They must have been trying to cover it up. It wasn't safe, Rob.'

'It's a disgrace,' he said. 'They know we're a family living up here. They should have double-checked everything before we moved in.'

'Our daughter could have... we could have lost her, Rob.'

'It doesn't bear thinking about,' Rob started pacing up and down. 'But don't worry. I'm going to sort it. I'll speak to them right away. Make sure nothing like this can ever happen again. I promise.'

Tears pricked Jen's eyes as she remembered seeing Ruby on the ledge. 'Thank you,' she said.

'You don't need to worry about anything. No matter what, I'll keep you and the kids safe. I've always looked after you, and I always will.'

Jen stood up. She had been pushing food round her plate but she didn't have any appetite. As she started scraping her meal into the bin, he came over and hugged her again. As he did she smelt a faint whiff of perfume on his collar, mixing unnaturally with the smell of his own aftershave. She recoiled slightly and looked up at him.

He looked exactly the same as he always did, his wavy dark hair slightly unruly, his shirt neatly ironed, collar protruding outside his navy jumper.

He was around other people all day; he often came back smelling of a mix of the scents of the city, but this seemed like something more. Someone must have got really close to him.

'Did you have a lot of meetings today?' she said.

'Yeah,' he said. 'The usual. New clients looking for properties. Some big investors wanting a piece of the UK property market.'

Jen nodded. The fragrance must have stuck to him after he met a client. As he leant in to greet a client, a strong perfume would have lingered on his collar. It was completely possible that that had happened, and yet something didn't feel quite right. Her instincts were telling her something was wrong.

She shook herself. Of course something was wrong – her baby had almost fallen from their balcony on her watch. It was probably just the stress of the day talking. Her nerves were shot and she felt wrung out.

'I'm going to have to go to bed and get some sleep,' she said to Rob.

'It's been a stressful day for you,' he said, squeezing her hand. 'But none of it's your fault. I'll call the building management now and give them a talking-to. Then I can clear up the dinner things.'

'Thank you,' Jen said softly, feeling a sliver of guilt about the thoughts that had just crossed her mind about the scent of the perfume. Rob always looked after her when it counted. He was her husband, her soulmate.

She poured herself a glass of water, and then waited for Rob to go to his study to make the call. Then she took the plastic bottle of pills out of the cupboard and tipped a couple into her hand. She usually only took one to get to sleep, but tonight she needed a bigger dose.

She downed the pills then went to the bedroom, got changed for bed and fell quickly into a dreamless sleep.

THREE

SEVEN MONTHS EARLIER

Mia ran her hairbrush through her silky, dark hair, checking her make-up in the cracked bathroom mirror. When Rob, her boss, had come over to her desk and knelt down beside her to ask her out for their second dinner together, it had felt like the stars were aligning. She'd spent most of the day preparing for her date with him.

Ever since she'd started working for Rob, things had been going better for her. Before, she'd had a series of temping jobs at uninspiring offices, after a spell trying to make it as an actress. The job at the estate agents was perfect for her. She liked the work, loved seeing all the huge houses, and loved the thrill of trying to close a sale. She was still just an administrative temp, but Rob had seen her talent for sales and let her get involved in that side of the business. She could see her future here. She wanted to stay and work her way up and become an agent.

It was Rob who made her excited about coming into the office each day; Rob whose rugged looks she admired from afar, Rob whose voice she listened out for, Rob whose jokes she laughed at. She'd known that he behaved differently with her compared to the others in the office. He always stood a bit too close and his hands seemed to seek her out; a hand on her shoulder when she was at the computer; a congratulatory squeeze of her arm when she'd managed to secure a tenant for a house.

He was attractive and charismatic and everyone in the office loved him. She'd never thought in a million years that he'd be interested in her, so when he'd said he wanted to take her out to dinner to celebrate a sale she'd made she'd thought he'd just been impressed by her sales skills. But when he'd leant in to kiss her outside the restaurant, her heart had melted. It felt like the whole world had stopped and they were the only two people in it. Everything had been about that moment, just the two of them, entwined. Lost in each other.

This was it. She was so sure of it. She'd been so wrong about men in the past, but this time she knew. Rob was the one.

Which was why it was so important to make this second date perfect. She had to impress Rob, to keep his interest. She couldn't mess it up. Mia had been to the shops earlier and maxed out her credit card on a red cocktail dress with a low-cut neckline. She'd paired it with new black heels and sheer tights. She'd even bought earrings and a red necklace to match the outfit.

Now, as she peered at herself in the mirror, she thought the dress might be a bit too much, that Rob might be frightened off rather than wowed. She grabbed a black shawl from her cupboard in the boxroom she rented and draped it over her shoulders. *That looks better*, she thought, studying her reflection.

She shrugged on a smart coat, then called an Uber, trying not to think about how much it would cost to get to central London. It was far too cold for her to walk to the station and wait on the chilly platform, all dressed up.

When the driver was nearly outside, she grabbed her bag from her room, locked the door and then went out of the basement flat she shared, climbing the steps up into the alleyway and walking past the big black bins to get to the street, shivering in the cold.

She smiled to herself as she climbed into the car. This relationship was everything. This was the relationship that would fix her life, make her the person she was always meant to be. As she looked out the window of the taxi at the world passing by, she could hardly believe how lucky she was.

FOUR

NOW

Jen hummed to herself as she made the dinner. It was Friday night, which had been date night in their house since they'd had the kids. But in the past year, since Ruby was born and Rob had been promoted at work, they'd both been too busy to commit to it. Rob often worked late and went on overnight business trips, which meant he was hardly ever home. When they did get the chance to speak they just went through a whole list of administrative household tasks, but they never really got the chance to talk properly, to connect.

It was time to change that. She'd explained to Rob that she wanted to start date night again, to prioritise each other and their relationship one night every week. And she'd promised to cook him Japanese food, the kind they'd usually order if they were going out. She was making chicken dumplings, ramen noodles and beef teriyaki. She'd researched the recipes and then driven to the Asian supermarket on the ring road and found exactly the right ingredients. The fresh ingredients had cost a fortune, but Rob had given her a budget of £100, and she knew it was going to be worth it.

The scent of home-made teriyaki sauce was making her

taste buds tingle. She looked around the kitchen and breathed a sigh of relief. For once, everything was under control. The children had had their baths, and the older two were in bed reading. Ruby was asleep in her cot. The living room was tidy. All she needed to do was finish cooking and get changed. She was going to dress up tonight, pretend they were going out properly, to a restaurant, like they used to. Rob was going to message her when he was on his way home and then she'd steam the dumplings, so they were fresh when he got in.

Jen reached across the hob for the bottle of red wine on the counter. As she did, she felt a warmth radiating from the electric hob. She frowned. It wasn't switched on. She checked the app on her phone that showed all the appliances in the apartment. She could see the hob was marked off. She hovered her hand a few centimetres above its surface. It was definitely producing heat.

She switched the isolator switch off and messaged the building engineer on the app. The same thing had happened last week, but when the engineer had come out he hadn't been able to find anything wrong. There had been so many teething problems with the apartment. She thought angrily about the gap in the balcony. Ruby could have been killed when she'd gone through. Rob had spoken to the building manager, who had been very apologetic and had promised that the glass panels on their balcony would be replaced as soon as possible, and that nothing like that would happen again.

Jen poured herself a large glass of wine. Despite the problems with the apartment, she knew how fortunate she was to live the life she had with Rob. When she was growing up, she'd never imagined she'd have such an affluent lifestyle. Jen was determined to give her kids a different childhood to the one she had. They'd never had to listen to the sound of the landlord banging on the door, shouting about unpaid rent. They'd never had to hear their father hitting their mother, feeling guilty because they hadn't intervened. They'd never had to think of lies to tell at school about where their father was when he'd been sent to prison.

Jen sipped her wine as she thought of her children growing up in the luxurious penthouse. She'd ensure all the problems were fixed, and she'd make this the perfect home for them.

Ruby's screams punctured her thoughts and she rushed into her bedroom, picking her up from her cot and holding her in her arms. Her nappy wasn't wet and she wasn't hungry. All she wanted was the warmth of Jen's body next to hers. She'd been unsettled since the incident on the balcony. Jen rocked her back to sleep, overwhelmed with love for her.

Ruby had been an accidental pregnancy. Not a mistake, as Jen had first thought of the tiny baby growing inside her, but a blessing. She loved her daughter and she couldn't imagine life without her. But there'd been a cost. Jack had been about to start school, and Jen had been really looking forward to going back to work, to starting her career again and becoming more independent. She knew she was lucky to be looked after by Rob, to not want for anything financially, but a part of her had wanted more. She'd loved being an estate agent, loved working, loved choosing how to spend her own money.

Jen put Ruby back in bed and looked at her watch. Rob should be home any minute, but he hadn't messaged to say he was on his way. She frowned and sent him a message:

How's your journey going?

In the meantime she'd better get dressed. She changed into the black lingerie that Rob had bought her for their last wedding anniversary and then went to her walk-in closet and pulled out a blue dress that she'd bought a few years ago, and had only recently managed to fit back into. Ruby had been a big baby and in her third pregnancy she'd seem to stretch and expand more than she had in her previous ones. It had taken a lot of work at the gym to get her pre-pregnancy body back, but she'd done it. She wasn't sure Rob had even noticed. He would tonight, she thought, smiling at herself in the mirror.

She was pleased with the reflection smiling back at her, her blonde hair shimmering and her make-up perfect. She'd made the best of herself. *She looked good. She felt good.*

Jen touched up her lipstick. She was completely ready. All she had to do was heat up the dumplings and then fry the teriyaki after they'd finished their starter. She looked at her phone and saw the message from Rob.

So sorry. A big client insisted on taking us all out for drinks in the city centre. I couldn't say no. This guy is a billionaire. Looking into buying a whole block of flats in central London. Think of the commission! We could make so much money. I'm on my way back now. Should be with you in 45 minutes. Xx

Jen read the message twice. Had he forgotten about their date night? A few days ago, she'd sent an invite to his work calendar so it was in his diary, and she'd reminded him about it just this morning. But she understood why he'd gone to the client drinks. Drinks with that type of high-rolling client were too good an opportunity to miss. Clients like that were only ever in London for a short time, and while they were here you had to put every effort into selling them the most expensive flats and apartment blocks. Jen looked over at the food she'd prepared and swallowed down her frustration.

OK. Looking forward to seeing you! Date night tonight and I've prepared some delicious Japanese food. Xx

He replied immediately.

I am SO sorry I'm late. I can't wait to have dinner with you.
Let me make it up to you when I'm home. Love you so much.
Please forgive my tardiness!! Xx

Jen took a sip of her wine. As a couple, they needed this evening to connect. Since Ruby was born, sometimes it felt like they were living separate lives. The evening could still be salvaged. They would still enjoy it together.

An hour later, Rob came through the door clutching a bouquet of roses, a bottle of champagne and a small box of expensive chocolates.

'I'm so sorry,' he said, putting down the champagne and chocolates, taking her in his arms and kissing her on the lips. 'Dinner smells absolutely delicious.'

'Thanks,' Jen said, as she took the roses from him. 'It's all your favourites.'

'What would I do without you?' Rob asked. 'I'm so lucky to have you.'

Jen smiled. 'I'm lucky too,' she said, taking the lid off the dumplings. 'Let's make a start on the food. These taste better when they're fresh.'

'I'll pour the champagne,' Rob said. 'There's so much to celebrate. This amazing penthouse. How well the drinks with the new client went.' He smiled at her. 'And how beautiful you look.' Her stomach flipped in happiness as he wrapped his arms around her. She grinned and pulled away, so she could remove the dumplings from the steamer and put them on the plates next to a small saucer of soy sauce.

She turned the hob off and then frowned, unsure if it was really off. She flipped the power switch.

'You know the hob switched itself on again today,' she said.

'Really?' Rob said, frowning. 'That's strange. I thought the engineer didn't find anything wrong with it?'

'He couldn't find the source of the problem, but it happened again today. The app said it was off but it was hot.'

'Are you sure it wasn't just hot from all your cooking? Or perhaps you left it on and it turned off automatically?'

Jen frowned. She supposed it was possible that she forgot to turn it off. Sometimes she was absent-minded. With three young children there was so much to think about all the time. 'I don't think so,' she said, doubtfully.

'Maybe best to always make sure you turn it off at the mains,' he said. 'Then there won't be an issue. Now, I can't wait to tuck into this delicious feast you've prepared.'

They sat down at the table and Rob picked up a dumpling with his chopsticks and examined it before taking a small bite.

Jen watched with bated breath, hoping all her effort had been worth it.

'These are divine,' Rob said. 'Even better than the restaurant. Just perfect.'

Jen smiled and started to eat. She was starving. Cooking all afternoon had filled the apartment with a host of delicious aromas, and it had taken all her self-control not to start tucking in before Rob got back.

'Those were just spectacular,' Rob said as he finished, and wiped his mouth with the cloth napkin.

'There's teriyaki beef next,' Jen said. 'I just need to fry it with the sauce.'

She stood up and went to the hobs. Rob stood up too, suddenly wrapping his arms around her from behind and squeezing her in a tight hug.

He spun her towards him. 'There's something else I'd like to do first,' he said, his eyes roaming over her body in her tight-fitting dress.

She smiled, recognising the hungry look in his eyes. She'd

first seen it when they'd both been at school together, him an attractive eighteen-year-old, who all the girls wanted to date, her a hard-working nobody in the year below, just trying to get by. That look in his eyes had been the start of everything.

Jen thought of the beef teriyaki she'd spent so long preparing. It could wait.

She let Rob carry her into the bedroom, her worries a distant memory.

FIVE

SEVEN MONTHS EARLIER

As Mia got out of the taxi, her heart pounded in her chest. This felt like such an important moment in her life, a turning point.

Inside the restaurant the lighting was dim, and candles adorned the thick tablecloths, laid with heavy sterling silver cutlery. Red velvet curtains divided the restaurant into smaller, intimate sections. Mia spoke to the front-of-house server, giving Rob's name, trying not to sound intimidated by her surroundings. As the waiter delicately pushed aside a curtain and gestured for her to go through, Mia saw Rob in the corner, looking down at his phone, dressed in a smart blue shirt and chinos. He'd come straight from work. Mia had had the day off today and had come from home.

She followed the waiter to his table, and he glanced up as she approached, his face breaking into a smile. She saw his eyes widen as he took in the full effect of her dress and he stood up. 'You look stunning,' he said, his eyes sparkling. As he leant over to kiss her on the cheek, their heads turned slightly as if synchronised and their lips brushed. An electric shock ran through her and she smiled.

The waiter pulled out her chair for her to sit down and Rob turned to him and ordered a bottle of champagne.

'Wow,' Mia said. 'But we have work tomorrow. I don't normally drink on a work night.' She blushed, immediately embarrassed. She sounded so unworldly, and for a moment she thought Rob must be imagining her all alone in the evenings, reading or watching TV in her dark basement room.

'Leading you astray, am I?' he said, laughing and taking her hand across the table and squeezing it. Under the table her leg brushed gently against his.

The waiter came back with the champagne. 'What do you think?' Rob said as she took her first sip.

'It's lovely, thanks,' she said, blushing once again. She'd never been anywhere like this before on a date. The closest she'd come were the bistros her mother used to take her to in France, but she was so young then, and they weren't anywhere near as luxurious as this.

The conversation flowed easily between them. She didn't think anyone had ever taken such an interest in her, asking about her childhood in France and her family. She wanted to tell him about her daughter, but she stopped herself. It was still early days. It might put him off.

Instead she talked about her school and then the various temping jobs she'd had in London. He seemed impressed by her upbringing, fascinated by the idea of an English-speaking boarding school in France, and entertained by her stories of her auditions for small TV parts when she'd first come to London.

'I was so naive,' she said. 'I really thought I'd make it in London. Become a famous actress. My teachers at school always said I was good.' She thought of Mrs Beddow, how she'd showered her with praise. 'But London – it's another world. It's so competitive. And so much of the time in acting, it's about who you know.'

'I can imagine. At least you tried to follow your dreams.' He looked into her eyes. 'That's so brave.'

'I haven't given up yet,' Mia said. 'I still go to the occasional audition.' It wasn't quite true. The last one she'd been to had been over a year ago and a complete disaster. 'I still might make it, I suppose.'

'That's what I like about you. You're so tenacious. You never give up.' Mia wasn't sure that was true, but she accepted the compliment. She couldn't believe she was on a date with someone like Rob, that he seemed to like her, to be impressed by her.

His curly dark hair fell across his eyes and he pushed it back with his hand. 'I'm glad you didn't make it as an actress,' he said.

'What?' Mia said, surprised.

'If you'd made it as an actress, I'd never have had a chance with you.' His hand was under the table, making its way up her skirt, and Mia felt a shiver of longing.

They were interrupted by the waiter bringing their main courses and Rob managed to engage in conversation while his hand massaged her thigh. The waiter didn't seem to notice the way he leant unnaturally forward.

Rob grinned at her as the waiter left, withdrew his hand and started tucking into his steak.

As they ate she asked him about himself, how he'd got into the estate agency business, how he'd worked his way up, what his childhood was like, his family. He talked about his sister and his parents, a happy childhood in West London. She didn't ask him about ex-girlfriends although she knew he must have them. He was in his mid-thirties and good-looking. He must have had a string of them.

Mia felt addicted to him, like she needed to know everything about him. He seemed to feel the same about her, hanging on her every word.

As their plates were being cleared, their eyes met again.

There was so much unspoken want between them, Mia could hardly stand it.

Mia was the first to look away. She reached for the water at the same time as he did. Their fingers touched and an electric shock jolted through her body. His fingers were on hers and he took the bottle from her.

'Don't worry,' he said. 'I'll pour the water. You run around after me enough at work. It's time I did something for you.'

She blushed and gulped the water down. They'd finished the bottle of champagne between them and she felt dizzy, her legs hollow and shaky when she stood up to use the bathroom.

In the bathroom, she studied her face in the mirror and topped up her lipstick. She smiled at her reflection. She couldn't believe how well this date was going. It was like she'd thought; Rob was the one.

'Do you want dessert?' Rob asked, when she got back to the table.

'I'm quite full but I could be tempted,' she said. 'I just don't want the evening to end.' She blushed, afraid she had revealed too much. It was only their second date.

He smiled, his eyes mischievous. 'How about we move on somewhere else? A friend recommended a good hotel. It's just up the road from here. We could go there.' He looked at her expectantly.

'Oh,' she said, her heart racing at the thought of them together in a hotel room. 'That sounds... well, that sounds good to me. I'm too full for dessert anyway.'

Rob's eyes sparkled, as he signalled to the waiter to get the bill.

He paid quickly and took her by the arm, leading her out of the restaurant. 'Let's go... I need you, Mia.' He looked deep into her eyes, his pupils wide with desire. 'I've wanted this since I first laid eyes on you.'

SIX

NOW

At the weekend, Rob played golf while Jen ferried Lottie and Jack to tennis and swimming and looked after Ruby. Jen didn't mind Rob taking some time to enjoy himself with his friends. She was just happy their date night had gone so well and that they'd managed to reconnect. But after a busy weekend with the kids, she didn't feel rested on Monday when she woke up to the sound of her alarm. The week went by in a flurry of school drop-offs and housework. She managed to get to the gym most days, and she felt grateful for the time to relax. By Thursday, she was still exhausted, but she woke up feeling happier as it was her favourite day of the week; the day she, Natasha and Amy volunteered at the cat shelter.

She took a quick shower and then left Rob getting ready for work while she went to the kitchen to make the children's packed lunches. She put a banana and some strawberries and raspberries into the smoothie maker, then added Rob's usual vitamin blend and blitzed it, before pouring it into his bottle for the gym. He went every day after work and always finished the session with a home-made smoothie. Jen used to make them for herself too, until she'd seen an article about how sugar was the new smoking and had given them up.

Soon the children were up and she started making their breakfast. Rob appeared from his shower, his hair still damp, and took a granola yogurt out of the fridge so he could have his breakfast at work. He grabbed his rucksack and she handed him his smoothie and kissed him goodbye as he left the apartment. He waved to the kids, and then Jen began the mad rush to get them to school.

Three hours after she'd got up, Jen dropped Ruby off at the crèche at the gym, waving goodbye as her daughter played happily with the toys. Ruby was used to it there now, and she liked the staff. They all knew her well as Jen dropped her off most weekday mornings.

It had taken Jen a while to realise that the benefits of the gym included up to fifteen hours of free childcare a week. Rob had been very clear that he wouldn't pay for any childcare while Jen wasn't working, but he was more than happy to pay for the gym. He always wanted her to look good. He would never say it out loud, but he liked to have a beautiful wife on his arm to impress clients. He wanted all the older men who were investing in the London property market to envy him. *The shortest skirts sell the biggest properties*, they used to say in the office when she'd worked as an estate agent. It had always made Jen cringe, as if they were belittling her performance. At that point in her career she'd earnt the most commission in the whole office; a lot more than Rob, who'd been working at the same agency.

Rob knew that the gym provided childcare, but he didn't realise she used it for more than just working out. On Thursdays she put Ruby in the crèche so she could volunteer at the cat shelter. If Rob found out, he wouldn't understand why she needed the time to herself. Apart from when she was exercising at the gym, it was the only time in the week she had without her children, the only time she had an identity beyond being a mother. And she loved caring for the cats and helping them find new homes.

As Jen walked down the street in the blazing sunshine, she smiled, her hands free of the buggy. She was still buzzing after the dinner she'd had with Rob on Friday. It had gone so well, and they'd felt like a couple again, rather than just parents. And she'd finally managed to talk to him about reconnecting, finding more time for each other. He was desperate to spend more time together as a couple too. He loved his job, but he was fed up with the long hours in the office.

'I've missed you, Jen,' he'd said, his hand squeezing her thigh as she sat eating the beef teriyaki in her lacy robe, her face still flushed from their activities in the bedroom. 'I love being with you. And you're so right. We need to make more time for each other.'

He'd suggested they go on a romantic weekend away together. His parents could look after the kids, down in their seaside cottage, and he and Jen could find a spa hotel to escape to.

He'd transferred £500 to her account and she'd agreed to book something. She'd spent the early part of this week organising the logistics and liaising with her in-laws to find a weekend that worked for them all. Finally, after the last hectic year looking after Ruby, Jen was moving out of the chaos and back into everyday life.

When she got to the cat shelter, Amy and Natasha were already there. Natasha was bottle-feeding a new kitten and Amy was cleaning out one of the litter trays. Jen said her hellos and then went to the computer at the desk to reply to the emails that had come through overnight from people looking to adopt a cat and people who had found cats that might need admitting to the shelter.

She'd been there four months now, ever since Natasha had suggested it at the school gate, when Jen had confided in her that she was worried about her skills getting out of date while she was a stay-at-home parent. Jen had always wanted a cat, but pets were forbidden in their apartment block. When Jen had complained about the policy to Amy at the reception desk, they'd got chatting. It had turned out that Amy loved cats too, and when Jen had told her about the volunteering opportunity she'd signed up straight away.

The morning went by quickly. Jen loved working there. It was always so varied. She put some posts up on social media advertising for new adopters, looked after and played with the cats and showed potential adopters round the shelter.

'The morning's really rushed by,' Natasha said, as they packed up to go.

'It always does,' Amy said, wistfully. 'I wish this was my paid job rather than just a volunteer role.'

Jen smiled at her. 'Work been bad lately?' Amy was always unflappable and calm, but Jen knew there had been a lot of problems with the building, and some of the other apartment owners could be very demanding and sometimes even rude to the reception staff.

Amy sighed. 'Just the usual. Lots of complaints. Showers not working, tiles coming off the walls, that kind of thing. Plus someone asking if the swimming pool could be moved to the roof.' She rolled her eyes and Jen laughed.

The three of them stepped outside into the sun. 'Anyone free for lunch?' Natasha asked. 'It's such a nice day. We should eat outside, make the most of the sunshine.'

'Sounds good,' Amy said. 'I could do with some sun.'

. . .

Half an hour later, the three of them were sprawled out on the grass in the park, eating supermarket sandwiches. Jen had collected Ruby from the crèche at the gym and then walked back to join them. Now Ruby toddled around them, a messy banana in her hand.

'So how was your meal on Friday night with Rob?' Natasha asked. Jen had told Natasha and Amy her plans last week.

'It went really well,' Jen said, smiling to herself as she remembered. I mean, he was a little bit late, but—'

'Work again?' Natasha interrupted, eyebrows raised.

'Yes, but—'

'You do a lot for him, Jen,' Natasha said gently.

'But that's what we agreed,' Jen said. 'When I gave up work, we agreed that I'd do all the housework and childcare. He has a busy job and I'm at home all day.'

Natasha sighed, picking the grass with her fingers. 'Hmm...'

'You've never liked him, have you?' Jen said. She'd met Natasha when she'd briefly been working at Rob's office. A temporary job that she'd soon left to become a carer for the elderly. Jen hadn't spoken to her much then; just seen her once in the office. But then when Lottie and Jack started at Natasha's daughter Matilda's school they'd quickly become friends. Sometimes Jen wondered if Rob had done something to upset her when they'd worked together. Natasha always seemed to criticise him.

'It's not that. It's just, he seems to take you for granted. A marriage should be equal. You should both feel the same way about each other. Care for each other.'

'We probably both take each other for granted,' Jen said. 'We've been married nine years, together since we were at school. We're used to having each other around. And I think it's normal for couples to grow apart a bit when they have children. Life is so busy and the children take up so much time. There's always so much to do.'

Natasha nodded. 'Maybe. I wouldn't know. Steve and I split when Matilda was two.'

Amy looked up. 'Marriages are hard work,' she said. 'You have to be completely compatible for it to last. Made for each other.'

'That's the thing,' Jen said, 'Amy's right. Marriages are work. Rob has been distant lately. He works hard and he's away a lot. But we can get the spark back.' She thought of how passionate their relationship had been on Friday night. 'I know we can. We just have to work at it. That's why I cooked him his favourite meal, that's why I work out what he wants and try to make sure he always has it.'

'But what about what you want?' Natasha asked.

'All I want is happy kids and a stable family.'

Amy nodded. 'I guess that's important. But surely that's just the basics. What about the fun bit? Are you still having sex?' she asked.

'Amy!' Natasha said. 'You can't ask that!' She laughed.

'It's OK,' Jen said. 'We're still having sex. That bit's always been good, actually. It's not the sex that's the problem. It's the talking, the connecting. We don't do that anymore.' She forced a smile. 'Like I said, I'm working on it.'

Natasha frowned again and put a hand on Jen's knee. 'I'm worried about you, Jen. Why do you think it's your responsibility to work on your marriage, not Rob's?'

Jen shook her head. 'It's not just mine. It's both of ours.' Although she knew that only she would be thinking about it. It was her who'd booked their romantic weekend away, her who'd arranged the childcare with his parents. As soon as Rob was back in the office, he probably hadn't given it a second thought.

She tried again. 'Look, I read a really good article in a magazine. "How to keep the spark in your marriage". It had so much good advice.'

'You have to stop reading those magazines. You can't

achieve everything they ask of you.' Natasha squeezed Jen's arm. 'The gym five times a week. Cooking three healthy meals a day. Always playing with your children and taking them to educational activities. Looking perfect all the time. Working to keep your husband. It's all just ridiculous.' Natasha glared angrily into the middle distance, as if imagining she was speaking to the editor of the magazine, telling them exactly what she thought.

Jen's brow crinkled. It felt like Natasha was ridiculing her whole life. Since she'd become a stay-at-home mum, those *were* the things that occupied her. Natasha was her closest friend, but sometimes it felt that she didn't understand Jen's life at all.

'I have to go,' Jen said, standing up and taking Ruby's hand. 'I'm visiting my mother at the home.'

Natasha stood up too. 'Do you want me to come with you?' she asked. Natasha knew a bit of Jen's history, and why she found it so difficult to visit her mother. She'd given her a lift to the care home once before, when Jen's car was being serviced.

'No, it's fine,' Jen said. She wanted to go on her own.

'Jen, I didn't mean to upset you. I'm too blunt sometimes, you know that.'

'You haven't upset me,' Jen said, reaching to hug her.

Natasha hugged her back, squeezing her tightly, their bodies pressed together. As she pulled away, she reached over and put some stray strands of hair behind Jen's ears. 'You know I only say these things because I care about you, don't you?' she said earnestly.

Jen nodded. 'It's OK,' she said. 'I'll see you tomorrow at drop-off.' She gave Amy a light hug, and then left.

As she walked home with Ruby in the buggy, Jen felt tears prick her eyes. She'd been so hopeful about her and Rob. She'd been sure she had everything sorted, that they'd get the spark back on their weekend away. But Natasha had a point. She was putting more effort into the marriage than Rob was. She thought of the perfume she'd smelt on Rob's shirt, all the late nights out drinking with clients. Sometimes she wondered if he really was where he said he was. She'd worked so hard to become the perfect wife, to support his career. But was he taking her for granted? Was she really living as empty a life as Natasha seemed to think she was? All she wanted was a happy family. She just had to make sure she did everything she could to keep that.

SEVEN

SIX MONTHS EARLIER

Mia smiled to herself as she let herself into the office. She was the first person in and she loved having the place to herself. In the dark early mornings, her boxroom in her basement flat felt miserable and claustrophobic, but when she got to the office early, it finally felt like she had her own space to stretch out and get on with things. In the empty room, full of computer screens, she could finally hear her own thoughts.

She always tried to make a good impression on her temping assignments, but on this one she was making more effort than usual, getting in early whenever she could. If Rob stayed late, she was always there, and he'd often take her to dinner. Their romance had proceeded at a rate of knots, and Mia could feel that wonderful sensation of losing control, of giving herself entirely to him. Finally she was accepted, she was part of something. Her and Rob were two halves of a whole.

It was him who'd insisted that she cover for his PA, Grace, this week, while she was on holiday. Grace's desk was right next to his office and now Mia had the excuse to pop in whenever she felt like it. And there were more reasons for her and Rob to go and have lunch together.

Rob had given her access to his emails and his diary and she loved having this level of involvement in his life. She was the one reading every email that came through, and deciding which ones he needed to respond to. When she had time she'd been going back through his old emails, reading anything that seemed interesting. There hadn't been a lot, really, just the usual you'd expect from an estate agent. It seemed like he deleted a lot of his emails after he dealt with them, and Grace had organised the old emails into folders. One of the folders had caught her interest. 'Penthouse, Riverview Apartments'.

It was strange, because all the other folders had generic names: 'House sales', 'Flat sales', 'Building sales'. She'd clicked into the folder and read a few messages before realising it was the apartment Rob had bought for himself. She found the sales leaflet and studied the beautiful penthouse, all modern furnishings and spectacular views. He hadn't taken her there yet, but she was sure he would soon. At the moment he was still focused on impressing her with expensive hotels with crisp white sheets and posh restaurants where she was served by waiters in black tie. She smiled as she thought of him living alone in his huge flat. Perhaps he hadn't invited her there because it was too messy and there was nothing in the fridge. He worked so hard he probably never had time to cook or take much care of the place. He was probably embarrassed and worried she would judge him. Maybe he was even worried she wouldn't be interested when she found out how he lived. But she didn't mind. She could help him with keeping the place in order. It would be the perfect place for the two of them to start their family together.

She'd spent a good twenty minutes yesterday studying the pictures of the penthouse in the brochure, imagining herself living in the flat with Rob, sharing a bottle of champagne in the hot tub on the balcony while they admired the view. She'd looked up the building on Google Street View and studied it from all angles. It was only a fifteen-minute walk from the office, and that evening she'd taken a detour after work and walked by, stopping to stare up at the top of the building, thinking of the views from the penthouse. She'd thought about ringing him and inviting herself in, but had then remembered he'd gone to the gym.

Now in the early morning at the office, she switched on the computer and sorted through Rob's emails that had come in overnight. There weren't many: a couple of offers that had come through for a new flat on the market, and there was a vendor wanting to sell his family home. Everything else was spam, which she quickly deleted.

She was soon up to date, so she went to the kitchen, unloaded the communal dishwasher and got herself a glass of water. After that, she sat down and went through Rob's diary. First she looked at this week. He had a series of meetings today: one with the team this morning, and several client meetings in the afternoon. She flicked through his calendar, absent-mindedly looking at the weeks ahead.

And then suddenly she stopped, her breath catching in her throat.

There was an appointment in Rob's calendar for next week, entitled 'wedding anniversary'. The invitation had been sent by someone called Jen. Mia felt vomit rise in her throat. This could only mean one thing. Rob was married. Jen must be Rob's wife.

EIGHT

NOW

Jen pulled into the car park of her mother's care home and quickly got out of the car. As she got Ruby out of her car seat, she shivered. She reached for the coats on the passenger seat. It had been hot earlier, but now the sun had disappeared behind a cloud and there was a light breeze tickling her neck.

It would be warm inside. They always kept the heating on high for the residents, even in the summer. She hurried across the gravel to the large brightly lit entrance. The home had formerly been a stately home, and even now it looked more like a hotel than a care home. When Jen had got the call two years ago to say her mother was in hospital because she'd had a stroke, she had rushed to her side. Her mother had only been fifty-five, but it had quickly become clear that she wasn't likely to regain her full capabilities. Even though Jen had lost contact with her mother years ago when she hadn't turned up to her wedding, claiming that the venue was 'too posh for the likes of her', Jen was still devastated at the prospect of her going into a home. Rob had held Jen while she cried and then he'd swept into action, pulling some strings to get her mother into the most sought-after care home in West London. Jen had cried with relief when he told her he'd found a place for her here. Jen had thought it would be too expensive, but Rob had told her not to worry, he'd take care of it.

The reception staff smiled and said friendly hellos to Jen and Ruby. Ruby waved back at them, giggling. Her daughter liked coming here, even if Jen didn't.

They made their way to her mother's one-bedroom apartment on the ground floor and Jen took a deep breath and then knocked firmly.

'Come in,' her mother called out.

Jen opened the door. Her mother was sitting in her armchair by the window, her frail body almost disappearing in the large chair. Despite visiting every week for two years, Jen always felt a fresh feeling of shock when she saw her mother like this. She was still in her fifties, but since her stroke she'd aged rapidly and now she looked much older.

'Oh, it's you,' her mother said, looking away from her and out of the window. 'I thought it might be the nurse. They sometimes bring round biscuits at this time of day.'

'I come every Thursday, Mum.'

'Well, you know you don't need to. Just after my inheritance. Waiting for me to die off.'

Jen swallowed. That was so far from the truth. Her mother had always rented her flat in East London, and had no money to her name. Rob was paying all her care home fees. But there was no point in saying that to her mother. She said she couldn't remember things because of her stroke, but Jen suspected her memory was just selective. There were things she didn't want to remember.

'Do you want me to make you a drink, Mum?'

'No, thanks, I've just had one.'

'Shall we go out for a walk round the building? There's a bit of a breeze, but we'll be warm enough with coats on.'

'That would be nice,' her mother said.

Jen helped her mother into her coat, and then offered her arm for her mother to hold on to. She was slightly unsteady on her feet and they walked slowly down the corridor. Ruby clutched onto Jen's other hand, trying to pull her along faster.

'Slow down a bit, Ruby,' Jen said, concentrating on walking at her mother's pace.

As they went by reception, her mother called out hello to the staff and they asked her politely about her day. 'I've had a lovely morning reading,' she replied. It was more than she'd said to Jen. At least she was happy here, Jen thought. That was all she could hope for.

'When do you think Harry will come and visit?' her mother asked, as they walked out the front door of the home and turned right towards the gardens.

'I don't know, Mum,' Jen said. 'You know I don't speak to Dad anymore.' They hadn't spoken since he'd been imprisoned for fraud when Jen was fifteen. He'd come out of prison a few years later but he hadn't been in contact with her or her mother since.

'Of course he doesn't speak to you,' her mother said, 'after what you did.'

'I was trying to protect you,' Jen said, but she knew it was pointless. Jen had called the police when her father had been hitting her mother. She'd been fifteen and she'd had enough of being scared in her own home. She'd been shaking when she called them, but they'd come quickly and arrested her father. Her mother was black and blue, but it had been Jen she had been furious with.

The police had tried to help her mother, but she'd decided not to press charges and had secretly let him back into the family home. Jen hadn't told anyone, because she hadn't wanted social services coming and taking her away. Instead she'd hung around outside of the house, in the library or the park, or at friends' houses, only coming home to sleep when she had nowhere else to go, and leaving early in the morning before her father got up.

'Your father was the love of my life,' Jen's mother said now. 'You ruined that. You destroyed our family. They never would have even looked at the fraud charge if you hadn't sent the police sniffing around in the first place.' Her mum's eyes started to get wild, and Jen could tell she was too worked up.

'Let's not talk about that now, Mum,' Jen said. Jen wished Natasha was with her. When she'd come to the home with her before she'd lightened the atmosphere by making small talk with her mother about the weather and the furnishings in the home. It had taken the pressure off Jen.

'It's because of you he doesn't visit. You haven't told him where I am.'

'I haven't heard from him for years. But if he gets in contact, I'll pass on your details.' Jen had started to think that maybe her parents deserved each other. For so much of her life she'd wished she had different parents, parents more like Rob's. Yet now her mother was frail, she felt a sense of connection to her. When she'd been young, she'd loved her unconditionally. Every now and then, Jen would get a flash of the mother she'd loved so much. The one who didn't live in the past and picked her up when she was down. She missed her.

'Thank you,' her mother said curtly. 'That's the least you can do.'

They continued walking round the gardens, and Jen began to point out the different flowers to Ruby, ignoring her mother. She remembered when she was seventeen and she had first met Rob, and he'd taken her to his parents' house. They'd had the most beautiful garden, and when she had got to know Rob's mother, she'd taught her all the names of the plants and how to care for them. She had been more of a mother to her than her own mother ever had been.

Jen walked round the garden with her mother and Ruby for fifteen minutes, chatting away self-consciously to her daughter, aware of her mother walking in silence beside her. Then Jen looked pointedly at the Cartier watch that Rob had bought her for their wedding anniversary. 'I need to go and pick the kids up from school.' As she said it, she realised her mother hadn't asked after them, not even once, and she hadn't bothered to engage with Ruby either. Jen felt a familiar aching for her mother's love.

'You'd better get going then,' her mother said. 'Just walk me back to my room first. You know I can't manage on my own.'

They walked back in silence, and Jen watched as her mother sank back into her armchair and then switched the telly on.

Jen went into the bathroom and checked the cabinet. She saw the rows of plastic bottles of pills the GP had prescribed. 'Are you remembering to take your medicine, Mum?'

'Of course I am. I haven't lost my mind yet.'

Jen reached into the cabinet and slipped a bottle of anti-anxiety pills into her bag. She was pretty sure her mother didn't need them anymore, and even if she did, it was easy to get medication at the home.

'Alright then, Mum. We'd better be off.' She came back into the lounge and leant over and kissed her mother's cold cheek. Her mother didn't react. Instead she just focused on the TV, as Jen let herself and Ruby out.

Often Rob had client meetings in the evenings, but tonight they were planning to eat together. Jen had prepared dinner and put Ruby to bed, when Rob messaged her at 7.15 p.m. to say he was just leaving the gym and about to head home. She started to heat up the dinner ready for him. But he wasn't back at 7.30, or even at 8 p.m., and as the time ticked on a bubble of anxiety started to form in Jen's stomach. She tried to call him but he didn't answer, so she sent him a text. She put her older children to bed and eventually ate her dinner on her own. At 10.30 p.m. she'd finished tidying up the flat and done the washing-up from her dinner. Usually, if Rob was out this late, Jen would go to bed by herself and see him in the morning. But it bothered her that he hadn't replied to her messages. Although he was often out in the evenings with his work, he always replied to texts. She stepped out onto the balcony, into the fresh air, and tried to ring him again. His number went straight to voicemail.

She looked again at the phone, wondered if she should call someone else to check up on him. He hadn't been in contact since he'd left the gym. Of course, he could have been waylaid by someone or something, but surely he would have let her know.

She stared out at the sparkling lights of West London below, watching the Thames flow gently below her. She'd stay up a bit later and see if he came back. He had work the next day, and unless there was a big event he was always home by midnight on a work night. Jen went back inside and picked up a book from her bedside table. She'd been reading it for the last month, only managing a few pages each night before the words started to blur on the page. Maybe she could make more progress with it tonight.

She switched on the balcony lights and sat on the rattan sofa, wrapping a blanket around her to protect her from the slight chill in the night air. She felt like she was on top of the world, West London spread out before her. She remembered saying that to Rob when she'd first seen the penthouse, when he was desperate for them to buy it.

'It doesn't just feel like we're on top of the world,' he'd

replied, his arm round her shoulders. 'It feels like we own the world.'

The apartment block was the most exclusive in the area and she knew Rob had done well to secure such a big discount with the developer. He'd sold most of the flats in the block to his clients, so the developer had been happy to help him. But Jen hadn't been completely sure about living here. It would have been perfect without the children, the kind of place she had fantasised about living in when she'd first worked as an estate agent. But a part of her wished the children had a garden to run around in, like they'd had in their previous house.

And now she was here, she appreciated the luxury of it all, but there had been a lot of issues with the building. She looked over at the place where Ruby had climbed out between the balcony panels. Amy had already organised for them to be replaced and there was no longer a gap. Jen shivered as she thought of what might have happened to Ruby if she'd fallen.

She looked at her watch again. *Where was he?* What had happened to him after he left the gym?

Her phone beeped and she rushed to pick it up. A message from Natasha.

Sorry if I upset you earlier. I didn't mean to. I just care about you, that's all. Hope it all went OK with visiting your mum. Xx

Jen messaged back.

Don't worry about it! Mum was her usual self. I never know what to say to her. Wish you'd been there with me! And now Rob's not home. We were supposed to have dinner together tonight, but he hasn't come back. Xx

Oh, Jen. But isn't that normal for him? He often works late.

He hasn't messaged to say where he is. I'm worried. Do you think I should do something?

Like what?

I don't know. I just feel like something might be seriously wrong.

Jen had a horrible twisting feeling in the pit of her stomach. What if something had happened to Rob? What if he never came home? What if, when she'd handed him his gym bag that morning, that was the last time she'd see him?

He's probably just out with his mates. Or clients. You know what he's like. Just go to bed. He'll turn up in the night.

Jen swallowed. Of course, Natasha was right. She went back inside the penthouse, locked the patio doors and put the key away, then got ready for bed.

She messaged Rob one final time:

Where are you tonight? I thought you were coming home after the gym. Let me know you're safe and well xx

Then she fell into a fitful sleep.

At 3 a.m., she was woken by her phone ringing. At first she thought it was her alarm, but then she realised it was a call. By the time she went to answer it, it had already gone to voicemail.

Missed call from Rob.

Her heart leapt. He was safe. Thank god. But what was he

doing calling her at this time? Her relief changed to irritation. He was probably drunk and hadn't realised the time. Typical of him. He could have just messaged her, instead of waking her up. But he hadn't. What was he playing at? She messaged him:

What's going on? Are you coming home? Xx

Where was he? Even the late-night bars and clubs were closed at this time. And he had to be at work in a few hours.

As soon as her message went through the phone started ringing again.

She picked it up. 'Rob?' She could hear the annoyance in her voice. 'Where are you?'

But it wasn't Rob on the other end of the phone.

'Who am I speaking to, please?' asked the female voice.

'Jen,' she said. 'It's Jen. Who are you?'

There was a brief pause. 'Are you Rob's wife?' she asked.

NINE

Jen's heart sank to the pit of her stomach, and she sat up straighter in bed. Why was another woman answering Rob's phone? And why was she asking if she was Rob's wife? She thought suddenly of the scent of an unfamiliar perfume on Rob's shirt the other day.

'Yes, yes, I'm his wife,' she said curtly. 'And who are you?' She had a feeling she didn't want to know the answer.

'My name is Priti. I'm a nurse at West London hospital.'

'What?' Jen said, trying to compute what she'd just heard. Her pulse raced. Why wasn't Rob calling her himself? 'Where's Rob?' she asked desperately. 'Is he at the hospital?' *He couldn't be dead, could he?*

'Calm down, Jen,' the nurse said. She sounded bored; these calls were just a routine part of her job. 'Rob's here in the hospital. He's fine now. He was found unconscious in an alleyway. We're not sure quite what happened to him. A passer-by called an ambulance and brought him to the hospital.'

'What?' Jen said. 'Had he been drinking?'

'The doctor thought so. We see so many drunks here. We usually just let them sober up and send them home. But he didn't seem drunk to me. And he said he didn't remember drinking or taking any recreational drugs. He had a complete blackout. He was confused and disorientated when he came round. Didn't know what was going on.'

'Oh my god,' Jen said. 'But he's OK now?'

'He seems to be. But he's definitely not well enough to get himself home. He'll need keeping an eye on for the next twenty-four hours. We're not sure of the cause of the blackout. We didn't find anything else wrong. He had slightly low blood pressure, but that's it. You should monitor him at home just in case. If you're worried about anything you can bring him straight back in.'

Jen swallowed. She was just relieved he was OK. 'I will do,' she said.

'Can you come and pick him up?' the nurse asked.

Jen thought of her sleeping children. She'd need to bundle them all into the car and drive to the hospital.

'I'll come over as soon as I can,' she said.

Jen hung up, and stared at the phone, adrenaline still pumping through her. *Rob was in hospital.* But he was OK.

She went into her kids' rooms and checked on them. They were sleeping so peacefully. She didn't want to wake them and drag them out of bed to go to the hospital. But she needed to see Rob, to check he really was OK, and get him home. It sounded like he'd blacked out for ages. What if the nurse was downplaying his symptoms?

Natasha had always said she could call her any time if she needed help. She knew her daughter was staying with her dad tonight so she wouldn't have any childcare responsibilities. And Jen had helped Natasha recently when her car had broken down, driving her to all her carer appointments that day.

Jen took a deep breath and called Natasha.

'Jen?' Natasha said sleepily, as she answered. 'What's wrong? Is it Rob? What has he done?'

'I'm so sorry to call you in the middle of the night. Rob's in hospital. He blacked out... And I need to go and pick him up. Would you be able to come and sit with the kids while I collect him? They're all asleep. You can lie on the sofa and rest.'

'Yeah, of course,' Natasha said. 'Let me get dressed and I can be there in fifteen minutes.'

Jen sighed with relief. Thank god she could always rely on Natasha.

When Jen got to the hospital and found Rob, she could see immediately he was in a bad way. He was still groggy and confused.

'He just needs some rest,' the nurse said. 'But if his symptoms get worse, please come back.'

'OK,' Jen said. Rob leant on her heavily as they walked out of the hospital, and he swayed from side to side. Jen was glad she didn't have the three kids with her. She wouldn't have been able to look after them at the same time as Rob.

She managed to manoeuvre him into the car and then drove him home, and took him up in the lift to the penthouse.

'Hi,' she called out softly to Natasha as they came in. 'We're back.'

'Hi,' Natasha said, as Rob slumped down onto the sofa.

'What happened to him?' she whispered to Jen.

'He blacked out.'

'Gosh,' Natasha said, eyeing him warily. 'Poor thing. Is there anything I can do to help? Do you want me to stay with you?'

Jen sighed. 'No, I'll be fine. They've told me to keep an eye on him today, make sure he's alright.'

She let Natasha out, and guided Rob into the bedroom, helping him out of his clothes and into bed. Then she crept in beside him and tried to get a couple more hours of sleep.

. . .

After Jen had taken the kids to school in the morning, she came back with Ruby to see Rob. She'd left him asleep but now he was up and dressed in his suit.

'I'm late for work,' he said, as if it was Jen's fault. 'My alarm didn't go off.'

'You can't go to work. The doctors said you had to rest.' His eyes were still bloodshot and he looked shaky. She touched his arm. 'I've been so worried about you.' She hadn't managed to sleep at all after he'd got home. She'd kept rolling over to check he was still breathing. She didn't understand what had happened. Rob had never had any medical problems before.

'But I can't rest. I have important meetings today. I need to get into the office.'

Jen shook her head. 'I've already emailed Grace to say you're not well. She sends her best wishes and says that she'll keep everything under control.'

Rob put his hand to his head. 'I have an awful headache. Perhaps you're right. Maybe I should stay at home. I can always answer some emails.'

'Just sit down on the sofa and rest,' Jen said, guiding him towards it gently. 'I'll make you a cup of tea.'

He sat down reluctantly, and then let his head flop onto the cushions. 'I'm still so tired,' he said. 'I don't know what happened. One moment I was leaving the gym, and the next I was waking up in A&E.'

'Had you been drinking?'

'No!' Rob said. 'I don't remember having anything to drink at all. Honestly. It's all so strange.' Jen frowned. The nurse hadn't thought he'd been drinking either. And even if he had, Rob could usually hold his drink.

Jen ran her fingers through his thick, curly hair. 'Nothing at all? Then what happened?'

'I must have blacked out after the gym. But the doctors checked me over in A&E and couldn't find anything wrong.'

'We need to follow this up,' Jen said. 'Go to the GP. Make sure you really are OK.' Her thoughts immediately went to her mum, and how her stroke changed her entire life. Her throat constricted at the thought of something like that happening to Rob.

'I don't need to go to the GP,' Rob said dismissively. 'The hospital's already checked me over, and besides, I'm fine now.'

'You need to go. Just in case it's something serious.'

Rob shook his head. 'I'm fine. Really. You can play nurse and look after me today. But tomorrow I'm going back into work.'

Jen looked at him, lying sprawled out on the sofa in his suit.

'Are you sure you're telling me everything about what happened?' she asked.

He nodded. 'Why would I lie to you?' he said, reaching for the remote control and turning on the television, making it clear their conversation was over.

TEN

SIX MONTHS EARLIER

Mia stared at Rob's calendar, not sure if she could believe what she was seeing. There was no denying the appointment in Rob's diary next week marked 'wedding anniversary'. *Rob was married. He had a wife.*

Mia didn't know how long she stared at the appointment, but the clock must have turned nine, because around her the rows of desks started to fill up and the office buzzed with activity as her co-workers hung up their coats and switched on their computers. Mia swallowed, ignoring the ringing phone on her desk. She felt like she might cry. After everything that she and Rob had done together. All the lunchtime trips to hotels, the secret rendezvous in the bedrooms of gorgeous brand-new apartments, the sweet words he'd whispered to her, the promises he'd made. He'd told her he loved her. He couldn't be married. He just couldn't be.

The phone kept ringing and she had to answer it. 'Hello, Davidson's Estate Agents. How can I help?' She made her voice sound professional, holding back her tears. All those years of trying to make it in the theatre had paid off. The woman wanted to view a local house and Mia booked it in the diary of one of the agents.

'Does anyone want a coffee?' she asked around the office. A few faces looked up at her from their computer screens blankly.

'I was going to go to Audrey's...' she followed up weakly when no one made a sound. She was told when she started how friendly the atmosphere here was, but it never seemed to extend to her.

She held back a sigh. She'd go and pick up a coffee for herself and for Rob too. Audrey's was his favourite coffee shop, and he always appreciated it when she returned with a steaming takeaway cup. By the time she got back from the coffee shop, Rob would be in his office preparing for the team meeting. It would give her the excuse to go into his office and talk to him. Ask him about Jen.

As she waited in the shop for the coffees, she thought about their relationship. It had all seemed so perfect: all the expensive meals out, the thoughtful gifts, the visits to upmarket hotels. He didn't always stay overnight, saying he preferred to go home and sleep in his own bed. But sometimes he stayed. Where had his wife thought he was?

Mia felt so stupid. Had she been used? Did the whole office know about his wife? He never wore a wedding ring at work, had never mentioned a wife or even a girlfriend. She'd just assumed he was single. How had she let this happen again? She'd thought Rob was one of the good guys; she'd thought he was 'the one'. But he was married. What did that mean? That everything he'd said about falling in love with her was a lie? It couldn't be, surely? No one could fake the feelings between them.

As she walked back to the office with the hot coffees her mind was spinning. She took a deep breath, then knocked on the door of Rob's office and let herself in, her heart racing.

He looked up and grinned, glancing at the coffee before his eyes settled on her breasts, accentuated by her low-cut top. 'Mia, you truly are the best,' he said as she handed him his drink. He put his free hand on her shoulder. 'I think you and I will have fun this week,' he whispered, glancing out of his office door to check no one could hear. 'On Friday I have plans to take you out for lunch at one of the best restaurants in London. There's a waiting list usually, but I know the owner.' He winked. 'And I also know a hotel nearby.'

'Who's Jen?' Mia blurted out, pulling away from him.

'Jen?' He walked swiftly across the office and shut the door.

'Yes, Jen. Is she your wife?'

Rob frowned. 'She's my ex-wife.'

'It says in your diary it's your wedding anniversary this week.'

Rob's face crumpled and he inhaled slowly. 'That's right. It would have been nine years. She put that appointment in my diary last year. I guess neither of us thought to take it out.' He looked Mia intently in the eyes. 'We're separated, Mia. For a year now.'

Mia tried to digest the information.

'I'm sorry if you got the wrong idea from my diary. You didn't think we were still together?'

She felt stupid. 'No, I—'

'Oh, Mia,' he said. 'I should have told you I'd been married.' He looked down at his feet. 'I should have been honest from the start, but I was worried it was too soon. I like you so much, I didn't want to scare you away.' He reached out and took her hand in his gently, raising his eyes to hers. 'There's something else I haven't told you that I should have. I have kids, three of them. I don't know why I didn't say, I'm sure you'd have found out from someone in the office soon enough. You're so young, and I just wanted you to get to know me first, so you could see what I was like. So my situation wouldn't put you off.'

'Kids wouldn't have put me off. I like children.' Mia thought of her own daughter. She swallowed and took a deep breath, ready to tell him about her.

'I should have known you'd be fine about it,' Rob said, before she could say anything. The moment was gone. 'You're just so lovely,' he continued. 'So perfect for me. My split from my wife was really painful. I really loved her, we had such a happy family. I had everything I wanted. But she cheated on me. I never thought I could trust someone again. But then I met you, Mia, and I can't explain it. I feel safe with you.'

He reached for her hand and squeezed it between both of his.

'Please don't abandon me, Mia,' he said. 'I think I'm falling in love with you.'

ELEVEN

NOW

Natasha and Jen walked together from the school, Jen pushing Ruby in the buggy, while the older children raced ahead to the park.

'How's Rob?' Natasha asked. 'Is he feeling better?'

'He seems fine,' Jen said. 'No sign of any long-term problems.' After his blackout last week, Jen couldn't help worrying, but Rob seemed like his usual self. There was no indication anything was wrong.

'Perhaps it was a one-off.'

'I hope so.' Jen felt a spot of rain on the bare skin of her arm, and looked doubtfully at the sky.

'The forecast said rain,' Natasha said, putting her hood up, 'but I think it will just be a passing shower.'

'Let's not risk it,' Jen said. 'Why don't you and Matilda come back to ours? The kids can play and then I'll make them some dinner.'

'It's my turn to host,' Natasha said. 'Why don't you come back to mine instead?'

Lottie, Jack and Matilda were running back towards them. 'Do you have an umbrella, Mum?' Lottie asked.

Jen shook her head. She hadn't expected it to rain.

'No, love. Why don't you get your coat out of your bag?' Jack and Matilda already had theirs on.

'I left it at school,' Lottie said.

'Not to worry. We're going to head home anyway. Matilda can come round to ours to play.'

'You should come to mine,' Natasha said quickly, 'although it is a bit of a mess.' She blushed. Jen had been round to Natasha's a few times before. Her one-bedroom flat was overflowing with Matilda's toys.

'But Muummm...' Matilda whined. 'Our flat is sooo boring.'

'Come to ours!' Lottie shouted. 'Please, Mum... can Matilda come to ours?'

Jen looked at Natasha. The rain was getting heavier. 'Our place is a bit nearer,' she said.

'OK,' Natasha said, with a smile. 'I'll host next time.'

When they got to the apartment block, they hurried inside. Amy came out from behind the reception desk to say hello.

'You look drenched,' she said to Lottie, who was shivering with cold. 'Didn't you have a coat?'

'I left it at school,' Lottie said again, looking at her feet.

Amy peeled off Lottie's wet jumper for her, and then gave her a hug, rubbing the little girl's cold arms. 'You'd better go inside and warm up,' she said. Amy had always been so good with Jen's kids, instinctively knowing how to comfort them. As they'd got to know her better she'd become like an auntie to them.

Someone approached the reception desk and Amy hurried away. 'I'll see you soon,' she said to Jen and Natasha, blowing them both a kiss.

Lottie, Matilda and Jack had already run over to the lift, and were arguing because Jack had got there first and pressed the button.

'It was MY turn!' Lottie screamed at Jack, giving him a push. Jack pushed her back.

'Stop fighting,' Jen said firmly, pulling the kids away from each other as she noticed the sideways look of a suited man, waiting for the lift beside them. She gave him an apologetic smile. Sometimes she missed living in their old house, where the children could be children as soon as they walked through the front door.

'Keep your voices down,' Jen said.

When the first lift came she let the man get inside on his own, and said they'd wait for the next one. It came within seconds and they all crowded in.

The button for the nineteenth floor was out of the kids' reach and she pressed it quickly to avoid arguments. The lift rushed up the shaft and Jen watched the numbers flash by on the digital display. At floor sixteen, the lift jerked to a halt and Jen tensed. Instead of the doors opening, it shuddered slightly, then dropped down a few feet. The lights went out.

'What was that?' Jack said.

'Nothing to worry about,' Jen said quickly. 'We'll get going in a minute.' She prodded the 'open door' button, but nothing happened. Maybe they were between floors. The electric display on the lift had gone blank. Had there been a power cut? She tried to keep calm, leaning against the wall for support. What if the lift fell all the way back down the shaft?

Jack started jumping up and down. 'Move, lift! Move, lift!'

'Stop that!' Jen said firmly. She felt faint, suddenly aware of the tiny metal box they were in, how high up they were.

Natasha was prodding at the alarm button. It didn't seem to be responding. Surely it should be ringing someone. Maybe it was doing that, just without sound.

'Are you alright, Jen?' Natasha asked suddenly, her face lit up by the weak emergency lighting. 'You look pale.'

'I'm OK,' Jen said. She suddenly felt faint, and she sank to the floor. 'I just need to sit down.' She'd never liked confined places. Not since she was a child. She always felt vulnerable and trapped. When she was little she used to hide in her bedroom cupboard while her father was beating up her mother, and enclosed spaces still made her heart pound.

'Is Ruby OK?' Jen asked. Ruby was suspiciously quiet in the pushchair.

'She's fine,' Natasha said. 'I'm going to call Amy, see if she can sort this out.'

'When are we moving?' Jack said impatiently.

Lottie sat down on the floor, shivering theatrically. 'I'm so cold,' she said. 'I just want to get changed.'

'We'll be out soon,' Natasha said. She was ringing Amy. On the other end of the line, Jen heard Amy pick up and the brief conversation between them.

'She's going to sort it straight away,' Natasha said to Jen, crouching down on the floor beside her. Natasha put her arm round Jen.

Jen blushed with embarrassment. 'I'm so sorry, I'm making such a fuss,' she said, trying to catch her breath. 'I just... hate being trapped.'

'Look, it's OK,' Natasha said, stroking her hair as if she was a child. 'Everyone's afraid of something.'

Jen thought of Ruby on the balcony, how close she'd come to falling. They were almost that high up now. They needed to get out of the lift as soon as possible. The building management had made a mistake with their balcony, installing the panels too far apart. What if they'd made a mistake with the lift too? What if it wasn't safe?

'It's alright,' Natasha said softly. 'Things like this happen all the time. Everything will be fine.'

Jen rested her head against Natasha's shoulder. She was so lucky to have a friend like her.

'Hello?' They heard a man's voice shouting from the other side of the doors. The children froze at the sound.

'Hello!' Natasha shouted. 'We're trapped in the lift.'

'Hang on,' the man said. 'I'll get you out.'

It didn't take the man long to return the lift to a floor, open up the doors and release them. Ten minutes later, they were up in the penthouse. Lottie was changing into fresh clothes, and Jen was putting out healthy snacks on the kitchen table so the kids could help themselves. She made Natasha a cup of tea, and then they went into the living room to chat while they watched the children play.

Natasha crouched down on the floor and played with Ruby, while the older kids ran around. 'I really miss Matilda being a toddler,' she said. 'It's such a lovely age.'

Jen smiled. 'It really is. But there always seems to be so much to do that I'm not sure I appreciate her properly.'

'I'd love to have another kid,' Natasha said wistfully. 'I always thought my family would be bigger, but when Steve left it put an end to plans for more children.'

'How many did you want?' Jen asked.

'Three. Maybe even four.'

'There's still time.'

'I'd have to meet someone with a bit of money,' Natasha said, and laughed. 'You can't bring up three or four kids in a one-bedroom flat.'

'You never know what the future holds,' Jen said. 'Maybe you'll meet someone.' Jen wondered if there'd been anyone since she'd split with Steve. She'd never mentioned anyone.

'Maybe I've already met them,' Natasha said softly, looking at Jen.

'Oh really?' Jen said. 'Who is it?'

'No one you know,' Natasha said, blushing. 'Forget I said anything.'

The afternoon rushed by as Natasha and Jen chatted. Natasha tidied away the kids' toys while Jen made them a quick dinner.

'Thanks for having us round again,' Natasha said. 'It's my turn next time.'

'It's no bother,' Jen said. 'Always a pleasure to see you and Matilda.'

'Well, I'd better get back and sort my dinner out.'

'Do you want to stay and have dinner with me and Rob? I was going to cook salmon. There's more than enough for three. I bought a whole fish. I was going to use the leftovers for pastas and salads.'

Natasha hesitated for a second, then smiled. 'Sure,' she said. 'I'd love to. Just let me know what I can help with.'

'You can keep an eye on the kids, while I get the dinner sorted.'

'It must be Ruby's bedtime soon. I can give her a bath and put her to bed if you like?'

'Yes, please,' Jen said, gratefully. Sometimes it felt like Natasha intuitively knew what she needed. Rob used to be the same, but these days he was so caught up in his work, he didn't pay so much attention to the rest of the family.

The doorbell rang and caught them by surprise. It was supposed to be impossible to get to the floor of the penthouse without a swipe card for the lift, but that swipe card function in the lift was another thing that wasn't working, and at the moment anyone could access any floor. Jen had had a video doorbell fitted, and she was about to check the app on her phone, but Natasha had already gone to the door.

'Hello?' Jen said, as Natasha opened the door to a young, dark-haired woman.

'Oh, hi,' she said. 'I'm here to see Rob. Is he in?'

'No, not yet,' Jen said. 'He's not usually back until 7.30.'

'Oh right.' The woman looked flustered. 'I... umm... I work with him. We left the office at the same time. I thought he'd be home by now.'

'He usually goes to the gym after work.'

'Yeah, I know.' The woman tucked her hair behind her ears. 'I just thought... well, I thought he said he wasn't going there tonight. I thought he was coming straight home. But never mind.' She held up a clear purple folder towards Jen, full of papers. 'I just came to give these to him. He left them in the office.'

'Right, thanks,' Jen said, taking the folder. 'I'll give them to him.'

The woman hesitated for a moment on the step, and for a second Jen thought she had something important to say. But all she said was, 'Great, thanks Jen,' and then she turned round and left.

Jen frowned. She had known Jen's name without her telling her, but she supposed Rob must have mentioned it in the office. Jen shut the door behind her and placed the folder on the kitchen table. 'That was weird, wasn't it?' she said to Natasha.

'Yeah, it did seem a bit odd.'

'Did you recognise her? From when you worked with Rob?'

Natasha shook her head. 'No, I don't think so. But then I wasn't there long. I don't remember everyone.'

Rob was home half an hour later, and he greeted Jen with a kiss and a smile. Natasha was still putting Ruby to bed. Jen could hear her reading her a story in her bedroom.

'Natasha's joining us for dinner,' Jen said.

'Oh right,' he said. 'Great.' Rob had always been as luke-warm about Natasha as she was about him. Jen wondered if it stemmed from when they worked together. Natasha would have been one in a long line of temps, whereas Rob had been in charge. Perhaps they'd never been able to let go of that power dynamic.

'And someone from your work dropped some papers off.'

'Papers?'

'Said you'd left them in the office.'

Rob tapped his briefcase. 'Oh, right,' he said. 'Of course. Where are they?'

'On the kitchen table,' she said.

He walked over to the table and picked up the folder. 'I'll put this on my desk and then get changed.'

As he walked towards the study, Natasha came out of Ruby's bedroom.

'Natasha!' he said. He leant forward to kiss her on the cheek. 'Nice to see you.'

Natasha blushed. 'It's good to see you too,' she said awkwardly.

Rob continued on to the study and Jen smiled at Natasha. She appreciated her making an effort with Rob, even if she knew she was only doing it for Jen's sake. Jen wanted them to get along. Maybe now Rob and Natasha weren't working together, they'd find some more common ground and they could all be friends.

TWELVE

FIVE MONTHS EARLIER

'Come into my office, Mia,' Rob said, and Mia's heart leapt to her throat. He was always so formal with her around the office these days, keen to make sure that no one had noticed their relationship. She wasn't convinced it was working. Her co-workers had never exactly warmed to her in the first place, but the whispers and snickering when she strode past them in the office seemed to be getting more frequent. Whether or not that was to do with Rob was unclear – she'd never quite got the hang of making friends.

'Sure,' she said, jumping up and following him through the door. 'What's up?' she asked as she closed the door behind her.

'I need to talk to you,' he said, and for a horrible moment Mia thought he might be about to end things between them.

'Oh?' she said, her voice small.

'Not here,' he said. 'Over lunch. I've booked a table for 1 p.m. At the Osteria. If you leave the office at 12.45, I'll leave five minutes later and see you there.'

'OK,' Mia said, her face spreading into a smile.

'Great,' Rob said, opening his office door and encouraging her out.

. . .

An hour later, Mia put on her coat and gloves and walked out of the office, deliberately keeping her head down as she passed Rob's closed office door. The weather had turned cold and as she walked down the street, she noticed the Christmas displays in the shop windows. Christmas had always made her feel sad, even when she was a child. Other people's families had seemed big and happy and fun, whereas hers had just been her and her mother, and a couple of token presents, never the ones she'd asked for.

When she got to the restaurant the waiter seated her near the back and she waited for Rob at the table, unfolding and refolding her napkin nervously. She didn't know what this was about. Rob had been more distant with her lately. He'd explained that it would look bad if people realised they were together. The others wouldn't understand that they had just fallen in love; they would think that he'd abused his power.

'Of course you haven't taken advantage of me,' Mia had said, shocked.

'I know. It just looks bad. I'm the boss and you...' he'd reached out across the table of the restaurant and tucked her hair behind her ear, '...well, you're very junior.'

Mia didn't like the new formality between them. In the office, her co-workers tended to ignore her, making their plans for evening drinks in front of her but never inviting her. She'd liked sharing secret glances with Rob, knowing that the others had no clue about what they were getting up to. It made her feel powerful. She was always waiting for the moment she could catch his eye, the shared looks between them. Now those looks were few and far between.

Eventually Rob rushed through the door of the restaurant ten minutes late, kissed her lightly on the cheek and sat down opposite her. Immediately, she could feel the electricity between them. She wanted to reach out and touch him, but he was busy calling the waiter over to order.

'You wanted to talk to me?' she said.

He grinned at her. 'Yes, I have a surprise for you.'

'You do?' Nervous excitement buzzed through Mia. 'What is it?'

'You know I'm going away for business after Christmas?'

She nodded. It was all everyone had been talking about in the office. In January, Rob was going to the Mediterranean to look for holiday homes for some of his biggest clients. He was acting as a middleman, speaking to the agents out there, looking at properties and trying to negotiate deals for his clients to add the properties to their portfolios. She had been working with Rob's PA, Grace, to contact the agents and book in viewings.

'Well,' Rob continued, 'I know your French is fluent. Grace has told me you've been the one speaking to the agents on the phone.'

'Yeah, it helps, growing up in France.'

'Well, I don't speak a word of French. I failed it at school. So I think I need you, Mia, on this business trip.' He was grinning at her, and she felt as if her heart was about to explode.

She thought of spending a week in the Mediterranean. It would be cold in January, but still magical. And it would be just the two of them, viewing huge houses overlooking the sea and then drinking champagne together in the evening before rolling into bed.

'I'd love to come,' Mia said, excitedly.

'That's brilliant,' he said, as the waiter came over with their drinks.

'Wow!' she said, giddily. She was on cloud nine and couldn't stop grinning. She wondered how she could possibly go back and work at her desk calmly after this.

'I can't wait to show you around,' he said, reaching across the table and squeezing her hand. 'I have a beautiful villa out there. But don't tell the others you're coming. I think everyone in the office wants to come on the trip. I've told them I'm going alone. I'll book your flights for you, and you'll still be paid, but I want you to tell everyone you're taking a week's holiday. Do you understand?'

'Of course,' she said, her eyes wide with excitement. She could almost feel the winter sun on her face already. The trip to the Med would be the start of their relationship deepening, becoming something more.

'Thanks,' he said. 'You'll love the villa. It will be too cold to use the pool at this time of year but it has a hot tub too and it's right by the sea. We'll have a brilliant time.'

'Wow,' Mia said, thinking of the two of them together out there, not having to hide their relationship. Spending every night together. 'I can't wait.'

She thought further ahead, imagining a future where they were in the Med together with all their children, a happy, blended family. It was the life she wanted, the life she dreamed of. And it finally felt like it might be within reach.

THIRTEEN

NOW

The estate agency summer party was in full swing, and Jen stood outside in the sun, sipping her wine, watching people mill around as she chatted to Rob's PA, Grace. The party was bigger than she remembered from previous years, with a couple of hundred people enjoying the free-flowing drinks. She hadn't been to the last party because Ruby had been so young, but this year she'd insisted on accompanying Rob. The parties were always fun, and it was good for her to have a night off from the children.

'I love working for Rob,' Grace was saying. 'He's such a good boss. Really kind and generous. I feel lucky.'

'I'm glad to hear that,' Jen said.

'You know he's presenting the company awards later? The MD has asked him to, as he's such a well-liked member of senior management.'

'He didn't mention it.' Jen looked across to where Rob was standing, propped up against the outdoor bar, chatting to a crowd of younger estate agents in cocktail dresses and suits.

'Rob's really popular with the younger ones,' Grace said. 'They all want to learn from him. He earnt double the commission of anyone in the company last year. It was mainly from the sale of all those flats in your apartment block. He just has a real knack for sales. They all want to be like him.'

'That's good,' Jen said, feeling a twinge of jealousy. She remembered when she and Rob had first started working as agents. They'd always been competing to see who could earn the most commission. Back then it had always been her who'd earnt more than him.

'I used to be an agent,' she said. 'But then the kids came along.' She shrugged, as if it didn't bother her.

'Oh, it must be lovely not to work. I have two kids, but I feel like I hardly see them in the week. I'm always rushing home to make sure I can pick them up from after-school club. Rob is such a good boss. He really understands that I need to see the kids every day. He always lets me leave at five on the dot. He thinks family is so important.'

Jen frowned, wishing Rob was as keen to get home to see his own children. She took a gulp of wine and looked around the room. Two years ago when she'd last come to the party, she'd known quite a few of the agents. But now everyone seemed to have left and been replaced by new, younger people. She caught the eye of a woman in her twenties in a bright red dress, queuing for the bar, and smiled. She was sure she recognised her from somewhere. The woman quickly looked away.

'It was such a shock when Rob was ill last week,' Grace was saying. 'So unlike him. I've never known him to miss a day of work. I got your email saying he was unwell, but he didn't tell us much, just said that you'd told him he needed to stay home and rest.'

'It was the nurse that said that,' Jen replied, quickly. 'He blacked out the night before. He was found unconscious and taken to A&E. We still don't know what happened.'

'Oh my god,' Grace said, her hand flying to her mouth. 'I

had no idea it was anything that serious. Do they think it's his heart?'

Jen shook her head. 'They didn't seem to know. Did you see him that day? Had he been drinking?'

'Not in the daytime,' Grace said. 'Like I said, I leave at five. I don't know about anything that might have happened after that.'

'I'm worried about him,' Jen said, thinking of her mother's sudden stroke. 'I tried to persuade him to go to see his GP. What if it is his heart, like you said?'

'It's probably not that,' Grace said, kindly. 'My mind jumps to the worst-case scenario sometimes. My brother died of a heart attack quite young. So it's the first thing I always think of.'

'I'll make sure he gets checked out,' Jen said firmly. 'Actually, I should go over and see him. I've hardly spoken to him all evening.'

Jen had hoped that tonight would be the chance for them to have a fun evening out together. But now Rob was more senior at the company, he seemed to always be surrounded by people who wanted his time and attention. As Jen nursed her now-warm glass of wine, she reminded herself that in just a week they'd be on their weekend away by the seaside. It would just be the two of them. She couldn't wait.

Later, Jen stood back in the evening sunshine and watched the awards ceremony. Her husband grinned as he presented the awards, leaning in to kiss the women on the cheek as he congratulated them, and shaking the men's hands. The ceremony seemed to go on forever, with Rob insisting on saying 'a few words' about each award winner, as well as all the others who he thought had done well in each category.

Finally it was the last award. *The Rising Star Award.*

'This one was a difficult choice for me,' Rob began. He

started to list the attributes of various young agents who were part of the team, showering praise on each one.

'Get on with it!' a drunken voice from the crowd shouted.

Jen looked at her watch. The party still had some time to run, but she didn't think she'd stay for the dancing. Rob would enjoy it more than her; he knew everyone. Jen was out of practice at staying up late, and she was looking forward to going home and sliding into her warm bed. Her mind started to wander. She hoped the children had been all right with the babysitter.

Rob was finishing his monologue. 'And now on to our Rising Star of the year. I'm sure you all know Lizzy. She's excelled in every area, but mostly in assisting me in selling the new flats in Riverview Apartments. Of course I helped out by buying the penthouse myself.' He laughed. 'But Lizzy has been tenacious in selling those flats, and it's really paid off. Thank you, Lizzy.' He smiled into the audience and the woman in the red dress who Jen had seen earlier climbed up the steps onto the stage to accept the plastic trophy. Suddenly Jen clocked where she knew her from. She was the woman who'd come to the house the other night with the papers for Rob. She almost hadn't recognised her all dressed up.

Rob kissed Lizzy on the cheek and then she held the award confidently in the air, to the cheers of the crowd. As she did so, her eyes met Jen's once more. She seemed to stare right at her as her expression changed from an elated smile to a worried frown. Lizzy's eyes dropped to the floor, and she quickly left the stage. It was hard to see clearly from where Jen was standing, but Jen could have sworn she was holding back tears.

FOURTEEN

FIVE MONTHS EARLIER

Mia watched as the others slowly left the office one by one, calling out 'Merry Christmas' to each other as they left. It was Christmas Eve, the last working day before the holiday, and she was sick of hearing how everyone else was going to spend the break with their families. No one had asked her what she was doing for Christmas, but if they had she would have told them she was spending it alone in her flat, and then visiting her mother for New Year.

It was 4 p.m. now, and dark outside. Christmas shoppers were walking by the window, umbrellas held up against the drizzle, determined to get the final bits and pieces before the big day.

The light was on in Rob's office and she knew he was still in there. Everyone else had left now and Mia had to keep waving her arms to keep the automatic lights on.

She supposed she should go home soon. She was planning to go by Marks and Spencer and pick up any reduced Christmas food to have for her lunch tomorrow. You could usually get lots of bargains if you left it this late; they were always overstocked on something.

She'd finish filing all the admin emails into folders and then she'd say goodbye to Rob and go. She knew he was spending Christmas with his children tomorrow. She understood that it was too early to introduce her to his kids, but she couldn't help feeling an aching longing to be there too, to be part of his family. Maybe next year they could all be together.

The door of Rob's office opened and he walked over to her desk.

'Still working?' he asked.

She nodded. 'Just finishing up a few bits and pieces before the break.'

'Good for you.' He glanced round the office, saw there was no one else in, then leant in to kiss her. She lost herself in him for a moment.

'I'll miss seeing you over Christmas,' she said.

'It won't be too long,' he said. 'We'll be in the Med soon, together.'

'I bet your kids are looking forward to tomorrow,' she said. Mia knew a little bit about his children. She'd found Rob's Facebook profile. It was private but his profile pictures were public and she'd clicked through them. They'd included two photos of his kids; one from a few years back and another from five years ago. She'd imagined his whole other life as a father, playing with his kids, taking them on day trips. She imagined herself being a part of their life, handing out packed lunches on trips to the seaside, wiping chocolate off dirty faces, hugging them close to her. She would try and be the best stepmother she could possibly be.

'The kids can't wait,' Rob said. 'They're still at an age where they believe in Santa. It will be magical.' He paused. 'Life as a single father can be tough though.'

'It must be,' she said. She thought of her own daughter. She was with her father on Christmas day too. Mia's heart ached

when she thought about it. She should have told Rob about her
daughter ages ago. She took a deep breath.

'I have a daughter, too,' she said.

'Oh?' he said, surprised.

'I'm so sorry,' she said, her stomach knotting. 'I know I
should have told you before, when you told me about your kids.'
She stared down at the floor, unsure what his reaction would be.

He reached out and took her hand. 'Don't worry about it,'
he said. 'How old is she?'

'She's five.'

'That's a wonderful age. You'll have a lovely Christmas
together.'

She felt tears running down her face and he reached for the
box of tissues on the desk, then came and crouched down beside
her, dabbing her eyes.

'What's wrong?' he asked. 'I don't understand.'

'It's just...' Mia didn't know how to explain. 'She's with her
father on Christmas Day,' she said finally. 'I'm going to miss her
so much.'

'Poor you,' he said, squeezing her shoulders. 'You'll miss her.
Of course you will. But it's only one day.'

'It's just so hard sometimes,' Mia said, her body shaking.
'I'm so sorry... I didn't mean to get upset.'

'Don't apologise,' Rob said, rubbing her shoulders. 'There's
no need.' Rob stroked her cheeks and then tenderly kissed her
on her forehead, soothing her.

'I bet you're an amazing mother. Your daughter is so lucky
to have you,' he said.

Mia sobbed harder. She'd been so nervous telling Rob about
her daughter. But he'd understood. She felt overwhelmed by
her love for him.

Rob went to the kitchen and got her a glass of water.

'Christmas is a hard time for single parents,' he said. 'I
understand.'

She nodded.

'Look,' he said. 'I have to get back now. But I don't want you to be alone when you're feeling like this. Why don't we go out and have one glass of wine to celebrate Christmas, before we go our separate ways?'

Mia nodded. 'That's just what I need,' she said.

Telling him about her daughter had felt like handing him the most fragile piece of her heart. Rob had treated it kindly; he hadn't broken her. And she was so grateful. As they walked towards the pub together, she reached for his gloved hand. She closed her eyes and for a moment let herself imagine that this was the beginning of their Christmas celebrations, that it was him and their children she was spending Christmas with tomorrow.

FIFTEEN

NOW

The kids squabbled in the back of the car as Rob and Jen sat in traffic on the motorway, travelling to see his parents on the south coast on Saturday afternoon. It was the end of the May half-term and Jen was exhausted from arranging new activities and playdates every day. They'd been to the London museums and the aquarium, explored local farms and woodland, and been swimming. Jen felt like she deserved her romantic getaway with Rob. She just hoped she didn't sleep through the whole thing.

They'd intended to set off for their weekend away in the morning, but just as they'd been about to leave the underground parking of their block, Rob had discovered they had a puncture, and by the time it was fixed they were two hours behind schedule.

When they finally pulled up outside Rob's parents' house, the kids were irritable and bored and Jen and Rob were losing patience with their arguing. As they got out of the car, the front door of the house opened.

'Hello!' Rob's mother exclaimed, holding out her arms as

Lottie and Jack ran into them. 'Gosh, you've both got even bigger. You'll be as tall as me soon, Lottie!'

Jen lifted Ruby out of her car seat and went to give her mother-in-law a hug. 'Good to see you.'

'Have the kids eaten?' her mother-in-law asked, as she leant over to pick up Ruby, smothering her in kisses.

'They had a late lunch at the service station, but they left most of it. I think they're hungry again.'

'OK,' Penny said. Jen followed her inside and Penny turned on the oven as Jen said hello to Rob's dad. 'I'll heat up some lasagne for them. I bet you'll be wanting to get away to your hotel. Just let me show you my garden first. The flowers are blooming.'

Her mother-in-law led Jen into the garden. There was a little path down to the sea at the end of it, which the children loved. Her in-laws had moved from West London eleven years ago, selling their big, detached house for a small fortune and using the money to buy this house by the sea, and the villa in the French Mediterranean, which the whole family used for holidays. Jen and Rob had gone on their honeymoon there, and now they went back every year in the summer holidays, with the kids.

'The garden looks beautiful,' Jen said, once they were outside. 'As always. You've always kept such a perfect home.' Jen remembered when she was a teenager, when Rob's house had been her sanctuary. She had always preferred his warm, comfortable, clean home to her chaotic one and she'd spent most of the summer holiday after she'd turned seventeen at his parents' house while they were at work. At that point, he'd been reluctant to introduce her to them because of her family's reputation. Everyone had known by then that Jen's dad was in prison.

They went back inside and found the kids in the kitchen. Lottie and Jack were spinning on the stools by the breakfast counter. Rob and his father were chatting in the sun-filled conservatory about the state of world politics.

'Lottie! Jack! Get down!' Jen said. She knew she would be blamed if they broke anything.

'I'll settle them down in the living room with a jigsaw puzzle,' Rob's mum said, 'and then we can sort out the dinner. Can you see if Rob and Hugh want a drink before you head off?'

Penny took the kids into the living room, while Jen got Rob and his father each a bottle of beer. It was always the way when she went to Rob's parents' house. Jen and his mother looked after the kids and cooked and cleaned while Rob and his dad relaxed. It was the way Rob had been brought up. Even though both his parents had worked, his mum had done everything around the house.

'How's it all going in your new place?' Penny asked Jen, as she prepared a salad to go with the lasagne.

'It's good,' Jen said, not wanting to tell Rob's mum about Ruby getting out of the balcony. She'd only worry.

'The kids seem happy.'

'They're glad to see you.'

'You're a good wife and mother, Jen,' Penny said softly. 'It must be harder, with your background. I can't imagine you had the best example from your own mother. But you've done well.'

'Thanks,' Jen said, not sure how to take the compliment. At the very beginning of her relationship with Rob, his mum had tried to stop them dating because of her background. The fact that it was forbidden had only fuelled their infatuation with each other. But once Penny had got to know Jen, they'd become close.

'You know Georgina is getting a divorce?' Penny asked. Georgina was Rob's sister.

'Rob mentioned it, yeah.' He'd been vague about the reasons why, but Jen had realised that her husband had cheated on her.

'You know, I'm really devastated. I don't know how she could do that. Just throw away her marriage like that. They've got kids! They need both their parents at home.'

'It's sad for them,' Jen said. 'But maybe it's for the best.' Georgina had a well-paying job, and could easily support her family without her husband.

Penny shook her head vigorously. 'I don't think so. Georgina's just being selfish. She needs to stick with him, understand the realities of a marriage. No marriage is perfect on its own. They take work. You need to look after your husband. I mean, look at you and Rob, he's taking you away for the weekend. You're both putting time and effort into your marriage.'

Jen smiled tightly. She didn't want to discuss her marriage with her mother-in-law. 'We'd better get going soon,' she said. 'We want to be there in time for dinner.'

'Men can be hard work,' Penny continued, as if Jen hadn't spoken. She looked out of the window into the garden. 'Hugh wasn't always faithful to me. But he worked hard. He provided everything I wanted. And I found that if I turned a blind eye, my life was a lot happier. None of it mattered really in the end. We're still together. And all his little flirtations fizzled out. None of that stuff is worth getting divorced over.'

Jen started to relax as she ate her dinner with Rob at the hotel's Michelin-starred restaurant. No one was making any demands of her or shouting 'Mummy'. It was finally just the two of them. After they'd eaten, they walked through the expansive grounds hand in hand, past an ornate fountain and down the path to the sea. They took off their shoes and held them as they crossed the sandy beach to the water's edge. The sea lapped over their bare feet as they walked on the wet sand, and Jen finally felt free. The light breeze lifted her hair, and she was grateful for the sun on her face. The hotel was in the middle of nowhere and they were the only ones on the beach.

'I'm so glad we got away,' Jen said. 'We needed this.'

'You're right,' Rob agreed, putting his arm around her waist. 'It's so good to be with you. And you've chosen the perfect hotel.'

Jen gazed out at the sea as they walked. For a moment she thought of Natasha, and the fears she'd voiced to her about her marriage that she didn't feel brave enough to say to Rob. If she trusted Natasha with her worries about married life, and not her own husband, what did that say about the state of their relationship? She looked over at him, the soft light shining on his windswept hair, and decided to take the plunge.

'Do you ever feel like we're drifting apart?' She looked away again, her pulse racing.

'No, not really. Do you?'

Jen felt dismissed, like he wasn't taking her concerns seriously. 'A little, maybe. Your time's taken up by work, mine's taken up by the kids, and it seems sometimes like our paths hardly cross.'

'We said we'd work on that, remember. That's why we're here.'

They came to a standstill and they both looked out at the horizon. Rob cupped Jen's face in his hands and he kissed her deeply. 'I love you.'

'I love you too,' Jen said, Penny's words still ringing in her ears. 'I don't have anything to worry about, do I? You haven't met someone else?'

'What makes you say that?'

'Just something your mum was saying. About Georgina's divorce. About how your dad cheated on her throughout their marriage.'

'I know he did,' Rob said, shaking his head in disapproval.

'He wasn't very secretive about it. But I'm not my father. I'd never cheat on you. You know that, don't you?'

Jen nodded. 'Of course. It's just—'

'Look, Jen. I know you, OK? I've known you since school. I know you didn't have the easiest childhood. And sometimes that can mean you find it difficult to trust men. But our marriage is our own. I'm not like your father. I'm not going to end up in prison. And I'm not my own father either. I'm not going cheat. You can trust me. You really can.'

'Of course,' she said. 'I'm sorry.' She knew he was right. She did find it difficult to trust. It was just her own anxiety making her think this way, nothing to do with him.

'This is supposed to be our time away together. It's supposed to be special.'

'I'm sorry,' she said again.

Rob grinned at her. 'Don't worry, you're forgiven. Now, do you want to go for a swim?'

She saw the look in his eye and started to run. But he was faster than her and he caught her and lifted her up easily. He paddled into the sea and she screamed with laughter as he held her over the waves fully dressed.

'Put me down, put me back on the shore!'

'If you say so,' he said. 'But only if you agree to come into the water with me.'

'OK!' Jen said. 'OK – you win. I agree.'

He placed her back on the beach, and started to strip off his clothes, his trousers already soaked to the knee. He had always had a good body, but looking at him now in the sunlight, Jen could appreciate the results of his work at the gym.

After looking behind her to check no one was about, she lifted her dress over her head, took off her underwear and chased him into the sea. Once they were submerged in the water, he embraced her, and she wrapped her body around him as his mouth met hers.

SIXTEEN

FIVE MONTHS EARLIER

Mia stretched out on the luxurious king-sized bed, her toes curling in happiness. The master bedroom of Rob's holiday home was just as spectacular as she'd imagined. They hadn't bothered drawing the curtains last night, and now she had woken up to the most amazing view of the sea beyond the windows.

She sighed contentedly. The first night in the Med with Rob had been better than she'd dreamed. He'd carried her straight to the bedroom and they'd spent the evening making love, before heading out to a local bistro to get dinner and then returning to the bedroom.

Now she could hear him humming to himself as he cooked sausages and eggs for breakfast.

She was so lucky to have a man like him. The office called him almost as soon as they got to the house, and Mia had had to fight back giggles as she heard him telling Grace not to worry, he wouldn't get too lonely. He needed some time to himself and he had a lot of work to do and deals to close.

They had a whole week ahead of them and Mia was determined to enjoy every minute. She eased herself out of bed, pulled a dress over her head and then wandered through the villa, her bare feet on the terracotta floor, peering into bedroom after bedroom. At the patio doors, she slipped her shoes and coat on and went outside, through the shaded barbecue area and past the hot tub. Rob had promised they'd get in later. She went down the steps to the swimming pool, covered up for the winter. She pictured her daughter here in the summer, splashing happily in the pool. She couldn't believe this was all Rob's. If things went well, the two of them would start a life together and all this would be hers, too. Finally, she'd leave the past behind and start her own life. The life she was always meant to have.

She continued down the path and across the garden to the clifftop. Looking down at the sea below, she felt a sense of freedom and power. Things were finally going her way.

A rustling sound behind her made her jump and she turned towards the land and took a step back. She didn't know why it had startled her, but she'd suddenly had the sense of someone behind her. There was no one there. She was just being paranoid. The sound came again and she realised it was just the breeze through the trees.

Turning back round to face the sea, she noticed she'd stepped dangerously close to the edge, and she took a quick breath as she backed away. All of this sneaking around was bad for her.

'Mia!' Rob shouted from the house, his voice carrying on the breeze. 'Your breakfast is ready.'

Feeling unsettled, she started walking quickly back towards the safety of the house.

SEVENTEEN

NOW

Jen woke naturally to the sunlight breaking through the crack in the curtains, and rolled over to see Rob beside her on his phone.

'What's the time?' she asked, stretching out her arms in the huge hotel bed.

'Eight thirty,' he said.

'Wow,' Jen said with a smile. 'I've slept all the way through the night. Without anyone waking me up. I feel so rested.'

Rob put down his phone and turned to face her. 'Me too,' he said. 'I feel completely refreshed.'

'We need to book our next trip away,' Jen said. 'It's not long until the kids' summer holidays. We'll have to book our annual trip to your parents' place in the Med. I've checked with your mum, the villa's free the first week of the school holidays. Have you booked the time off?'

'I haven't, but it won't be a problem. That time of year's always quiet. I'll just block the time out in my diary.'

Jen picked up her phone and browsed the flights to France. Four return British Airways flights would set them back £2,000 that week. Luckily Ruby was still young enough to sit on her lap. Jen showed Rob the price on her phone.

'Go ahead and book those,' he said. 'I'll transfer you the money now.'

'Thanks.' Jen waited for the notification to come through, and saw that the money was in her account. 'I'll book them later today.' She pulled Rob towards her, and drew him into a kiss. 'We've still got a few hours before we have to go and pick up the kids,' she said.

'Actually, I've booked in nine holes of golf,' Rob said, pulling away gently. 'I hope that's OK. One of the best courses in the UK is right next to the hotel. It was too good an opportunity to miss. I'm meeting an old friend there.'

'Oh,' Jen said, disappointed. She'd thought they'd spend the morning together.

'There's a spa at the hotel,' Rob said. 'I've booked you in for a massage.'

'Thanks,' Jen said. 'A massage sounds like a lovely end to the weekend.' She never got the chance to have one normally. But a part of her still wished they could just prioritise being together.

'Or you could always come and join the golf,' Rob said, with a cheeky grin.

Jen smiled. 'You know I'm rubbish at golf. I'd only embarrass you.'

'I'll be back in time for lunch,' Rob said, getting out of the bed and heading towards the shower. 'We can eat here and then go and collect the kids. Mum's messaged me to say they've had a great time.'

Jen felt love for her kids welling up inside her. Now she'd had a proper night's sleep, she couldn't wait to see them again and give them all a big hug.

'That sounds great,' she said. 'I'll relax at the spa while you're on the golf course. Make the most of our time here.'

. . .

Jen had her massage and then went for a swim, lying leisurely on the cushioned sunlounger afterwards and finally finishing the book she'd had on the go for over a month.

Once she was dressed, she went for a stroll around the hotel grounds. She passed the fountain and went through old stone arches, down to the gardens below, which led to the edge of the cliff. There was no one about and she felt a shiver pass through her as she looked out down to the sea below. She was beyond the area with the beach, and here the sea bashed angrily into the cliffs. It was a long way down. It reminded her of Rob's parents' villa in the Med. That was perched on a clifftop, too.

As she walked along the path she had the sense that she was being watched. But when she turned, all she could see were a few dog walkers and a young woman taking selfies, none of them looking her way. She wasn't sure why she was so on edge; she'd felt so relaxed in the spa. But something didn't feel right. It was like her body thought it was under threat; it was going into fight-or-flight mode, her heart beating faster, her muscles tense. It was probably just anxiety. Rob was right, she had felt anxious recently, worried about their relationship. And Ruby escaping from the balcony had really scared her. It had reminded her that life could change in an instant.

Thankfully they had the holiday in the Med to look forward to. The five of them all together, proper family time. She'd booked the flights before she went to the spa. Jen continued down the clifftop path and found herself walking along the edge of the golf course. She looked out for Rob, but couldn't see him. He'd probably finished his game by now; he'd be in the clubhouse.

She walked on until she found the clubhouse and went inside. She saw him standing in the corner of the room on his work phone, pacing up and down, a frown on his face as he spoke.

'I can't come and speak to you today,' he was saying. 'I'm not in London. I'll see you this week.'

He was silent for a moment.

'Look, I'll come round this week. We can talk then.'

She tapped him on the shoulder and he spun round.

'I have to go now,' he said down the phone. 'Bye.' He turned to Jen. 'How was your massage?'

'It was wonderful,' she said. 'What was your call about? It sounded stressful.'

'It was one of the owners of the apartments in our block, Richard. He's someone I sold a flat to.'

'Oh?'

'He just wanted my advice on a leak in his kitchen.'

'That doesn't sound good,' she said, thinking of all the problems there'd been with the apartment block.

'I know,' he said. 'Another teething problem. But it will be sorted as soon as I get back.'

Rob's phone started ringing again.

'Excuse me,' he said to Jen, as he looked down at the number. It was a number that wasn't stored in his phone.

'Hello,' Rob said, answering the phone. 'I'm afraid I'm busy. I'll have to call you back later.' He hung up.

'Sorry about that,' he said. 'More of the same. Another flat owner. Kevin this time. Not much I can do right now. We need to enjoy the end of our break from the kids. Shall we go to lunch?'

'Sure,' Jen said, frowning. She knew it hadn't been Kevin on the phone. The voice on the other end had definitely been female.

EIGHTEEN

FOUR MONTHS EARLIER

Mia stood in the corner of the boutique thumbing through the row of dresses. She needed to buy a new one for her dates with Rob; she'd come to rely too much on the two 'posh' dresses she had, which she recycled over and over, pairing them up with different layers and accessories in the hope he didn't notice. But looking at the price tags, she really couldn't afford anything. For the moment she'd just have to browse.

She ran her hand over the silky material of a midnight-blue dress, imagining accompanying Rob to a party in it. Their relationship was still a secret from everyone else in the office, but she was sure it wouldn't be long until it was out in the open. She understood his reticence about announcing anything too early. He hadn't introduced her to his kids, and until he did they had to take things slowly. When you had kids it was really important you waited until you were completely sure about a relationship before you introduced a new partner. Soon they'd be able to announce their relationship, and she'd be able to introduce his kids to her daughter and they could all be part of a happy blended family.

They'd only come back from their trip to the Med a few

weeks before, and that trip had made Mia even more sure than ever that they were made for each other. He seemed to understand her so deeply, in a way that no one else did. She'd been able to tell him everything about her past, about her daughter. All the secrets she'd kept buried inside her. She'd felt so ashamed, but he'd just listened to her, and accepted her for exactly who she was. He still loved her. And she loved him.

Mia pulled out the blue dress and held it against her figure, moving back and forth. She could tell it would fit perfectly. The cut was just right. Maybe Rob would buy it for her. As she looked in the mirror, she saw someone out of the corner of her eye and gasped in delight. As though she'd summoned him, Rob was there. It shouldn't have been a surprise. She was only a few hundred metres from his apartment block.

She turned towards him, smiling. He was on the other side of the shop window, accompanied by his children. And next to him was a woman with neat blonde hair, pointing at a dress in the window.

Mia stood frozen to the spot. He hadn't seen her. The woman was holding the handle of the buggy. She said something to Rob, and then he took the buggy from her. One look at their body language and Mia knew exactly who she was. She was his wife.

At that moment, Rob caught Mia's eye. He frowned at her, and started to steer his wife away from the shop. She protested for a moment, and then he must have made a joke because she laughed, the smile lighting up her face, and then took the children's hands and started to walk away with him. They looked every inch the happy family.

Mia felt like she might throw up. Her pulse raced. Rob had been lying to her. How could he? She'd trusted him, told him all her secrets, even told him about her daughter. How could he have betrayed her like this?

It wasn't fair. How could Jen have everything? Rob, her

happy little family. As Mia watched them walk away laughing and holding hands, all she wanted to do was run after them and rip them apart.

NINETEEN

NOW

It was raining when Jen arrived at the cat shelter, and she called out a cheery 'hello' as she walked through the office and out the back to where the cats were kept. She saw Amy kneeling down beside Coco, a pregnant tabby cat, stroking her softly.

'Coco's about to give birth,' Amy whispered. 'Natasha will be disappointed she missed this.'

'Where is she?' Jen asked, kneeling down beside Amy.

'Matilda's off school, sick, so she's stayed home.'

'How's Coco doing?'

'She's coping OK. She's having contractions.'

'Oh wow,' Jen said.

Amy continued to run her hand over the cat's fur, soothing her. 'She's doing so well.'

Jen nodded. 'Do you need my help?'

Amy shook her head. 'Not really, but you should stay nearby, to see the kittens.'

Jen started cleaning out a nearby litter tray.

'How was your weekend away?' Amy asked.

'It was good,' Jen said. 'Very relaxing. We needed to spend some time, just the two of us.' She thought of how Rob had spent the Sunday morning playing golf without her and the odd phone call he'd received in the golf clubhouse. Surely it had been nothing?

'I'm glad it went well,' Amy said.

Jen sighed. 'I still get worried sometimes. About our relationship. But I think I'm just paranoid. My own childhood wasn't the best. And now I just want the kids to have happy, stress-free lives.'

Amy nodded. 'That makes sense,' she said. Then her eyes widened. 'Oh my god – look! The kittens are coming.'

They watched as Coco pushed the first kitten out and then began to lick it clean.

'Wow, it's so tiny,' Jen marvelled.

'There are more coming,' Amy said. They both watched, entranced, as the cat continued to work to deliver her litter. An hour later, there were three little kittens, one tortoiseshell and the other two black.

'She's still contracting,' Amy said.

The cat pushed once more and a final kitten appeared, but this one wasn't moving.

'I'll call the vet,' Jen said nervously, picking up her phone, as she watched Coco vigorously lick the tiny kitten. It still wasn't moving. After a few minutes she seemed to give up, and she left it alone, her attention shifting to her other kittens.

Amy picked the tiny thing up and stroked it. 'It's not alright,' she said, her eyes wide. She bundled it into a towel and rubbed it again and again, anxiously trying to revive it. 'Come on,' she whispered. 'You can make it.' But its limp body didn't respond.

'It's not working,' she said, finally. Tears ran down her face. 'I think it's gone.'

'The vet will be here soon,' Jen said desperately. 'Maybe he can revive it.'

Amy shook her head, wiping her tears with the back of her hand. 'It's left us.'

'It's so sad to see,' Jen said, putting her arm round Amy. 'Poor Coco.'

'Just part of life, I suppose,' Amy said. Her body started to shake with sobs.

'Amy, what's wrong?'

'It just reminds me of when... when I gave birth. I lost the baby.'

'Oh Amy,' Jen said sympathetically, stroking Amy's back. 'When was that? What happened?'

'I was young. Only seventeen. The pregnancy was an accident. Not something I planned or wanted. I didn't know I was pregnant for ages. And then when I found out, it felt like a kind of punishment at first.'

'Punishment for what?'

'Seeing the wrong man, I suppose. He was a lot older than me and we'd always kept our relationship secret. We knew that others wouldn't approve, that they'd judge us. So at first I didn't want to be pregnant. But then I started to get used to the idea. I liked the idea of having a child who would love me unconditionally, simply for being me. I imagined buying things for her, playing with her, the two of us being a little team. Us against the world.'

'You poor thing,' Jen said, feeling choked up herself.

'I lost her just after she was born. And I had to put all those dreams aside. Just continue with my life as if nothing had happened, as if she'd never even existed.'

'I'm so sorry, Amy. I can't imagine what that would be like.'

'I still remember the last time I held my daughter,' Amy said, staring off into the distance.

'What was her name?' Jen asked gently.

'Gemma,' Amy said, stumbling over the name. 'Her name was Gemma.'

'Do you have any photos of her?'

'Not with me,' Amy said. 'I have them at home. I don't like to take them out. They feel too precious somehow. I don't want them just shoved inside my purse.'

'I'd love to see the photos sometime,' Jen said. 'If you ever feel like sharing them.'

Amy nodded. 'Maybe one day. I've never shown them to anyone before. They feel too personal.'

'I understand,' Jen said, squeezing Amy's hand.

'I can't believe I lost her,' Amy said softly.

'She'll always be with you,' Jen said. 'In your heart.'

'If I got pregnant now, I'd treasure every day of the pregnancy,' Amy said. 'I wouldn't take the life inside me for granted.'

'Do you think you'll have kids with Jonathan?' Jen said, realising Amy was trying to move the conversation on from Gemma.

Amy nodded. 'I hope so. I think I'd like three. Like you. Or perhaps even four.'

Jen squeezed her arm. 'I hope it works out for you,' she said.

'I want us to get married first,' Amy said. 'But if I got pregnant now, it wouldn't be a problem. I'd feel lucky.'

The vet arrived then, far too late. He picked up the tiny kitten and checked it over. 'I'm afraid this one hasn't made it,' he said. 'I'll leave it near its mother for now, so she has time to adjust. I'll just check over the others.'

He glanced up and saw Amy's tear-stained face. 'Why don't you two go and make yourselves coffee?' he said. 'I can take over here.'

In the kitchen, Jen made coffee for them both. 'I'm sorry I unburdened on you like that,' Amy said, as she took her mug from Jen. 'It was nice to have someone listening to me.'

'No problem at all,' Jen said. 'Any time.'

'Thanks,' Amy said. 'You know you can talk to me too, don't you?'

'Yeah,' Jen said, 'of course I do.'

Amy smiled. 'We'll always be there for each other,' she said.

Jen nodded. 'To friends,' she said softly, raising her mug at Amy.

That evening, Rob came home early with a bunch of flowers and a bottle of wine.

Jen smiled at him in surprise. 'I thought you had a client meeting today?' she said.

'Oh, it was cancelled. I thought I'd come home and help out. Do you want me to look after the kids?'

'I would love you to,' Jen said. Tomorrow he was leaving for a golf weekend and Jen liked the idea of having some time to herself before she spent the weekend ferrying the kids back and forth to their various activities.

She planted a kiss on Rob's cheek. 'I think I'm going to go for a swim,' she said. The small pool in the basement of the apartment block was ideal for an evening swim.

'I'll put the kids to bed,' he said, 'and then cook dinner.'

When Jen got to the pool area it was eerily quiet and the automatic lights flicked on as she walked down the corridor to the changing rooms. A solitary man swam up and down one side of the pool, and Jen eased herself in on the other side. The water ran smoothly over her body, and she put her face beneath the water and focused on her breathing, letting the stress of the day fade away.

When she got to the end of the first length she saw the man had got out of the water and she was alone. A few lengths later and he was gone completely, the lights in the changing rooms automatically switching off so that only the pool was lit up, with Jen in the middle of it. She kept swimming, back and forth, back and forth, relaxing as she concentrated on her stroke.

When she emerged at the end after twenty lengths, she

noticed the lights on in the women's changing room and prepared herself to be joined by someone else. She swam another length, then a few more, but still no one appeared. It must have just been a cleaner.

Jen got out and dived into the water, then swam along the bottom, seeing if she could get to the end holding her breath. She almost made it, coming out within a foot of the end, gasping for breath. She reached for the side, and looked up to see a pair of woman's legs, standing above the lane.

She jerked her head upwards, startled. The whole pool was free. Why had someone chosen to stand just there? They must have been waiting for her.

Above her she saw a tall woman, in a swimming cap and goggles, her hands on her hips. Jen's pulse raced. What did she want?

'Jen!' the woman said, loudly. 'I thought it was you.'

It look Jen a moment to recognise the voice, and then she relaxed.

'Oh, Natasha, hi! What are you doing here?' Jen had no idea how she'd got into the pool. It was only for residents.

'Rob lent me a spare keycard for the pool when I was over at your flat the other day,' Natasha said calmly. 'He said I could use it whenever I wanted. I think I'd just been moaning about not being able to afford a swim at that fancy gym of yours.'

'Oh right, I see,' Jen said. It was the kind of thing Rob would do. He always liked to be generous and share his things. And Jen had asked him to make more of an effort with Natasha. He was probably trying to get on her good side. For a moment, Jen felt guilty that she'd never thought of sharing her own keycard with her. 'We should swim together sometimes, then,' Jen said. 'Although I don't get the chance to come here often.'

'I only come when Matilda's with her dad,' Natasha said. 'It gives me a chance to clear my head.' She blushed.

Jen tried to conceal her surprise. Natasha used the pool more often than she did.

'And I love this pool, and this building,' Natasha continued. 'It's so quiet. You're so lucky to live here, Jen.'

Jen smiled. 'Sometimes I have to pinch myself,' she said.

'It's amazing,' Natasha said. 'I wish I could live here too.' She smiled. 'Maybe one day,' she said, before diving into the water and swimming off.

TWENTY

FOUR MONTHS EARLIER

Mia watched Jen as she came out of the gym with her daughter, Ruby. She was dressed in chic pale trousers and a bright patterned shirt, like Mia had seen in an old edition of *Vogue* she'd flicked through in the waiting room when she last went to the doctor's. Mia followed Jen at a distance as she walked along with Ruby in the pushchair, chatting to her daughter. Ten minutes later Jen and Ruby disappeared into the hairdresser's. Inside Jen talked happily to her stylist while another member of staff took Ruby off to a small play area.

Mia felt a twinge of jealousy. Jen really had a charmed life. She had the entire day to do whatever she wanted, all the while spending Rob's money. Mia would never be like that. She'd always paid her own way, ever since school. Always had a job. Even when she'd been trying to make it as an actor, she'd waitressed. Jen was lazy. She didn't deserve the life she had.

But Mia couldn't help but feel a grudging admiration. Jen had landed Rob. And for some strange reason, he'd stuck with her. Mia just had to work out why. Jen was older than Mia, and definitely heavier. But she had something about her; she was calm and organised and in control. Mia wished she could be more like her.

She knew she shouldn't be following Jen like this, but ever since she'd seen Rob out with her and their happy family, she couldn't stop thinking about her. At first she'd been shocked to see the two of them together, but the next day in the office, Rob had called her in to see him.

'I have something to tell you,' he'd said, and she could see the worry in his eyes. 'The situation with my wife is a bit complicated. The thing is, we still live together. Not as a married couple, but in the same place.'

Mia stared at him. She understood why he hadn't mentioned that before. She'd assumed 'separated' meant they lived in different homes. She thought of the perfect week she'd spent with him in the Med, the number of times he'd told her he loved her, how he hoped they'd always be together. Surely he wouldn't have taken her to his family's holiday home if it wasn't serious?

'What do you mean?'

'We're separated in the ways that matter. We don't have sex. The thing is, I fell out of love with her years ago. But she has mental health problems. She had a difficult childhood. Her father was in prison. It still affects her today. I just can't leave her. I don't know what she'd do if I did.' His eyes went dark, and he looked regretful. 'I'm trapped.'

When Mia had got home that day, she'd felt a visceral rage build inside her. It wasn't right that Jen got to keep him. She'd spent the evening googling Jen and Rob, finding out everything about them including all their previous addresses on the electoral roll and any social media profiles. She'd already studied all the publicly available information on Rob's Facebook profile in detail. Jen had Instagram and Facebook, but the Instagram account was hardly used, and showed pictures of places she'd been rather than people. Her Facebook account was completely private except for her profile pictures. Nine years ago, Jen had a wedding day picture as her profile photo, and each time the family had grown she'd updated her picture to include the new baby. Mia had found out the names of each of their children from the congratulations comments left under the photos. Rob's sister, Georgina, had an entirely open profile and she'd been through every photo, saving any that contained Rob. There was a photo of a barbecue with Jen and Rob in the background, where they appeared to be arguing, which she'd studied for ages, trying to guess how serious the argument had been from the severity of their frowns.

Even after all that, she didn't feel like she knew Jen at all, or understood why Rob had stayed with her. She wasn't sure she believed that she had mental health issues. So she'd decided to follow her. If she could just figure out what Jen had that she didn't then maybe she could change enough for Rob to leave Jen for her.

As she watched Jen in the hairdresser's from across the street, Mia realised how much she craved Jen's easy life. She never wanted for anything, never had to work. She had her children with her every day, and could spend every moment with them if she wanted. And Rob came home to her each evening. But Jen didn't appreciate any of it.

It was a life Mia wanted for herself. A life Mia deserved one hundred times more than Jen did. And she was going to make sure she got it.

TWENTY-ONE

NOW

It was Friday night, and Jen sat on her living room sofa opposite Natasha and Amy and helped herself to a big a slice of take-away pizza. She was glad to have a night off cooking, while Rob was away on his golf weekend with his clients.

'This has got to be my new favourite pizza place,' she said to Natasha. 'Thanks for recommending it.'

'No problem,' Natasha said, eyeing up the last pieces of pizza. 'Thanks for inviting us round. How long's Rob away for?'

'Until Monday. It's a business golf trip.'

Natasha raised her eyebrows. 'That sounds a bit more like play than work.'

Jen shrugged. 'It's all about entertaining the clients. Rob needs to make the right connections. These guys are foreign businessmen investing in the London property market. When they're over in the UK, they like to be shown around, treated like kings. And they like to play golf at the best courses.'

She saw Natasha and Amy exchange a look.

'What?' she asked.

'It's just that he's away a lot,' Amy said.

'It's just his job,' Jen said. She didn't want to think too hard about it. Her marriage meant everything to her. 'So what are everyone's plans for this weekend?' she asked brightly, changing the subject.

'I'm working,' Natasha said. 'Matilda's with her dad, so I've taken on a few extra shifts. How about you?'

'The usual,' Jen said. 'Taking the kids to their swimming and tennis lessons. Maybe a trip to one of the parks on Sunday.'

'I've got a date,' Amy said.

'Ooh, is this with your "future husband"? Natasha and Jen had always teased Amy about how much she liked Jonathan.

Amy blushed. 'Yep. We're going to the theatre, then staying at a hotel.'

'Sounds perfect,' Natasha said. 'I wish I was young again and life was exciting. I never date anymore. I feel like a shrivelled-up old maid.'

Jen looked at her, surprised. Natasha was naturally beautiful, with perfectly symmetrical features and shiny dark hair. The kind of woman everyone wished they looked like. She was sure she'd have a queue of interested men.

'You've never seemed interested in dating,' Jen said.

Natasha blushed. 'I guess it's just about finding the right person. It's hard to know if someone feels the same sometimes.' She met Jen's eyes, then looked away, and Jen got the hint of something deeper behind the words, something she wasn't willing to say.

Jen nodded. 'I get that. I was lucky to meet Rob so young.'

'How was your romantic weekend away?'

'It was brilliant,' Jen said, hesitating slightly.

'Jen?' Natasha said, noticing her hesitation.

Jen sighed and took a gulp of wine. She had been longing to get her friends' opinion on Rob, just to put her mind at rest. 'Something a bit strange did happen. He lied to me about a call he took. He said it was a man he'd sold a flat to, but I could hear the voice on the other end of the phone. It was a woman.'

'Oh Jen,' Natasha said, putting her hand on her knee. 'I'm sorry.'

'I don't think it means anything,' Jen said quickly. 'He's allowed to talk to other women.'

'But he lied about it,' Natasha said gently. 'Told you it was a man.'

'I guess it could be nothing,' Amy said. 'But it could be something... do you have any other reasons to be suspicious?'

'Not really,' Jen said. She thought of her conversation with Rob on the beach, how he'd told her she was just anxious.

'Not really?' Natasha said. 'What about him disappearing the other week?'

'He'd blacked out. He was in A&E!' Jen said.

'He does work away a lot,' Amy said. 'If he wanted to cheat, he'd have the opportunity.'

Jen put her head in her hands and pressed on her temples. She felt so disloyal talking about Rob in this way. 'He told me he hasn't cheated,' she said.

'You asked him?' Natasha said, incredulous.

'Yes.'

'So you must have suspected something.'

'Not really. I—' It was hard to explain how she felt. It wasn't like she suspected something specific, more that things didn't feel quite right between her and Rob. It felt like they were drifting away from each other.

'I have to believe him, don't I?' she said. 'I have to trust him, he's my husband.'

'You could check up on him,' Amy said suddenly.

'You could check his phone,' Natasha said, warming to the theme. 'See if there are any more messages between him and another woman.'

'He has his phones with him. Both his work phone and his personal phone.'

'What about his laptop?' Amy asked. 'Is it here?'

'It's in his study.' Jen took another sip of her drink. As much as she thought she shouldn't snoop around in Rob's study, there was a part of her that desperately wanted to check. She'd been feeling so insecure recently. She just wanted to be sure he wasn't lying to her.

'Right,' Amy said, getting up from the sofa. 'Let's have a look. That might give you some answers.'

'I don't have his email passwords,' Jen objected.

'He might already be logged in,' Amy said.

Natasha giggled tipsily and followed Amy into the study. Jen came in reluctantly behind them, trying to suppress her guilt about hacking into her husband's emails. She was sure they would never get in, anyway. The whole thing was pointless.

Jen watched as Amy and Natasha attempted to guess the password to get into the computer.

'You're going to get him locked out,' Jen said. 'Stop. He'll know I've been trying to get in.'

'Hmm...' Amy said. 'I did a degree in computer science. I think I know a way round this. Hang on a sec. Let me just take the account details. I need his email address. And then I just need to check something on my phone.'

Amy went to get her phone from the living room.

'I'm just looking up how to do it,' she called out. 'It's a bit complicated.'

'She doesn't know how to do it,' Natasha whispered to Jen. 'She's just trying to impress you.'

'Look,' Jen said, trying to calm things down. 'I don't think we need to do this at all – I can just speak to Rob myself. I don't think I should read his private emails.'

Suddenly Amy was back. 'I've figured it out,' she said. 'Pass me the laptop.'

Natasha passed it over, and Amy sat down on the floor

against the wall and stared at the screen intently as she typed and clicked.

'I'm in!' she said excitedly, a couple of minutes later.

Jen swallowed.

'Why don't you have a look?' Amy said as she handed the computer to Jen. Jen took it over to the sofa in the living room and sat down, her curiosity and her guilt fighting each other. She knew she shouldn't look through Rob's emails, but she couldn't help opening them up. She wasn't expecting to find anything. It wouldn't hurt if she just had a quick look.

As Rob's email account loaded, a new email came through. It didn't have a subject and the sender's email address was just a combination of letters and numbers which meant nothing to Jen. It was probably junk.

Jen clicked on it.

Then her hand flew to her mouth as she gasped in shock, hardly able to comprehend the words on the screen in front of her. She read them over and over, trying to understand.

Just a reminder that I love you! I'm so excited for us to be together for good. When are you going to tell your wife? I can't wait for you to be rid of her!! xxxxxxx

TWENTY-TWO

Jen stared at the email, the words blurring in front of her eyes.

I'm so excited for us to be together for good. When are you going to tell your wife?

She couldn't be reading it right. It wasn't what it looked like.

But she couldn't ignore it. The words were there in black and white.

'Is everything alright?' Amy said, her voice breaking through Jen's thoughts. 'You've gone pale.'

Jen moved her hand across the screen. She couldn't have them witnessing her humiliation. It was too much.

'What is it, Jen?' Natasha said softly, squeezing onto the sofa beside her. 'Show me.'

Jen didn't know whether to cry or scream. 'It was what you thought,' she said to Natasha. 'He's been cheating on me.'

'What?' Amy said. 'Is there an email? What does it say?'

Jen realised there was no point in hiding it from them. She uncovered the screen.

'Oh my god,' Amy said. 'That's awful.'

Jen looked at the message again.

Just a reminder that I love you! I'm so excited for us to be together for good...

'Just a reminder'. As if their love was so normal, so much a part of their everyday lives that they needed to be reminded of it.

She had never thought that Rob would cheat on her. He wasn't always completely honest, she knew that. He'd always stretched the truth at work, exaggerated things to sell properties. But she'd always thought his lies were for other people. Not for her.

They were a team. They took on the world together. They had both always done what was best for their partnership. She'd sacrificed her career for him. How could he have betrayed her like this?

'I'm so sorry, Jen,' Natasha said, putting her arm around her. 'This is horrible. I know it is.' Natasha had told her before how painful her split from Matilda's dad had been. How difficult it had been for her to make ends meet after her break-up. And now she had to share custody of Matilda, facing some weekends completely alone without her child. Jen didn't want the same thing to happen to her. It couldn't be happening to her.

'Poor you,' Amy said. 'I can't imagine how this feels.' She reached for the prosecco bottle and topped up Jen's glass. 'It's a lot to take in.'

'I don't know how he could do this to me. I thought he loved me.' Jen burst into angry tears. She'd planned her whole life around him. She'd stopped working, become dependent on him. And it was all for nothing. She had counted on his loyalty. But she didn't even have that.

She gulped down the prosecco and Amy topped up her glass once more.

'What am I going to do?' she asked. The alcohol was coursing through her body and she wasn't thinking straight. She felt drunk and disorientated. 'I never thought he'd do this.'

'It's alright,' Natasha said firmly, squeezing her shoulder. 'We can help you.'

'I was so stupid to trust him.'

'Of course you're not stupid. He married you. He promised to stay with you. He's let you down.' Natasha stroked her arm. 'Look, I know it feels like the end of the world right now, but it doesn't have to be.'

'Natasha's right,' Amy said. 'You can start again.'

Jen shook her head. 'I've been with Rob since I was seventeen. He's all I've ever known. We have three kids. I can't just start again.'

'Maybe we're getting ahead of ourselves,' Natasha said. 'The first thing we've got to work out is what you're going to say to him.'

'What do you mean?' Jen said. When she thought of Rob, all she could imagine was screaming at him. He had let her down so spectacularly. But a part of her desperately wanted him to tell her it was all a mistake, that there was some kind of innocent explanation.

'Maybe the email went to the wrong person?' Jen said feebly.

'It went to his work address,' Natasha said.

'I don't think someone would have got that wrong,' Amy said gently, reaching out and stroking Jen's back. 'I'm so sorry.'

Jen's mind spun. She wondered what this woman must be like for Rob to choose her over Jen. Was she younger? Better dressed? Sexier? Cleverer than Jen? Did she have a better career?

Jen couldn't help thinking of all the ways she felt she was lacking.

'Maybe I'm not good enough for him,' she said. It was what she'd always thought when she was a teenager. They had always seemed mismatched. Jen with her run-down flat and a father in prison and Rob with his big, detached house and attentive parents. It had never made sense, him choosing her. Maybe he'd finally realised. This charmed life wasn't for her.

'Of course you're good enough. He's just an idiot,' Natasha said.

'What should I do?' Jen asked. 'Should I call him?' She imagined interrupting his evening drinks at the golf club, screaming down the phone at him.

'No,' Natasha said firmly. 'First you need to gather as much information as possible, see where you stand. Is there anything else in his emails?'

Jen glanced down at Rob's laptop in her hands. 'I don't think I want to see any more.'

'I'll have a look,' Amy said. 'If you don't want to.'

'OK,' Jen said, cringing at the thought of the lies in her marriage being exposed. But she handed the laptop to Amy.

Amy scrolled through the messages. 'There're a few other messages between them,' she said.

'What do they say?'

Amy frowned. 'Just more of the same. This has been going on a long time.'

'How could he?' Jen whispered. She felt tears welling up in her eyes as she thought of her children sleeping in their bedrooms across the hallway. How could he be willing to tear their family apart?

'We had such a lovely trip away. I don't understand.'

'She called him on the trip away, though, didn't she? This woman...' Natasha said.

'I think she must have done,' Jen admitted. 'But he said he loved me. I even asked him about an affair when we were away. He told me I was just anxious. This can't be right. And we've got our trip to the Med coming up soon. How are we going to go and pretend that everything's fine?'

'You don't have to go,' Natasha said. 'If you don't want to.'

'But I do want to go,' Jen said. 'I'm not losing out on my

holiday because of him. I'm looking forward to it. If anyone's not going, it should be him.'

'You're right,' Natasha said. 'You should tell him he can't come. But will you really be able to cope on your own? Isn't it in the middle of nowhere? It might be a bit depressing, just you and the kids.'

Jen's mind was spinning. Natasha was right.

'Why don't we come with you?' Amy said suddenly. 'We could make it a girls' holiday instead. Really enjoy ourselves. And me and Natasha could help with the children.'

'That's a great idea,' Natasha said. 'We could all go and have a brilliant time. That would show him.' Natasha slurred her words slightly.

'Yes,' Jen said, suddenly feeling a bit brighter. 'That would be amazing.' She imagined the three of them sitting on the terrace in the sun, toasting her freedom.

Amy was scrolling on her phone. 'What date are you going again?'

'Twenty-seventh of July. First week of the school holidays.'

'My ex has Matilda that week,' Natasha said. 'I'm free as a bird.'

'Where are you flying into?' Amy asked. 'There are some totally bargain flights to Marseille at the moment. They're only £50 each return. Flying out on the twenty-eighth.'

'We always fly to Nice airport,' Jen said. 'But you can drive from Marseille.'

'Book them,' Natasha said, giggling. 'Just book them.'

Amy nodded. 'It would be silly not to.' She laughed. 'But I think I'm probably at my credit card limit.'

'I'll pay,' Natasha said. She handed her card to Amy. 'I really need a holiday. And this will be a bargain. Plus we'll all have loads of fun together.'

Jen smiled at her friends. She was lucky they were so

supportive. She giggled drunkenly. The room was spinning, but she was starting to feel better about things.

'Have you booked?' she asked.

'Yes,' Amy said, grinning. 'All booked.'

Jen raised her glass, alcohol slopping over the edge and onto her cream sofa. She didn't care anymore. 'Here's to us,' she said. 'To friends.'

'To friends,' the other two said, as they clinked their glasses against hers.

TWENTY-THREE

THREE MONTHS EARLIER

Mia sat in the coffee shop next to Rob's apartment block, mentally preparing herself for her job interview. It had been nearly a week since she'd left the estate agents. The woman she was covering was coming back from maternity leave and they no longer needed her. Rob had done everything he could to try and find her another role in the company, but there were no vacancies.

She sipped the bottle of water she'd bought as she looked out of the window at the people passing by. It had been the cheapest thing she could find in the shop, but it was still £3, and she'd felt resentful as she handed over the money.

She'd been spending too much recently. After her temping contract at Rob's office had finished, she'd been at a loose end in the daytime and had taken a luxurious trip to the same hairdresser that she'd seen Jen go to. She'd watched as the hairdresser cut off her long dark locks, leaving her hair shoulder-length, before dyeing it the same shade of blonde as Jen.

Since leaving the estate agency she'd applied for every job she could find that was office-based, but she'd had no responses yet and the temp agency didn't have anything local on their books.

She'd been shocked when she'd seen this job advertised online. At first she couldn't believe it, and had to read it twice:

Receptionist required for upmarket apartment block in West London

Customer service experience a must

Would suit someone presentable and hard-working

Immediate start

Please email dominic@riverviewapartments.com

Riverview Apartments was where Rob lived. It would be perfect. She'd still be able to see him. She thought back to last week when they'd sneaked out together on their lunch break to a huge empty manor house that they had been instructed to sell, and made love in the rainforest shower. It wouldn't be as easy to coordinate their dates now she wasn't in the office, but at least if she worked in Rob's apartment block, she'd be near him. She just needed to get the job.

Mia had remembered that all the documents associated with the building and Rob's purchase of the penthouse were in his emails. She'd been given access when she'd filled in for Grace, when she was away. At the weekend, she'd gone through everything, including the glossy brochures advertising the apartments and the architectural plans for the building. She felt she knew everything there was to know about the block.

Now it was time to go in and show them that she was perfect for the job. She smoothed her navy pencil skirt, checked her make-up in her compact and stood up. Head held high, she left the coffee shop and strolled confidently into the apartment block reception next door.

'I'm here for a job interview,' she said to the woman behind the desk.

'And your name is?'

'Amelia,' she said. 'Amelia Harrison.'

When she'd come to London she'd shortened her name to Mia, as she thought it sounded more cosmopolitan, a better name for an actor. But now it was time for a fresh start. She smiled warmly. 'But please, call me Amy.'

TWENTY-FOUR

NOW

'Mummy! Mummy!'

Jen rolled over in bed and opened her eyes slowly, her head pounding.

It took a moment before she realised Jack was calling her from his bedroom.

'Mummy – is it morning?'

Jen lifted her phone from the bedside table. It was 7 a.m. She knew she should get up but she couldn't face dragging herself out of bed straight away. She'd had far too much to drink last night.

'It's not morning yet, Jack,' she shouted, and closed her eyes again.

There was a stirring from the floor. 'I'll go and see him,' Amy said, from an air bed they must have pumped up last night. Jen could vaguely remember insisting that Amy shouldn't sleep on the sofa, that it was too uncomfortable. She remembered them drunkenly trying to fit the air pump into the air bed, giggling hysterically.

'Thanks,' Jen mumbled, as Amy left the room.

She rolled back over and saw Natasha sprawled over the bed beside her, still fully dressed.

Jen's head hurt as everything from last night came back to her.

The emails. Rob. Another woman.

In the cold light of day, it was hard to believe that it was possible.

But she knew she hadn't imagined it. Now she just wanted to hide away, not accept that it was true.

Jen could hear Amy getting the kids their breakfast in the kitchen and she forced herself up and into the shower. She was so grateful to have her friends around today to help. She didn't think she could have faced the kids alone. As the hot water ran over her, she wished she could wash away everything that had happened last night. A part of her wished she'd never seen the email, never had to face the truth. She could have just continued to live in blissful ignorance.

Her brain whirred with the effort of putting together the pieces of what happened last night. She remembered lying in bed when the others had dropped off to sleep, writing a long message to Rob, calling him a lying bastard, asking who the woman was, asking if she, Jen, wasn't good enough for him. She'd typed the message through tears.

Jen jumped out of the shower, grabbed a towel and checked her phone. As soon as she opened her messages she saw a garbled stream of autocorrected and misspelled words she'd sent to Rob in the middle of the night.

Oh god. She'd done exactly the thing Natasha had told her not to do. She'd contacted Rob before she'd had time to think things through.

He'd tried to call her while she was in the shower. He was calling again now. Jen's stomach dropped.

Natasha rolled over in the bed beside her. 'Your phone's ringing,' she said.

'It's Rob,' Jen said, picking up the phone.

'Don't answer it!' she said, jumping up and taking the phone out of Jen's hand. 'Don't speak to him until you've had something to eat and time to think.'

'OK,' Jen said uncertainly.

'God, my head hurts,' Natasha said.

'I think we had a lot to drink.'

'What do you have for breakfast?'

'Not much, just toast. And kids' cereal, if you fancy that.'

Jen's phone beeped with a message.

I'm on my way home. We can talk then. I love you.

Half an hour later, Amy and Natasha had finished their toast and the kids were settled in front of the TV.

'I've got to take them to their tennis lesson in an hour,' Jen said miserably. 'And I guess I should tidy up before Rob gets back.'

Natasha looked at her like she was crazy. 'Why would you do anything for him?'

Jen surveyed the empty wine bottles and pizza boxes on the floor of the living room. 'It's for the kids as much as Rob,' she said.

'I'll help you,' Amy said, 'and then I've got to get going.'

'What time's Rob back?' Natasha asked. 'Do you want me to stay?'

'He shouldn't be too long,' Jen said. 'But I don't need you to stick around. We should talk in private.'

'Are you sure?' Natasha asked.

'Yeah, go home and enjoy your day.'

'Actually, I've got work,' Natasha said. 'But I'm happy to pull a sickie if you need me to.'

'I'm fine,' Jen said. 'Really. And thanks for everything.'

'No problem.' Natasha got up and put her shoes on. 'I'd better go back and get changed. I'll message you the name and number of my divorce lawyer later.'

Half an hour later Amy left too, and Jen sat down at the kitchen table and looked around her perfectly designed penthouse, the sun streaming through the floor-to-ceiling windows. Soon she would lose all of this. She knew neither of them could afford to keep the penthouse if they split up. They were mortgaged up to the hilt as it was. They'd both have to move somewhere smaller.

She heard the key in the lock and jumped up from the table. Most of the mess from the night before had gone, but the house wasn't anywhere near as clean and tidy as normal.

Rob came through the door, dressed in smart chinos and a pale blue polo shirt.

'Jen,' he said. 'What's going on? You sent me an incomprehensible message in the middle of the night. Were you drunk? I was so worried. I had to come back.'

She looked at Rob, trying to reconcile what he had done with the man standing before her. The world had shifted beneath her feet since he'd left the penthouse yesterday morning. Now, when she looked at him, she felt like she was looking at someone she hardly knew at all, almost a stranger.

She swallowed. 'I found emails,' she said, trying to keep her tone neutral and stop the well of emotion bubbling up inside her. 'Between you and another woman. She sent you an email last night, telling you she loved you. Asking when you were going to tell me about the two of you.'

Rob reached out to touch her. 'It's not what it looked like,' he said.

Jen recoiled. 'What do you mean? What else can it be?' Jen's voice got louder, and out of the corner of her eye she saw

Lottie glancing over at them from the sofa. She'd always promised herself she'd never fight with Rob in front of the children. Her childhood home had been full of arguments and fights. She wanted theirs to be different.

'Let's talk about this in the bedroom,' she said.

She double-checked the children were OK in front of the TV, strapped Ruby into her Jumperoo, checked the balcony was locked and then went with Rob into the bedroom, leaving the door slightly ajar so she could listen out.

'I can't believe you'd do this to me,' Jen said. 'I loved you. I gave you everything I had to give, without a second thought... I've always put what you wanted first. Your career. Your life.'

'Look, Jen, just let me explain about the email. There's this girl. Very young, who used to work with me. A very naive young girl. And she's got a huge crush on me. Sends me these messages saying we're meant to be together. She's completely obsessed. But it's not reciprocated at all. It's completely one-sided.'

'But—' Jen's mind spun. There was more, she was sure of it. The perfume on his shirt, the call he'd picked up from the unknown woman when they were on their romantic weekend break. 'I don't believe you,' she said.

Rob sighed. 'What's this about, Jen? Because you know that I love you. I thought we were happily married. But lately it's like you've convinced yourself something is wrong. And to be honest, it makes me worried about you. It makes me question whether you're OK. Maybe the stress of having three young kids is getting to you.'

Jen frowned. 'It's not that,' she said. She put her hands to her head. Her hangover was raging. She wished she hadn't had so much to drink last night. She thought of the number Natasha was sending her for the divorce lawyer. How sure they'd all been last night that Rob was cheating on her. Could they have got it wrong?

'Do you want to throw away everything we've built together?' Rob asked.

'No,' Jen said. 'But—' She thought of the family life they had together. The children were settled and happy. She didn't want to take that away from them. They'd made so many plans as a family. They were throwing a birthday party for Lottie next weekend, and they were due to go on holiday to the Med soon. So much of her wanted to bury her head in the sand and pretend everything was OK, but her instinct said it wasn't.

Rob wrapped his arms around her, and started to kiss her forehead with light, feathery kisses.

'Get off me,' she said, pushing him away.

She needed time to think. She looked at her watch. 'Lottie and Jack need to leave for their tennis lessons,' she said. 'Why don't you take them? Take Ruby with you. She can watch.'

'OK, sure,' Rob said. 'If that's what you need.'

Jen nodded. She needed space so she could work out what on earth she was going to do. Her head was spinning. She'd been so sure that Rob had betrayed her, but now his words had confused her. Was it possible he'd been telling the truth about an obsessed young woman? Should she trust him, or was he lying through his teeth?

TWENTY-FIVE

Amy walked slowly back to her flat, appreciating the feel of the pavement beneath her feet and the bright morning sunshine. Unlike Jen and Natasha, she wasn't hungover, and she felt fresh and ready for the day ahead. Today was the start of something. A new beginning. Not just for her; for all of them.

Now Jen knew the truth about Rob, she would finally realise that he didn't love her and she'd leave him. Even Jen had admitted things had been bad between them lately. It was clear they weren't the right fit for each other. Amy was just helping Jen see that. Of course it would be hard for Jen at first. But Amy was sure she'd soon accept things. After all, they were well off – she'd have enough money for her own place.

And then, in a couple of months, Amy could move in with Rob, and they'd be together, like he'd promised. Amy hoped Jen would accept their relationship. She genuinely liked Jen. She'd become one of her closest friends. And she had always seemed reasonable. She would understand that Amy and Rob were soulmates. It might just take a bit of time. Once she got used to it, Amy knew she'd be happy. She was sure she'd quickly meet someone else who could love her in a way that Rob just couldn't anymore.

Amy had enjoyed making the kids' breakfast this morning, as Lottie and Jack happily chatted away to her. Once Jen found out about her and Rob, she would know she'd make a good step-mum. In fact, once Jen had fully accepted that she and Rob were over, she would probably be pleased that he was with Amy, rather than a stranger.

Amy smiled at the thought of their family holiday to the Med. She'd be there too. By then Rob and Jen would have split and it would give them the chance to all be together, to start life as a blended family.

Amy thought wistfully of the future, imagining her, Rob and Jen sitting round the dining table in the penthouse at Christmas with their children, a beautifully decorated Christmas tree behind them. She'd never had a proper family Christmas before. It had always been just her and her mum, and she'd always got the impression that her mum was counting down the hours until she could send Amy back to boarding school. Once she had even spent Christmas with her teachers, Mr and Mrs Beddow, as her mother had decided to go to America for Christmas without her. That had been the first time that Christmas had felt really magical and special. They'd treated her like royalty, buying her lots of presents, and she'd helped them make the Christmas dinner.

Amy thought of her daughter, Gemma. Christmas had been painful without her by Amy's side. She was still living with her father in France, but if Amy had a stable home in the UK, maybe he would split custody. Amy's heart leapt at the thought. Next Christmas it would be different; Gemma might be with her.

Amy smiled as she opened the door to her flat. She'd done the right thing, showing Jen that email. Rob had needed pushing along to cut the cord with his wife. Now she and Rob could finally get started on their future together.

TWENTY-SIX

As soon as Rob left with the kids, Jen went straight to his study. She needed to clear her head, look for any information she could get her hands on, and work out what to do. Despite what Rob had said about an obsessive stalker, Jen knew in her heart that he must be cheating on her. There was only one way to read that email. And there'd been so many signs; all the late-night dinners, the work nights away, the smell of another woman's perfume on his shirt.

Suddenly the future flashed before Jen's eyes. Neither of them could afford to live in the penthouse alone. They'd have to sell it, split the money and each buy their own place. Assuming she was entitled to half. She knew the penthouse was entirely in Rob's name. Something to do with the contract he'd signed, directly with the builders.

Natasha was right. She needed to work out what money she was entitled to from Rob before she told him she wanted to split up. She should have done it before she'd confronted him about the affair. Rob had always controlled their bank accounts, only giving her money if she asked for something specific. She had no idea if they had any savings. The only money she could access was the kids' university funds, but she wouldn't dream of touching those.

Jen started going through the drawers in the desk in Rob's study. She felt a fresh surge of fury wash through her as she thought of the other woman. She'd ruined everything. Who was she?

Suddenly it came to her. Lizzy. The woman from his office he'd given an award to at the office party. She'd been giving Jen strange looks that night. It must be her. She saw him every day at work. It would be easy for them to have an affair, without Jen having a clue.

Jen thought of the time she'd come round to the penthouse to drop a folder off. She must have been checking up on Rob, seeing what her competition looked like. Jen smiled to herself. Clearly Lizzy had no idea that Rob would pretend she was just an obsessed admirer who meant nothing to him.

Jen riffled through the drawers, looking for the purple folder Lizzy had dropped round. She'd said it was work-related, but what if it wasn't? What if it contained mementos of their relationship; hotel receipts and love notes? What if Lizzy had wanted Jen to see what was in it?

The folder was at the bottom of the middle drawer. Opening it up, she pulled out a pile of papers. When she flicked through them, they were all to do with the sale of the penthouse: the deeds, safety certificates and details of the sale.

Jen sighed and went through the other drawers. They were full of council tax bills, energy bills, printer cartridges and paper. Nothing interesting. No bank statements.

She wasn't giving up. She went to the hallway and felt through the pockets of Rob's coat. There were multiple receipts for meals at expensive restaurants, but they didn't necessarily mean anything. Rob took a lot of clients out to dinner. The final receipt was from a jewellers, dated two months ago, for a necklace that Jen had never received. Clearly for Lizzy, not Jen.

Jen's heart sank. This was it – the proof. Rob wasn't the man she thought she'd married. She felt sick. But they couldn't split just yet. She needed to get her affairs in order first. Besides, Lottie's birthday party was next weekend. Lottie had chosen her cake and invited her whole class. Jen wouldn't let anyone ruin it for her. If Rob left now, Lottie and Jack would be devastated. Even if he still came to the party, the upset it would cause would completely overshadow the day.

After the birthday party, she'd tell Rob to leave. It was the only solution. She didn't want to uproot the kids from their home. He would have to move out.

Jen knew she was mentally stronger than Rob. Her dad had been in prison and she'd grown up in an unstable, violent home. She'd had to become hard. And although she'd softened over the years, underneath it all she was still strong. If it came to a battle between her and Rob, she knew she would win. But in the meantime, she would pretend to be a perfect wife while she got everything in order. Then she'd take him by surprise.

TWENTY-SEVEN

The following weekend, Jen was at the health club where they'd hired part of the garden to host Lottie's party. When Rob had got back from taking the children to their tennis lesson last weekend, she'd pretended she'd believed him about his obsessive stalker, made out everything was fine. Then she'd spent the week looking into his finances. She hadn't found any evidence of savings, just an unimaginably huge mortgage. The stress of it all was starting to affect her and she hadn't been able to sleep without a double dose of her mother's pills. Her brain felt foggy, but she knew she had to keep putting on the show of a happy family. At least for today. For Lottie.

Everything was set up and ready for the party. Rob's parents had driven up that morning and Jen had put the party bags together with Rob's mum. Jack was jumping up and down crazily on the bouncy castle, while Lottie attempted to cartwheel across it. Beside the castle, there was a pink and white balloon display, spelling out 'Lottie'. At her daughter's request there was also a nail technician sitting by, waiting for the kids to arrive, so she could paint their nails, like they had at one of Lottie's classmate's parties.

The sun shone through the trees, and Jen could already feel a film of sweat forming on her skin. Lottie was lucky to have a summer birthday. The weather was usually good, and in previous years they'd always had her birthday party in the garden of their house. This year that hadn't been an option, and she'd been glad the health club did birthday parties.

Jen took lots of photos of Lottie, Jack and Ruby all dressed up. She wanted to make happy memories today, that her kids could look back on. The day was bittersweet; she felt like this was the last time they would all be happy together. She knew she would tear their lives apart by splitting up with Rob.

The parents started to arrive with their children, who handed over their gifts and then ran to the bouncy castle. Natasha appeared with Matilda shortly after the party had started, and Jen felt a wave of relief. She always felt better with Natasha by her side.

'I'm so sorry I'm late,' she said to Jen. 'Her dad was late dropping her back.'

'No problem,' Rob said. Natasha smiled tightly at him. Jen had explained to her that for the children's sake she was pretending everything was fine between her and Rob. Despite the tension between them, none of the kids seemed to have noticed a change. It was important that Natasha didn't give anything away.

'Do you want a glass of champagne?' Jen asked.

'No, thank you,' Natasha said. 'Last time we all had fizz the evening didn't end particularly well.' She looked pointedly at Rob, and Jen flushed, thinking of their girls' night in.

'Come on, Natasha,' Jen said, 'I'll introduce you to some of the other parents.'

The party passed by in a rush of activity, Jen constantly running after Ruby and checking that all the other kids were OK. With thirty kids there was always at least one who wanted something. As Jen directed yet another kid to the toilet, and lifted Ruby up into her arms to stop her eating another biscuit from the table, she glanced over at Rob and saw that he was chatting happily to one of the younger mothers. Rob threw his head back and laughed at something she said, then reached out to touch her arm.

Normally Jen hardly noticed how affectionate Rob was. He'd always expressed himself physically, kissing new acquaintances on the cheek and hugging people he'd met before. Jen had thought it was all part of his charm. But now watching him with the young mother, his behaviour was starting to bother her. He looked like he was flirting.

Jen marched over to him and handed him Ruby. 'I think she needs a nappy change,' she said. She turned to the woman. 'Did you want another drink?'

When Rob came back with Ruby, his parents wandered over to join them, clutching full champagne glasses.

'The nappy was dry,' Rob said to Jen, bemused.

Jen shrugged. 'I must have got it wrong.'

'Easily done,' Penny said. 'It's a wonderful party. You've really outdone yourself, Jen. The children are having a fabulous time.'

'Thanks, Penny.'

'I've tried to get some photos of the kids, but it would be good to get one of you two with Ruby. Jen – why don't you lift Ruby up?'

Jen obediently lifted Ruby up, and stood stiffly beside Rob. She felt his arm fall over her shoulders.

'Move a bit closer to each other,' Penny instructed, and they both shuffled in. 'Now smile for the camera.'

Jen beamed at the camera as Penny took the picture. 'That's

lovely,' her mother-in-law said, looking at her phone. 'Such a happy family.'

When Jen was looking through all the photos that evening, the ones Penny had taken and the ones she'd taken herself, she paused on the photo of her, Rob and Ruby. They were all smiling happily. There was no sign at all that anything was wrong. She was a better actress than she thought.

She pulled together the best photos of Lottie's birthday to put on social media, at the last minute adding the one of her, Rob and Ruby. She didn't normally post much, but today she wanted to. It was a special day for Lottie. And she hoped that if she tagged Rob, then Lizzy would see the photos. Jen had found out she was his friend on Facebook, and she followed him on Instagram.

Celebrating our lovely daughter's 8th birthday. Such a happy family day!

That would show Lizzy, she thought. Just because Jen was planning to leave Rob, didn't mean Lizzy needed to know that. Until Jen had her plans in place, it was better if it looked to the outside world like their marriage was perfect. She wanted the other woman to see just how much Rob loved his family and how little he cared about her.

TWENTY-EIGHT

Amy sat in her room on her bed on Saturday night staring at Jen's Instagram post. She hadn't posted for months, and now suddenly there she was, beaming out at Amy, surrounded by her family.

Such a happy family day!

It seemed so wrong. Jen had been devastated about Rob's affair just a week ago, and now she was pretending that everything was fine? It didn't make any sense. Had she forgiven him? As far as Amy could tell, he hadn't moved out. When they'd been working at the cat shelter on Thursday Jen had been quiet, refusing to talk about it. Natasha had told Amy that Jen was just trying to get everything sorted before she left him, but Amy wasn't so sure. She thought Jen might want to stay married to Rob. After all, she was used to the life of luxury his work allowed her.

The sound of a man and a woman laughing as they came through the door of her basement flat brought Amy back to reality. She quickly found some music on her phone and shoved in her headphones. Since her housemate Leanne had split up with her boyfriend, she'd started bringing the men she met online back to the flat.

'Much safer to bring them back here when you're in, than it is to go back to their place,' Leanne had told Amy. 'After all, they could be anyone.'

From the room next door, Amy heard bedsprings creaking, louder than the music on her phone which was already on the highest volume. Amy wondered if she should go out and do something, anything, to get away from the noise.

A phone call interrupted the music blaring through her headphones and she saw it was her mother. She almost let it ring through to answerphone, but then thought better of it. She hadn't spoken to another human being all day.

'Hi, Mum,' she said.

'Oh, Amelia, darling. How are you? I've been meaning to call you for absolutely ages. But things have been so busy. You know the garden's a real nightmare at this time of year. Everything just grows so fast. It's hard to keep on top of.'

'I wouldn't know. I don't have a garden.'

'I thought you had a terrace. Haven't you put some plant pots on it, or something like that? Livened it up a bit.'

'No, I haven't.' Amy paused, not wanting to mention that the plants would attract the rats that lived in the bins. Her mother already thought London was overrun with rats.

'Well, that is a shame, isn't it? It's important to make your house a home. How long have you been living there now? Six months?'

Amy stared up at the bare light bulb above her bed. 'Two years.'

'Gosh – really? Where does the time go? It just speeds by when you get older. You'll find that out for yourself one day. I really must come and visit you. I've been putting it off. You know I don't like London. It's so dirty. I thought you might come back and live in France so I don't have to visit.'

'Maybe one day,' Amy said, her mind wandering to Rob's house in the Med. She suddenly felt guilty that she'd been in France, but hadn't even thought of visiting her mother. 'I did come back at New Year to see you. And Easter,' she said, justifying it to herself. Her mother always expected it to be that way round. She never thought to visit Amy. But then again, Amy thought, looking round her dingy room, why would she? It was hardly like she could stay here.

'What's that noise?' her mother asked, and Amy realised that the creaking of Leanne's bedsprings in the room next door was loud enough for her to hear.

'Oh nothing, Mum. It's probably the radiators. They're a bit clunky here.'

'The radiators? Why have you got the heating on? It's warm outside. Are you made of money?'

'No, Mum. Never mind.'

'Because if you need more money you won't be getting it from me. Not since you dropped out of school.'

'That was five years ago. You don't need to keep bringing it up. And I don't want any money. You called me.' Amy sighed. The truth was she could do with the money. She'd run up a big credit card bill buying new clothes to wear for her dates with Rob.

'I was just calling to see how you are. Have you made any new friends?'

'I'm not nine years old. You don't need to ask me that.'

Her mother sighed. 'So, no, then? I guess people never change. I thought you'd grow out of your shyness when you got older.'

'I've got a boyfriend,' Amy blurted out, before she could stop herself. She thought of Rob, how when she was with him the world felt like a better place, how she felt like she was interesting and worthy of love.

'You've got a boyfriend? Well, that's a surprise! Where did

you meet him? Not on that Tinder, I hope?' Amy could almost see her mother's disapproving scowl down the phone.

'No, I met him at work. When I was working at an estate agents. He's in charge of a whole chain of agents.'

She thought her mother would be impressed by that but she simply brushed it aside. 'How old is he? He must be old to be in that job.'

'He's a bit older than me.'

'Was it an office affair? Is he married? They usually are. Lots of them about, these lecherous old men who chase younger women at the office.'

'Mum – it's not like that. He loves me. He took me on the most amazing holiday...'

'Ah!' her mother said, triumphant. 'I knew he was married.'

'I didn't say that!'

'But he is, isn't he?'

'He loves me. He's told me a thousand times. He's leaving his wife for me.' Amy heard the shake in her voice. She thought of Jen's post on Instagram about Lottie's birthday party, showing off her happy family.

'They all say that,' her mother said. 'This is just history repeating itself for you. He won't leave his wife. Do you remember that silly schoolgirl crush you had on your history teacher, Mr Beddow? I think you thought you'd end up with him when you were a teenager.' She laughed.

Amy felt tears prick her eyes. It hadn't been a silly crush. They'd been in love. Their relationship had had to end when she left the school, but he hadn't wanted it to.

She thought of her daughter, Gemma. Amy hadn't seen Gemma since she'd left her with Mr and Mrs Beddow a few weeks after she was born. Their comfortable house on the school grounds had seemed like the best place for her to grow up. Amy had never told her mother about the pregnancy, about how she'd lost someone so precious. But she couldn't think about that now. It made her heart ache.

'I'm older now,' Amy said. 'I'm sure you'll really like Rob when you meet him.'

Her mother sighed. 'Why do you always make such bad decisions? It's like nothing I say will stop you. This will only end in tears.'

'It won't, Mum,' Amy said, and she hung up the phone, throwing it down onto her bed angrily. Her mother knew nothing about Rob.

In the room next door, Leanne was groaning noisily and the creaking had reached a frantic rhythm. Amy found herself wiping away the tears that had started to fall down her cheeks.

TWENTY-NINE

On Monday, Jen sat in the meeting of the management company for their block of apartments, Ruby crawling around by her feet. She looked at the concerned faces of the other residents and wondered why she was even here. She might not be living here much longer. She'd booked an appointment with Natasha's divorce lawyer for later in the week. She needed to find out if she could force Rob to move out so she could stay in the penthouse with the kids. Or, if he wouldn't move out, if she was entitled to money from him to rent her own place. She imagined moving somewhere smaller, Ruby sharing a room with Lottie. She knew Lottie would object at first, but she'd soon get used to it. Jen could make it a proper home, and then buy somewhere for herself once they'd sold the penthouse and split the proceeds.

The chair of the management company was going through a long list of problems that had been reported with the flats: damp, draughty windows, issues with the smart electrical appliances, problems with the lift, and some structural issues with the building. It went on. Jen could see some of the other residents looking at her and she felt uncomfortable, knowing that Rob had sold the flats to so many of the owners.

'We're just getting quotes for how much it will cost to fix everything,' the chairman said. 'But, just to manage your expectations, the costs are looking to be a minimum of £100,000 per flat.'

People around the room gasped. Jen felt faint. There was no way she and Rob could afford that. Even if they sold their penthouse, she knew that the equity they had in the property wasn't much more than that. Rob had done a deal with a broker he knew that had allowed him to take out a huge mortgage. If they had to pay their share of the costs, they'd have nothing left. Neither of them would be able to afford another place.

'That's ridiculous!' a man shouted angrily.

'But these flats have just been built,' the woman sitting next to him said. 'Shouldn't the building company be paying for this?'

The chair nodded. 'We can try and get the money from them, of course. But it might take time. And in the meantime, we will really need to start fixing things, especially the structural issues.'

'How can a new building have structural issues?' someone asked. 'Is it even safe?'

'Yes, don't worry about that. It's safe. It was all signed off properly when it was built. These are just unforeseen issues.'

Jen had heard enough. She left the meeting before the question-and-answer session, scooping Ruby into her arms and sneaking out the back door.

She needed to speak to Rob and find out what he knew about the problems with the block and what they were going to do about their share of the costs. She put Ruby in her buggy, deciding to make a surprise visit to see him in the office.

. . .

As she walked it started to rain, and she put the hood down over the pushchair, opened her umbrella and wheeled the pushchair with one hand. She thought of Lottie and Jack, who were at school, and wondered if they'd be inside at playtime. She'd been worried that they'd notice the atmosphere between her and Rob since she'd discovered his affair, but she'd worked hard to hide it and act like the perfect wife and mother. She was still pretending she'd believed Rob when he said the email he'd received had been from an obsessed stalker. But Rob must have known he hadn't got away scot-free, as he'd been making more effort with her. He was getting home earlier from work most days, coming back straight after he'd been to the gym and avoiding the evening drinks. He was even giving the kids their baths some days. All in all, he was being a better husband. It was just a shame it was all too late.

She arrived at Rob's office and stood outside for a moment, looking in. Before he'd been promoted he'd worked out on the open-plan floor and had a seat by the window. She'd always wave at him whenever she walked by with the children. But since he'd been promoted he'd been given his own office at the back.

Jen opened the door and held it awkwardly as she lifted the buggy up the steps and inside.

'Hello?' A young male estate agent jumped up to greet her. 'Can I help you?'

'I'm here to see Rob.'

'I'm sure I can help you. Are you looking to rent or buy?' He looked down at Ruby, who had picked up a set of keys from his desk and was playing with them. 'She's adorable,' he said.

'Actually, I'm not looking for anything. Rob's my husband. I just came in to see him.'

A look of confusion flashed across the agent's face. 'Oh,' he said. 'Well, nice to meet you. I'm Damian. I started here six months ago.' He reached his hand out and shook hers. 'I can see if he's free. Do you want to sit down?'

Jen sat down in one of the soft leather armchairs opposite his desk and put Ruby on her lap.

She saw Grace sitting in the corner by her husband's office and tried to catch her eye, but she didn't look up. It seemed odd. She'd been so friendly at the company awards evening. Maybe she knew what was going on.

Across the room, Damian knocked on the office door, but there was no answer. She saw him poke his head round the door and then close it again.

'Where's Rob?' she heard him ask Grace.

'I don't know. I didn't see him leave his office.' She looked over at Jen then and quickly looked away. Jen shifted awkwardly in her seat.

Then she heard the sound of Rob's booming laugh from down the corridor. He rounded the corner, holding a mug of coffee, a young female colleague beside him, giggling at something he'd said. *Lizzy.*

Grace got up as he walked towards his office.

'Rob – your wife's here,' she said, indicating where Jen was sitting. 'With your daughter.'

'Jen!' Rob said, pulling away from Lizzy. 'What a lovely surprise. And Ruby, too.' He picked his daughter up and tickled her. 'What can I do for you?'

Jen hesitated for a moment, her mind full of questions. Rob and Lizzy had looked like more than just colleagues.

'I need to talk to you, Rob,' she said. She noticed that Lizzy was still standing there, staring at her.

'Oh, OK, of course. Is something wrong? Why don't we talk in my office?'

He led her inside, still carrying Ruby, and she noticed how soulless it was. Aside from his laptop and monitor, a pad of paper and some pens, and a pile of apartment brochures, the desk was empty. No family photos.

She shut the door behind her. As he passed Ruby back to her, she noticed his left hand.

'Where's your wedding ring?' she asked.

'Oh,' he said, blushing. He went over to his desk, opened a drawer, pulled it out and slipped it back on his finger. 'You wouldn't believe what happened this morning. We're selling a lovely flat in central London. Huge space, amazing views. Had a viewing booked with a very interested buyer. And guess what? The tenant had only gone and blocked the toilet. There wasn't time to call a plumber, so who do you think was on his hands and knees unblocking it?' Rob grinned at her. 'Me, of course. Oh, the glamour of this job. I took my wedding ring off before I went over. Didn't want to lose it to the sewers.'

Jen raised her eyebrows. She didn't believe a word.

'There was a meeting of the management company at our apartment block this morning,' she said calmly, changing the subject. 'There are a lot of problems with the flats. They think it's going to cost at least £100,000 per flat to fix them.'

'Oh...' Rob paled.

'How are we going to afford that kind of money, Rob?' she asked.

'Look,' he said, looking nervously at the door of his office, as if he was worried about someone listening in. 'Things have been complicated... with those flats. There's been lots of issues.'

'Did you know how much it was going to cost?'

Rob shook his head. 'I hoped it wouldn't be that much. But listen – I don't want to talk about our financial affairs in the office. But I have a plan. Can we talk about it at home tonight?'

That evening, Rob came home and helped her put the older children to bed, before they sat down for dinner together.

As Jen cooked, she thought about how living apart from Rob seemed less and less of a possibility. They didn't appear to have any savings. And now they had these extra costs to contend with. How would either of them afford to move out?

'You said we could talk about the money for the repairs for the flats,' she said. 'Everyone was angry in the management meeting this morning. The cost has been a huge surprise.'

Rob put his head in his hands. 'The building company has really screwed us over. I get complaints from other flat owners all the time. The block wasn't built properly. They took lots of shortcuts.'

'Did you know that, when you bought the penthouse? Is that why you got the discount?'

'I had no idea.'

'How are we going to find £100,000 to pay the bills?'

'We can't, Jen. All my salary goes straight into the mortgage and your mother's care home fees. There's a bit left over for the gym and everyday expenses, but not much. We've put a lot on credit cards.'

'We need to cut down then,' Jen said. 'I can quit the gym. I don't need to go to the hairdresser. The kids can stop some of their activities.'

'It's never going to be enough,' Rob said. 'We simply can't afford the £100,000 without selling the penthouse.'

'So we have to sell up?'

'It's not as easy as that. We'll have to tell any buyers of this new charge and all the problems with the building. Lots of people in the block will be trying to sell. There won't be any buyers.'

'So what does that mean?' Jen asked, knowing what was coming.

'It means we'd be pretty much bankrupt. We won't have a penny to our names.'

Jen put her head in her hands. 'You said you had a plan. What plan could you possibly have to solve this?'

Rob looked at her solemnly and topped up her water. 'I know it will sound crazy, but I want you to hear me out. We need to be a team for this, to work together.' Jen felt a sense of dread building inside her. He was the last person she wanted to work with. She didn't trust him at all.

'What is it?' Jen said, her heart beating faster.

'About six months ago, when things were looking a bit uncertain, I took out life insurance,' Rob said.

'OK,' Jen said, her brain struggling to work out how this was relevant.

'I thought I could disappear.' He met her eyes.

'What do you mean?'

'I've been thinking about this a lot,' Rob said. 'If I disappeared one day, like, while swimming in the sea on our holiday, well, that would clear up a lot of problems for us, wouldn't it? If I was presumed dead, then you could claim on that insurance.'

She couldn't believe was she was hearing. 'What?' she asked, trying to work out if he was serious.

'Jen, if I just disappeared, this could all be fixed.'

THIRTY

Jen started to laugh. 'You'd pretend you'd died?' she said. 'How would that work?'

Rob frowned. 'It's like I said. I'd go swimming in the sea and never be seen again. You'd report me missing and then claim on the life insurance. After everything calmed down you'd share the insurance money with me.'

'You mean, like the man who disappeared in the canoe near Hartlepool?'

'A bit like that, yes.' Rob shifted in his seat uncomfortably.

'You know he and his wife were found out by the police?'

'Yes, but I'd be cleverer than that. *We'd* be cleverer than that.' He reached out to touch her hand, but Jen pulled away and stood up. She went to the fridge, took out the bottle of wine and poured herself a glass. She took a huge gulp.

'You're completely crazy,' she said.

'Jen – just think about it. It could be a solution to all our money problems. If we don't do it then we'll be bankrupt. We won't be able to afford our own home.'

'We could rent. We'll still have your salary.' Jen thought of her plans to split up. She wouldn't be able to afford to live if he didn't have any money to share with her. She could get a job, but unless she could find something that was only in school hours, she'd hardly be able to cover childcare costs, let alone rent.

Rob sighed. 'We might not have my salary. I'm not sure I'll be able to keep my job if all the people I sold the flats to complain. Lots of them already have.'

Jen took another sip of wine.

'Think about it, please, Jen,' Rob said.

'What about the kids?' she asked.

'What about them?' Rob looked confused and Jen realised they hadn't crossed his mind at all in his ridiculous plan.

'They'll think you've died.'

'But I won't have, will I? When it's safe to meet again, we'll work something out. I'll see them again. It just might not be for a while.'

'But I'll have to tell them you're dead. Imagine how traumatising that will be for them. They love you.' Jen felt tears prick her eyes when she thought of telling them their father was dead.

'They'll see me again. I won't be gone forever.' He looked at her pleadingly. 'Please consider this, Jen. It's the only way we can give our children good lives. If we do this they can continue to live in an expensive home, and want for nothing. If we don't, they'll have nothing at all. We could end up on the streets.'

The next day, Jen dropped the children off and then walked to the cat shelter, her mind spinning. She hadn't realised what a dire financial situation they were in. Even so, Rob's plan had seemed so absurd, so ridiculous. He seemed to think he could just disappear into the sea, and then travel across Europe with a fake identity. But if Jen didn't go along with it, they could lose everything. They'd be homeless. Jen thought of her mother. They wouldn't be able to afford her care home fees anymore.

They'd have to move her. Rob had made such a huge mistake buying the penthouse and running up so much credit card debt. He'd let her down. She clenched her hands into fists, furious with him.

She arrived at the cat shelter and pushed open the door, calling out hello. Natasha and Amy were already there, cleaning out the cages. Jen went over to help.

'How's it going?' Natasha asked gently.

'OK,' Jen said. 'I'm getting by.'

'How are things with Rob?' Amy asked.

'They're... strange,' Jen said, unsure what to say. Everything had changed last night.

'What do you mean?' Natasha asked.

'I'm trying to figure everything out, what's best for the kids.'

'It's no good for kids to live with unhappy parents,' Amy said.

'I'm still thinking things through. For the moment, I'm pretending everything's fine. For the kids' sake.' Jen knew that if she was going to go along with Rob's plan to disappear it would be better to minimise the problems in their marriage. But could she do that? Could she pretend to still love him? She needed to bide her time, work out what to do.

'Have you spoken to my divorce lawyer yet?' Natasha asked, as she took a mop and bucket from the corner and started mopping the floor.

'No, not yet. I've got a call scheduled later this week.' Jen wondered if she should cancel it.

Natasha put the mop down and put her arm round Jen's shoulders. 'I know it seems hard to split up, but you'll look back and realise it's the best thing that could have happened. I certainly feel that way about Matilda's dad.'

Jen nodded.

'Sometimes people just stop loving each other,' Amy said. 'It's not anything anyone's done wrong. Just something that happens. And then it's best to move on to a new life. To start again. I'm sure you'll meet someone else.'

Jen laughed. 'I think I'll be sworn off men for a while,' she said.

Natasha squeezed her shoulder. 'Well, we're going away next weekend, aren't we? Me, you and the kids. Time away will give you the chance to clear your head.' She and Natasha were taking the kids for a weekend mini break to a theme park in the Midlands. Natasha had managed to pick up reduced-price tickets and had found a cheap hotel where the kids could all share a room, and they would have an interconnecting 'adults' room' next door.

Amy smiled. 'I think a break is exactly what you need. You can work out how to tell the kids in the least disruptive way.'

'And when we get back, I can help in any way you like,' Natasha said. 'If Rob leaves the flat I can cook, clean, help with the kids, whatever. I can be there to help you get back on your feet.'

Jen nodded. 'You sound like you'd be a better husband than Rob,' she said, laughing.

Natasha blushed. 'Honestly, anything you need, I'll be there.'

Jen felt tears prick her eyes. She wanted to make a clean break from Rob, but everything was just so complicated. She didn't think it was possible.

'It's OK,' Amy said, fishing a packet of tissues from her pocket. But as she walked across to Jen, she lost her footing and slipped on the wet floor.

'Ow,' she cried out, as her ankle gave way underneath her.

Jen crouched down beside her and offered her an arm to help her up. 'Are you alright?'

'I'm fine,' Amy said, embarrassed, standing up quickly, without Jen's help.

'Take it slow,' Jen said. 'Lean on me.' She walked Amy over

to a bench and lowered her down. She examined her ankle gently. There was no obvious sign of trauma, but it was hard to tell if it was injured. 'Have a rest here for a bit, before you try and walk on it. I'll get you a cup of tea and a biscuit.'

When Jen returned with the tea, Natasha and Amy were talking about Amy's date tonight.

'Amy's supposed to be going to the Ritz for dinner with Jonathan tonight,' Natasha said.

Jonathan always seemed to take her to the most amazing places. *The first flush of love*, Jen thought, a little bitterly. But she knew Amy deserved to be happy. From the small pieces of her past Amy had shared with her, Jen knew she'd had a difficult childhood.

'Wow,' Jen said. 'That will be spectacular. Rob and I went once, years ago.'

'Typical of me to twist my ankle today of all days,' Amy said, blushing.

'Does it still hurt?' Jen said. 'I can drive you over to the walk-in doctor's clinic if you like, after I've collected Ruby.'

'It does hurt a bit,' Amy said. She stood up slowly and walked awkwardly across the room, trying not to place weight on her ankle. 'But I think I should be alright. I'll take a taxi there tonight.'

'Good idea,' Jen said. 'I wish I was going to the Ritz,' she said, wistfully. 'I guess those days are over for Rob and me.' She felt tears prick her eyes. She was starting to realise that any love in her marriage was gone. Rob must have known he didn't love her for a long time; he'd had an affair. But falling out of love with him was a slower, more painful process.

'Oh, Jen,' Natasha said.

'Sorry,' Jen said. 'Seeing other people enjoying themselves just brings it all home.' She turned to Amy. 'I'm happy for you and Jonathan. I just wish Rob still did things like that for me.

He used to always surprise me with extravagant presents and dinners.'

'People change,' Amy said sympathetically. 'But I'm sure you'll feel much better in a few weeks' time. Once you have your own space.'

Jen nodded, distracted.

'It's not long until we're coming to the Med with you,' Natasha said. 'We'll all be able to relax then.'

Jen forced a smile. Rob would be in the Med, too. He was planning to disappear there. If she went along with his plan then the life insurance money would cover everything: a home for her and the kids, her mother's care home. Maybe it was the only solution. She'd have to stay with Rob for now and pretend to be happy, pretend she still loved him. It was important everyone thought they had the perfect marriage.

THIRTY-ONE

Amy got dressed in her room, sliding into a low-cut evening dress. Rob was taking her out tonight, for dinner at the Ritz. She deserved it. After staying with Jen for so long, despite everything he'd promised, he owed her.

Amy had made the reservation in his name, and then messaged him to say she'd see him there at 7.30 p.m. He'd tell Jen he was at a client dinner, although a part of her hoped that he'd tell her the truth, make it clear they were well and truly over.

She felt a sliver of guilt about lying to Jen earlier at the cat shelter, pretending it was the imaginary Jonathan she was going to the Ritz with. But it hadn't been the right time to tell Jen. Not yet. Jen was finding it so difficult to even accept that Rob didn't love her. It was just going to take a bit more time before she'd be ready to accept Amy.

Amy looked at herself in the mirror and smiled at her reflection. She was younger than Jen, and thinner. Possibly Jen was prettier, although Amy had spent enough time with her now to learn how to do her make-up like Jen's and make the best of her own features. It was inevitable that Rob would always choose her over Jen. More important than looks or age, they had a connection. It was like the air changed in a room when they were together. It fizzed with energy. Amy had never felt like that before.

Amy's ankle was still hurting so she called an Uber she couldn't really afford and then went outside to wait for it. She thought about how kind Jen had been to offer to take her to the doctor. She'd never had a friend like that before.

She didn't like lying to her, waiting in the shadows until she and Rob could make a clean break. She wanted Jen to know about them soon, so they could all get on with their lives.

She'd speak to Rob tonight, ask him to push things along a bit. She knew he was putting on a brave face for the kids, but really he and Jen needed to get their act together and end the relationship. She thought of her daughter Gemma, living with her father in France. If Amy had a happy, stable home with Rob in the UK, then maybe she'd be able to bring her back to live with them.

As she took the taxi across London, looking at the sights, she tried not to think about how much it was costing. Soon her life would be perfect. She wouldn't have to worry about money. She'd live in a happy blended family with Rob and his children, and her precious Gemma. She'd be surrounded by love. It was all she'd ever wanted. She just needed to make sure Jen and Rob split up for good.

THIRTY-TWO

Jen rolled over in bed to the sound of her alarm. She sat up, surprised to see Rob still sleeping beside her. Lately he had started going into the office early, and he was usually up before her.

She shook him awake. 'Rob, you've slept through your alarm.'

He rolled over. 'What? Oh, I didn't set it. I'm staying home today. I've decided to take the day off, spend it with my family.'

'Oh, really?' It was hard to spend time with him these days without confronting him about his affair. She was still giving the impression she believed his lies, but it was difficult to keep it up face to face.

'Yeah.' He sat up in bed and smiled at Jen. 'I thought it was about time I prioritised you. I've been working so hard since I've been promoted. And I've been so stressed it's been making me ill. I need a bit of a breather.'

She thought of what he'd said about the angry residents of the flats complaining to his work. Was that why he was stressed? Was he going to lose his job?

'OK,' Jen said. Regardless of the reason, she should make

the most of it. This was the first time she could remember that Rob would be around in the morning to help with the school run. 'I'll go and have my shower,' she said. 'Can you get the kids up?'

'Sure,' Rob said. 'I'll get them up and do their breakfast. I can take them to school later if you like?'

'Yes, please,' Jen said. She knew he had an ulterior motive; he wanted her to agree to his plan to disappear.

'And I could look after Ruby today. Then you can do something for yourself. Have a spa day, go to the hairdresser's, get your nails done. Anything you like.'

'How can we afford it?' Jen asked.

Rob shrugged. 'We can't. But if we're going to go bankrupt, we might as well spend as much as we can before it's all taken away from us.'

Jen swam up and down the pool in the gym. Rob had given her £200 for a day at a spa, but it hardly seemed necessary when she already had access to her expensive gym. She'd pocketed the money instead. She needed to start saving for herself. The water felt good as it embraced her body, and Jen tried to let her mind empty. When she'd had enough of swimming, she lay down on a lounger and tried to read her book. Rob had told her to relax, but it was almost impossible. She couldn't stop thinking of his plan to disappear, what it would mean for her, what it would mean for the kids.

Jen put her book down, picked up her phone and started to flick through photos of her kids. She felt so grateful for her family. Whatever happened, she would still have her children.

She looked through the photos of Ruby she'd taken since her birth, watching her change from a baby into a toddler. She stopped at a photo of Ruby on the beach, next to a sandcastle that the older children must have built. Her mother-in-law had sent it to her when she was looking after the kids, while Jen and Rob had their weekend break. Ruby was smiling cheekily as she clutched a spade. She was a gorgeous child. Jen looked at the background of the photo, trying to work out where exactly on the beach it had been taken. She saw the beach café some distance behind Ruby and managed to place the spot. She smiled. She'd taken the kids down to that beach with Rob before, when they'd been staying with her in-laws.

Then a figure caught her eye. A blonde woman in a flowing summer dress, standing about ten metres away from the children. At first Jen had thought she was looking out to sea, but when Jen zoomed in, she could see that she wasn't, that she was looking at her children. And she could have sworn the woman was Amy.

When Jen finished her swim, she went to the library and used the computers. She wanted to look up what it would mean for her and the kids if Rob went bankrupt. What she discovered terrified her. They really would lose everything.

When she got back to the apartment block, she looked for Amy on the front desk, but realised she must have finished her shift. Jen would have to ask her about the photo later. It probably wasn't her, but if it was, it was a coincidence that she'd gone down to the coast the same weekend as Jen and Rob.

As soon as Jen got out of the lift on the penthouse floor, she smelt the delicious aroma of freshly baked bread. She could almost taste it. Rob was making a real effort. She put her key in the lock and walked in.

Inside, the penthouse was spotlessly clean and tidy. A vase of red and white roses sat on the dining table. Rob came through from the kitchen.

'I'm treating you tonight,' he said. 'Because I want to say sorry for the way I've behaved lately. I've been working too hard. And, well, I haven't treated you the way I should have. I'm so lucky to have you.' He kissed her deeply, but Jen couldn't concentrate.

'Where are the children?' she asked. They were never usually this quiet.

'They've gone to an overnight babysitting service.'

'A what?'

'There are babysitters who can take them overnight. All above board and criminal record checked. In fact, I think one of the babysitters used to teach at their school.'

'Why didn't you tell me?' Jen felt a rush of worry. She didn't like being apart from them. She wished she could kiss them goodnight, like she did every night.

'I thought it would be nice to have some time just the two of us.'

Jen heard the noise of pans clanking from the kitchen. 'What was that?' she asked.

'Oh, that's Pierre, the professional chef I hired. He's cooking us a three-course dinner. I think the first course is nearly ready. Butternut squash soup with home-made bread. He'll leave after dessert, and we'll have the place to ourselves. No kids waking up. No interruptions.'

'How much did this cost?' Jen asked, shocked by the extravagance that she knew they really couldn't afford. He could have just prepared a home-cooked meal, like she did every day.

'Don't you worry,' Rob said, putting his hand on her shoulder. 'We've got to live for today. Who knows what tomorrow might bring.'

'If you say so.'

'I've paid a cleaner to clean the place from top to bottom too,' Rob said, pleased with himself. 'And I've put a new dress on the bed for you. You can go and get changed.'

'Can I speak to the kids first?' Jen said. She didn't like the thought of them being with strangers she'd never met.

'Sure,' Rob said. He dialled a number on WhatsApp on his phone and started a video call.

The babysitter appeared on the screen and Rob introduced Jen. Then the babysitter panned round to the children. They were all fine, playing a game with other children in a huge garden.

'It's a high-end childcare service,' the babysitter explained. 'The kids think of it as an overnight camp. They love it here! For them it's a holiday.'

Jen asked to speak to the children, but they were too busy playing their game. At least she could see they were happy.

She went into the bedroom and lifted the slinky red dress from the bed, running her hands over the soft material. It reminded her of the red dress Lizzy had been wearing when she'd first seen her at the awards party. The thought made Jen feel nauseous, but she steeled herself. She had to pretend everything was fine. She changed into lingerie and then pulled the dress over her head. It fit her perfectly, clinging in all the right places.

'You look amazing,' Rob said when he saw her. 'Let me pour you some champagne, and then I think our starters will be ready.'

The butternut squash soup was delicious, and afterwards Jen savoured every bite of the perfectly cooked beef wellington. This was one of the things she'd loved about Rob when they'd first met – his sheer decadence. Now, it alarmed her that he was still willing to spend so much money when they were on the verge of bankruptcy.

After the chef had served a chocolate cheesecake as the final course, he topped up their champagne glasses and left. Rob held up his glass. 'To us,' he said to Jen. 'Long may we continue.'

Jen clinked her glass against his. 'To forever,' she said, smiling. She didn't know how he could behave like this when he'd been cheating on her. She was beginning to think they were only still together so she could claim on his life insurance and give him half the money.

'I thought,' he said, 'that when we go to the Med, we could renew our marriage vows. It's been nearly ten years. And I know I've not been easy lately.'

Jen nearly spat out her champagne. Did he really think she didn't realise he had cheated on her? 'Are you feeling guilty about something?' she couldn't stop herself asking. It was such a cliché to renew their vows after an affair.

'No, of course not. You're not still worried about that email you saw, are you? I explained about that. There was a younger woman at work...'

'Obsessed with you?'

Rob grimaced. 'Yeah. I couldn't get rid of her.'

'And now you want to renew our vows?'

'Yeah. I thought we could do it on our holiday to the Med. The hotel just down the coast from the villa does weddings and I've spoken to them, and they said they can do vow renewals too. I've seen the pictures in the brochure. It's a beautiful venue.'

'And then, afterwards, you'll disappear into the sea?'

'A couple of days later, yeah. But only if you can help me, Jen. I need you to claim the insurance money.'

Jen took another sip of champagne. She'd been thinking a lot about his plan, and the more she thought about it the more it made sense. She wouldn't face bankruptcy or be made homeless. She'd be able to continue her life as before with the kids. 'OK,' she said, 'I can do that.'

'Great,' Rob said. 'That's great. And I think the vow renewal will help too.'

'Make us look like we're in love, you mean?'

Rob clutched Jen's hand. 'But we are in love. I love you so

much. And the renewal's something we can do as a family. With the kids there watching. To demonstrate our love for each other.'

'I guess it might be a good idea,' Jen said, coolly. It couldn't do any harm. It would be a nice memory for the kids of her and Rob together and it would show their commitment to each other before the disappearance. For a moment Jen imagined Lizzy seeing the photos online, realising that Rob had chosen Jen. She smiled to herself.

'OK then, I'll go ahead and book.'

'Great,' Jen said. She squeezed his hand back across the table.

Suddenly she remembered that Natasha and Amy were also coming to the Med.

'I've got a couple of girlfriends who are coming to stay with us too, on our holiday.'

'Oh,' Rob said, frowning. 'Normally it's just family, isn't it?'

'Yes, but I invited them. And they've booked flights. Besides, they're really looking forward to it.' She smiled at him reassuringly. 'Don't worry, it won't interfere with your disappearance.'

Rob brightened. 'You're one hundred per cent sure you want to go ahead then? You'll help me disappear?'

Jen smiled. His plan was totally dependent on her cooperation. She liked the feeling of being in control. If she chose to, she could leave him in the lurch. It felt good to be the one holding all the cards for a change.

'Yes,' Jen said. 'I'll help you.'

THIRTY-THREE

Jen felt a sense of relief when the weekend came around and she got in the car with the kids and drove down the motorway to the hotel by the theme park where they were spending the weekend with Natasha and Matilda. She was acting her heart out pretending to Rob everything was fine, but her anger about his affair was eating her up inside. She hoped it had stopped now, that her discovery of the email had scared him enough into ending it. He was certainly spending less time at late-night dinners. But she couldn't be sure it was over. She hated the thought of him with another woman.

She knew she had to be pragmatic. If it wasn't for their money issues she'd have split up with Rob already. As it was, he'd be out of her life soon enough, when he disappeared in the Med. She just had to be patient. It was for the best that she didn't let her anger boil over, that she acted like everything was normal between them and focused on their plan.

When Jen arrived at the hotel, Natasha greeted her with a hug, her eyes sparkling. Lottie and Jack ran past her to where Matilda was watching the television, Ruby toddling after them.

'You look well,' Jen said, taking in her shiny hair and glowing skin.

'You do, too,' Natasha said quickly. Jen knew she was lying. Her carefully applied make-up couldn't hide the bags under her eyes. Her mother's pills helped her to sleep, but they made getting up in the morning like pulling herself out of a fog, and she never felt truly rested.

'I know I'm not looking my best at the moment. It's the stress. But it's lovely to get away.' It felt a bit like coming home when she saw Natasha. She always felt safe with her, like she could be completely herself.

'Sometimes you need to get away to have space to think,' Natasha said. 'And we're going to have a brilliant day all together. Honestly, who needs men?'

Jen laughed. She couldn't help thinking how carefree and relaxed Natasha seemed. She was proof that people could bounce back after divorce, be happy again.

Jen had been anxious about taking her three kids to the theme park, but it was easy with Natasha by her side. The kids got on well, and there was only minimal fighting. And Natasha and Jen split the workload, Natasha playing with Ruby while Jen took the others on the rides, and then swapping round again. They seemed more like a team than she and Rob had ever been.

Jen loved seeing Lottie and Jack let go and enjoy themselves. Lottie's party hadn't made much of a difference for her friendships with the other girls in her class, and she was becoming even more withdrawn. Jen wondered how much of the tension in her parents' marriage she'd picked up on. At least now she was having a good time.

'I'm so glad you could come with us,' Natasha said later when they got back to their hotel and they'd put the kids to bed in their bunk beds in the adjacent room. 'It can be a bit boring on my own with Matilda. It's much nicer to do things with a friend.'

Jen nodded. 'It's better for me, too. I take them to places on my own all the time. Rob's parents sometimes help out, and... well, you know how things are with my side of the family.' Sometimes Jen saw other families with grandparents in tow and longed for the same closeness with her own mother. But it would never happen.

'Great that we've found each other then,' Natasha said. 'How are things with Rob now?'

Jen looked away, knowing she couldn't tell Natasha the truth. 'A bit better, actually,' she said. 'He treated me to an amazing chef-cooked meal earlier this week.' She forced a smile as she thought of the money Rob had wasted. Money they didn't even have.

Natasha raised her eyebrows. 'You deserve to be looked after,' she said. 'The amount you do for him. But when are you going to leave him?'

Jen sighed. 'I don't know,' she said. 'I just keep thinking about how much us separating would devastate the kids. I think I need to stay.' She longed to tell Natasha that Rob was planning to disappear in the Med, ask her if she thought the plan was realistic, if he could pull it off. Jen still had doubts in the back of her mind about whether it would work. But she knew she couldn't confide in her. She and Rob were planning to break the law. She couldn't risk Natasha telling the police about the insurance fraud after Rob was gone.

'What?' Natasha said, her mouth dropping open. 'After everything he's done?'

'I'm not sure there even was an affair. He said that email was just from a young girl who was obsessed with him.' She tried to keep a straight face while she repeated Rob's lies.

'And you believe him?'

Jen sighed. 'I want to,' she said. 'And I think he deserves a second chance.' She hated lying to her friend, but she had to.

'Rob's making a real effort,' she continued. 'He wants to start afresh. He wants us to renew our wedding vows.'

'Jen, you can't be serious?' Natasha said angrily. 'Why would you recommit to him?'

Jen sighed. 'Rob and the children are my life. Without him I don't have anything to my name.'

'You have us! Amy and I, we'll make sure you and the kids are OK,' Natasha said. 'I don't understand,' she continued. 'I thought you were getting everything together so you could leave him. I said I would help you.'

'I can't really leave,' Jen said truthfully. 'There's no money. The mortgage is worth nearly as much as the flat, and there are some unexpected bills too, to do with the building. We can't sell the penthouse. We'd be left with nothing. I wouldn't be able to get my own place. We'd be homeless. And then, how would the kids feel? Without their father, without a home. We just can't split up.'

'You could move in with me,' Natasha said.

'That's really kind, but I know you're short on space as it is.' Natasha's one-bed flat was cramped with just her and Matilda.

'You could all sleep in the living room. We could put air beds on the floor. Honestly, if you want to leave him, Jen, I'll find a way to help you make it work. I promise.' Natasha stared intensely into her eyes.

All Jen could think about was their financial trouble. It wasn't so simple; Natasha would never understand just how deep they were in.

'I'm sorry,' Jen said. 'I want to try and make it work with Rob. For the sake of the kids, it's the best thing.' She laughed lightly. 'He's not so bad.' When Rob went ahead with his plan to disappear, she wouldn't see him anyway. They wouldn't be together. It was only a matter of time.

'"Not so bad" is hardly the love story of the century,' Natasha said.

'I don't think it has to be. I just want the kids to have a stable home. I hardly see Rob anyway, and when I do we get on OK.'

'You mean like friends?' Natasha said. 'You don't love him?'

'We need to work on our marriage,' Jen said. 'Our holiday to the Med will give us the chance to do that.'

Natasha sighed. 'I thought he wasn't coming to the Med. It was going to be a girls' holiday. I was really looking forward to it.' Matilda was staying with her dad that week, and Natasha had told Jen how delighted she was to have something else to do the first week of the school holidays.

'It's a chance for us to spend time as a family,' Jen said. 'I think we need to take it.'

'I think Amy and I should still come,' Natasha says. 'I hate to say it, Jen. But I want to be there to pick up the pieces if he hurts you again. He could still be having an affair.'

Jen nodded. 'I understand,' she said. 'But it won't be quite the girls' holiday we imagined.'

Natasha nodded. 'Amy's keen to come too,' she said. 'You know she grew up in France? She still has relatives over there. I suppose the two of us could do a bit of a road trip to visit them.'

'That sounds like a good idea,' Jen said. She reached out to touch Natasha's arm. 'And Natasha, I really value your friendship. I've never had as close a friend as you.'

Natasha's eyes met Jen's and she leant in closer. 'You know,' she said, 'if you're just staying with Rob for the sake of the kids, well, maybe you deserve some fun too.'

'You mean, cheat on Rob?'

'Yeah,' Natasha said, 'if you find someone you want to be with. Then why not? He cheated on you.'

Jen smiled. 'I don't think anyone's shown any interest whatsoever since I've had the kids.'

'That can't be true,' Natasha said. 'You're beautiful, Jen. Your smile lights up a room.'

Jen flushed, embarrassed. She looked into Natasha's eyes, not quite understanding what she was trying to say.

And then Natasha cupped Jen's face in her hands and kissed her.

THIRTY-FOUR

Amy shivered as she heard the clunk of the door unlocking, running her hand over the smooth handle. She'd never broken out the master key from reception before, but with Jen away for the weekend she could let herself into the penthouse undetected. She'd taken the key shortly before the end of her shift, gone to the coffee shop across the street and waited until the entrance to the apartments was crowded, then slipped back inside and into the lift. One by one everyone else got out, until she was the only one rising up to the top floor.

She'd been to see Jen in the penthouse lots of times before, but she'd never been there on her own and she felt a buzz of excitement. As she went through the door, she imagined Rob calling out to her, welcoming her home.

She had the place to herself as she waited for Rob to come back. Amy wandered round the flat, running her hands over the luxurious surfaces. While Jen was away they had to take every opportunity to be together. Amy smiled as she made herself a coffee with their machine. She took it outside and sat on one of the chairs on the balcony and drank it, looking out onto the river.

This apartment would be hers one day. And the villa in the Med. She could start her life with Rob, the life she was meant to have. Her, Rob, his kids and Gemma. A happy family. Jen just needed to accept the way things were and let go.

Amy went back inside. Rob would be back soon. She wanted to be ready for him. In Rob and Jen's bedroom, she marvelled at the views from the floor-to-ceiling windows. She looked down at the neatly made bed and imagined Jen making it before she left. The sheets were white and looked freshly ironed. On the bedside table there was a single book, by a famous crime fiction author, next to a collection of perfumes. Amy tried spraying one on her wrist. It smelt unfamiliar, not the one Jen used every day.

Amy opened the walk-in wardrobe and browsed through Jen's dresses. She had so many. She picked a few out and tried them on in front of the mirror. She smiled at herself. With her hair the same colour and style as Jen's, and in Jen's dress, she could almost be her.

Stripping off Jen's clothes, she eased herself between the white sheets, feeling the cool cotton against her skin. She felt a rush of elation. She was in Rob's bed, between his sheets. He'd be back soon and she couldn't wait.

THIRTY-FIVE

Jen pulled away quickly from Natasha's kiss, her lips tingling.

'I'm sorry,' Natasha said quickly, flushing. 'I just thought...'

'It's OK,' Jen said, trying to control her confusing rush of emotions. 'I mean, it just took me by surprise. I had no idea you felt that way.'

'Didn't you?' Natasha said. 'I thought I'd hinted enough times. I was starting to feel it was all in my head, but then I got this feeling that you might feel the same way too. I must have got it wrong. I'm sorry.'

Had Jen known? Had she even suspected? Jen didn't think she had, but there was an uncomfortable and new feeling unfurling inside her, one she didn't want to address.

'Don't be sorry,' Jen said. 'You're my best friend, and I love you. I just... it's a lot to process, that's all.' With everything else happening, this felt like one thing too many. Jen's mind wouldn't stop spinning.

Suddenly, she understood why Natasha's loyalty was so unwavering, why Natasha was so desperate for her to leave Rob. Jen hugged her friend, feeling the comforting warmth of her body. 'Let's just forget about it for now,' she said. 'Enjoy the rest of our break.'

'Sure,' said Natasha. 'I can sleep on the floor tonight. You have the double bed.'

'Don't worry,' Jen said. 'We can still share the bed.' She flushed, unsure how to navigate the conversation. 'Let's just stick to our own sides.'

'Definitely,' Natasha said. 'And I'm sorry again. I obviously misread things.' She smiled. 'I think I need a drink after that humiliation. Shall we crack open the minibar?'

When Jen got home the next day, she was still thinking about Natasha, trying to digest what had happened. She'd never thought about her that way before, and yet now she couldn't stop thinking about her, analysing every interaction they'd ever had, an unfamiliar excitement building inside her.

As she went through the door of the penthouse she called out to Rob. 'Hello?'

He appeared from the living room.

'Daddy!' the children cried, running up to him and throwing their arms around his waist.

Rob hugged them tightly and Jen couldn't help thinking about how he planned to disappear, to leave his own kids.

Natasha was worlds apart from Rob. She was unfailingly loyal, always putting Jen first. After Rob disappeared, Jen would be able to start her life again exactly how she chose. She thought of the way Natasha had kissed her and a shiver went up her spine. She'd pulled away in shock and yet it had awakened something in her she hadn't realised was there. There was something intoxicating about it.

She pushed those feelings aside; she didn't have time for any more complications right now. She had to focus on pretending that she had a happy marriage. Rob had been putting a lot of effort in lately, at least on the surface. If they were going to pull this off she couldn't be caught slipping.

That evening, Jen went into the kitchen and downed a couple of her mother's pills before she went to bed. Every morning she told herself it would be the last time, and then every night she found herself with them in her hand. Her mind just wouldn't rest without them.

As Rob cleaned his teeth in the bathroom, Jen slid between the sheets. She could tell Rob had slept there because the bed hadn't been remade to the same standard. The sheets had been tucked in but not smoothed over.

As she stretched her legs out under the covers and turned over to one side to get comfortable, her foot hit something. A piece of material.

She reached under the covers to fish it out with her hand.

Holding it up, she could hardly believe what she was seeing. A pair of lacy red knickers. And they weren't hers.

Jen felt sick. It was bad enough knowing he had had an affair. But to continue it after she had confronted him? He'd brought the other woman here, into their home, to what was once their safe place reserved just for them.

This was it. Blood pounded in her eardrums and her fists shook. Any sliver of love she'd still had for him was completely gone. He'd betrayed her again, even when he was asking so much of her.

She listened to him in the bathroom for a moment, humming as he washed his face. He had been lying to her all this time, keeping secrets. He always had the upper hand, knowing everything, while she was in the dark.

Well, she could keep secrets too. Holding the knickers by the edge of the lace, she went out of the bedroom, into the kitchen and found a plastic bag. She put them inside, took a photo in case she needed evidence later, and then threw the bag in the bin.

'Everything OK?' Rob called from the bedroom.

'Yeah, fine,' she called back. But inside, she was seething. Someone had left the underwear there deliberately. Lizzy? Or someone else? Jen was going to make sure she found out who it was. And whoever it was would soon know not to mess with her again.

THIRTY-SIX

Jen lay awake while Rob slept peacefully beside her. He'd brought someone back here to her home, to her bed. She felt sick with rage. As she lay there she realised he couldn't have even washed the sheets.

She jumped out of bed, grabbed some fresh bedding from the cupboard and went to sleep on the sofa. She needed to know who it was who had been here, if it was Lizzy. For a moment, she thought about messaging Amy and asking if she'd seen anyone there last night, but she didn't work at the weekends, so it was pointless.

She just wanted someone to confide in, to explain all the awful things that had happened. She thought about contacting Natasha, but she just couldn't. If she told her about the lingerie in the bed, Natasha would be even more convinced Jen should leave Rob right away. And that would ruin the plan for him to disappear in the Med.

Jen started to doubt he was even capable of disappearing without messing it up. The plan was so risky. If Rob wasn't clever enough to double-check the bed after he'd slept with someone else in it, it seemed unlikely that he'd be able to disappear without being found.

She wanted to tell Natasha so badly, to get her opinion on Rob's plan. But she'd ruin everything if she had the wrong reaction. Amy cared about her too, but not in a romantic way. Maybe Amy was the one to confide in about the lingerie in the bed. She always seemed more pragmatic and less emotional. And perhaps she'd heard rumours about Rob from the other receptionists. Amy's shifts were always when Rob was at work, but she might have heard something on the grapevine.

Jen bit the bullet and messaged her.

Hey Amy. Just a quick question. Did any of your colleagues mention any visitors to the penthouse over the weekend? Xx

Amy messaged back immediately, even though it was past 11 p.m.

Someone did say something about Rob going up there with a woman. I wasn't sure how to tell you. I knew it would upset you. I'm so sorry. Xx

Jen stared at her phone. Something about the message seemed odd. She hadn't really expected Amy to know anything. She hadn't been on shift all weekend, and she'd never seemed that friendly with her work colleagues. One of them must have messaged her. But it just didn't seem likely that one of them would message her with something like that.

Amy messaged again.

Are you OK, Jen? Do you want me to come over? xx

No, I'm fine. I'll see you tomorrow. Xx

OK. Well, I'm here if you need me. Try to get some sleep xx

Will do. See you soon xx

Jen stared at her phone, remembering the photo of the woman who looked like Amy on the beach, standing behind her kids. She'd never asked Amy about that.

She remembered her video doorbell. She'd disabled the notifications on the app, but it recorded whenever it sensed movement outside the door.

Heart pounding, she opened the app on her phone and flicked through the recordings it had captured. The first few were of her and the kids leaving on Saturday morning. Later that morning it had captured a cleaner hoovering in the corridor. And finally, in the afternoon, she saw a woman at their front door, looking back towards the lift, as if she was worried someone might be behind her.

Amy.

Jen swallowed, and kept checking the footage. It couldn't be. There must be a mistake. She was convinced Amy would turn back around, sure she'd just been popping up to their floor to check the radiator in the corridor and that she'd leave any moment.

Jen watched open-mouthed as she opened the door to their penthouse, all the while checking over her shoulder.

Rob must have given her a key.

Half an hour later, Rob got home.

It was another hour before Amy left, her hair dishevelled.

THIRTY-SEVEN

Jen couldn't get to sleep; all night her mind was spinning with what Amy had done. She had thought they were friends, but Amy had completely betrayed her. How long had it been going on? Jen had only known Amy since she'd started working on the reception desk earlier in the year. Despite the age gap, they'd always got on easily. Was it possible her relationship with Rob had begun when she started working here? Had she met Rob in the building? The whole thing he'd said about an obsessed girl in his office must have been a complete fabrication to keep Jen off the trail.

She thought of all the secrets she and Amy had shared, the group chat messages, the times they'd laughed until they couldn't breathe. Had it all been a cover? Amy and Natasha were the two people she relied on most. But Amy had been lying to her all along.

She remembered Amy finding the email on Rob's computer. The email she must have sent herself not long before. Her whole plan had been to get Jen to leave him, so she could have him for herself. Jen kicked herself for being so easily manipulated.

Jen rolled over on the sofa and looked at the time. It was already nearly 6 a.m. Rob would wake up soon. Her hatred for him overwhelmed her, as she listened to his gentle snores coming from the bedroom. How could he sleep so peacefully? She thought of his plan to disappear. She'd be rid of him soon anyway. As long as he managed to successfully pull it off. She thought of the life insurance money, the happy life she'd be able to live with the kids.

Jen got up and cleared the sheets off the sofa so that Rob wouldn't know she'd slept there. Then she went into the bedroom and had a quick shower, before going to the kitchen and starting to make Rob and the children's packed lunches and Rob's smoothie for the gym. She could pretend to be the perfect wife for a little while longer. She'd just think of the money and put on the performance of a lifetime.

Amy was working at the reception desk when Jen got back from the school run. Jen had managed to get through the early morning making the briefest conversation with Rob, but she wasn't sure if she could stand to talk to Amy.

'Hey,' Amy called to her, eyes full of sympathy. 'How are you doing?'

Jen felt her body tense up, but she put on a smile. She thought of last night when Amy had been so keen to tell her there'd been another woman in her flat. Jen knew that Amy wanted her to be falling apart, to be ready to leave Rob for good.

As much as Jen wanted to punch Amy, she wasn't going to give her the satisfaction of knowing that she'd affected her. 'I'm really well, thank you,' she said, as she walked past the desk.

Amy waved her closer. 'I'm sorry about what I told you last night,' she said in a whisper. 'I just thought you should know that Rob had a woman in the flat.'

'Thanks, Amy,' Jen said, with a fake smile. 'I appreciate it.

But luckily it turned out to be nothing. Rob said it was just a delivery woman dropping off a package.'

Amy looked shocked, her sympathetic smile slipping from her face. 'Really? Do you believe him?'

'Why wouldn't I?'

'Oh – it's just – you messaged me so late last night. I thought you were upset. I thought something had happened between you and Rob.'

'No,' Jen said innocently. She knew what Amy was doing. She wanted Jen to tell her about the underwear she'd found, the underwear that Amy had deliberately left. 'Actually, Rob and I are better than ever. Things have been going well lately.'

'Really?' Amy said, her eyes wide.

'Yes,' Jen said, starting to enjoy herself. 'Rob even wants us to renew our wedding vows.'

'What?' Amy went pale. 'That's quite a change of heart,' she said, her voice small.

'Is it?' Jen said, sticking the knife in. 'I mean, he always denied any affair. He said it was just an obsessed younger woman. He wants to make it clear how much he loves me.'

'Right.' Amy nodded awkwardly.

'And how's Jonathan?' Jen asked. She had realised that Jonathan didn't exist. He had always been a cover for Rob.

'Oh, he's great. I spent the weekend with him,' Amy said. 'We had a brilliant time.'

'Oh, wonderful. Do you think an engagement is on the cards then?' Jen asked casually.

Amy blushed. 'I'm not sure yet,' she said. 'We'll have to see.'

'I hope you do get married someday. It has its ups and downs, but in the end you're stronger together.'

Amy forced a smile. 'I'm glad things are better,' she said.

· · ·

When Jen got back up to the penthouse, she stripped the bed in the master bedroom and shoved the sheets in the wash.

Then she started to turn the penthouse upside down, looking for more evidence of Rob's affair with Amy. Once again it felt like she was in the dark. Rob was living a completely separate life. She went through each drawer in Rob's desk in the study to check there wasn't anything she'd missed last time. Then she continued in the bedroom, going through Rob's bedside table, chest of drawers and wardrobe. As she swept her hand over the top shelf of his wardrobe her fingers ran over a ziplock bag, with what felt like a phone inside. She pulled it out.

Sitting on the bed, she tipped out the contents. A wad of cash, a passport and a phone. She opened up the passport and looked inside. It was a convincing fake, with Rob's name and date of birth changed. She wondered if it would work at border control. She supposed it wouldn't matter if he stayed in Europe. He'd be able to cross borders without it.

He'd told her they would reunite when it was safe to do so, that in a year or two's time he'd reappear in his new identity and they could continue being a family. She didn't think he meant it. It would be too risky. Once she'd given him the insurance money she might never see him again. That wouldn't bother her if it weren't for the children. The children deserved a relationship with their father. But Jen knew Rob wouldn't think twice about taking that away from them if it suited him.

She put the passport down and counted the cash: €5,000. She ran her fingers over the notes. She could just take it now and run away with the kids. But it wouldn't last her very long.

Next she picked up the phone. Rob had told her he was going to get a burner phone so that he could contact her while he was away. He'd told her not to expect to hear from him for at least six months. He'd been sure his parents would lend her money for the first few months, before she claimed on the insurance.

She switched it on, and was surprised when it came to life immediately. It had already been charged.

Guessing at the password, she tried his birthday and then Lottie's. To her surprise, it worked. She started to look through it. There were no contacts stored. But when she went into the messages she saw a series of texts back and forth. The first ones were in the middle of the night a week ago.

I had a great time yesterday xxxxxxx

Me too xxxxx

Are you all ready for the adventure? Xxxxxx

Yeah. Everything in place. Got the passport now. Soon we'll start our new life together xxxxxxx

God it's crazy! Can't believe this is happening – so exciting! Xxxxxx

Jen swallowed. So they were planning to run away together. After Rob 'disappeared', he'd reunite with Amy. Suddenly Jen felt stupid, gloating to Amy about the vow renewal. Amy must already know it was just a cover for Rob's disappearance. They must have planned the whole thing together. Jen was just a pawn in their game. They only needed her so she could claim on the life insurance. She imagined them laughing at her behind her back, and grimaced. She remembered Amy inviting herself to the Med with them. She'd be there, ready and waiting to run off with him into the sunset, after he disappeared.

There was a pause and then more messages from a few days ago. Jen couldn't believe Rob had been lying in the bed beside Jen while she slept and messaging Amy.

Looking forward to seeing you this weekend. Glad your wife is away! Xxxxxx

We can discuss everything then. Finalise plans. Xxxxx

Awesome. The main thing is your wife. Everything else is sorted. Xxxxxx

Then Jen saw the last message. She stared at it in shock, her mouth dry.

Leave my wife to me. I'll deal with her. I promise. Xxxxxx

Amy had sat in the pub on her own for most of the evening, nursing a Diet Coke. She was in Soho and the pub was buzzing, with several groups of people looking enviously at her table by the window that she occupied by herself.

She checked her phone again. She'd messaged Rob three times now to tell him she was here, but he hadn't responded. She was so confused. They'd had such a brilliant time at the weekend in his penthouse. There'd been an electricity between them as he'd stripped off his clothes and she'd pulled him towards the bed. Even though she had been in Jen's home, in Jen's space, it had felt so completely right. Jen was on borrowed time with Rob.

Amy knew Rob didn't want to tell Jen the truth, but she felt she needed to know. Amy thought of Jen finding the underwear she'd left. It must have been a shock, and yet this morning she'd been all bright and breezy, pretending everything was fine. She was completely deluded. Rob didn't love her anymore. He loved Amy.

Even so, Amy couldn't help but feel a niggling doubt about their future. She needed to check in with Rob, just see him again, to know everything was OK and it was Jen who was crazy. The estate agency still hadn't taken her work email address off their system, so she could still log in and see Rob's diary. He was going to a client meeting in central London, and had blocked out time to go to the branch of the gym in the city. She'd suggested they meet in the pub across the road from the gym, where she was now, but he'd never replied. So she'd turned up, sat down at a table with a view of the entrance to the gym and waited.

She thought she'd seen him go in at around 6.30 p.m. in a long stream of office workers, but she still hadn't seen him come out.

It was getting late now. He should have already been at the client dinner. Perhaps she'd missed him when he left the gym. Amy tried to ring him again. No answer. She thought about the holiday to the Med in a few weeks' time. By then she hoped that Rob would have resolved things with his wife.

As Amy sat in the pub, she became more and more frustrated. How could he ignore her like this? They'd planned their whole future together.

At 11 p.m. she decided to call it a night and head home. There was nothing else she could do. She'd have to speak to Rob tomorrow.

As she came out of the pub, she crossed the busy street, weaving round a taxi which had stopped to drop its passengers off. She turned to walk towards the station, feeling completely alone in the crowds of friends and couples. She passed two police officers patrolling the streets in fluorescent vests, chatting as they did. As she neared the station, she glanced down each side street, still hoping that she'd somehow bump into Rob. She passed a dark alleyway and saw two men down there, standing over someone lying on the ground. She shivered, her instinct to walk away, to get out of danger. But something stopped her. The man on the ground's trousers had come up at the ankle revealing brightly coloured striped socks. Rob had a pair like that. He wore them when he was meeting particularly big clients. He called them his lucky socks. She recognised the polished shoes, too. She was sure it was Rob. She hesitated. There'd been so many times she had seen people in the street and been convinced it was him. She saw him everywhere, even when he was nowhere to be found. It could be anyone. Or anything. Gang-related. A drug deal gone wrong.

Amy came to her senses and turned back round, looking for the police officers. She spotted them further down the street and ran over.

'There's a man on the ground in an alley,' she said. 'I think he's hurt.' The police officers hurried after her as she led them to the alley. She was half expecting the men to have left, but they were still there.

'I think he's drunk,' one of them said when he saw the police officer. 'We found him like this. He won't get up.' Amy looked at the men in the dark coats more closely and could see they were just businessmen, not the potential criminals she'd first thought.

Amy took a step closer, as the police officer leant over the man, shaking him gently. 'Are you OK, sir?'

The man lifted his head groggily and Amy gasped. It was Rob.

'Oh my god,' she said. 'Rob – are you OK?'

Rob turned his head towards her and then let it fall back down. 'Mia?' He seemed suddenly aware of his surroundings, looking around him at the alley and trying to get up.

'Are you injured, sir?' the police officer asked.

Rob still looked confused. He shook his head slowly. 'I don't think so...' he said groggily. Amy wondered how much he'd had to drink at the client dinner, how he'd got into such a state.

'Can you get up, sir?' the policewoman said, somewhat impatiently. She gave her colleague a knowing look, and Amy realised that this was a regular part of their job when they did evening patrols.

The other police officer offered Rob her hand and helped pull him up. 'Can you walk OK?' she asked. He stumbled forward, and Amy reached out to steady him.

The police officer turned to her. 'Do you know him?' she asked.

'I'm his girlfriend.'

'And do you think you can get him home safely?'

Amy nodded. 'Yes, of course.'

'OK then, we'll leave him with you. Have a good night.'

The policewomen went back off down the alley, and Amy walked with Rob towards the underground station, with him leaning heavily on her. When they got to the entrance he stumbled and Amy realised he wouldn't be capable of getting on a train home.

'What happened, Rob?' she asked, as she tried fruitlessly to hail a taxi.

'I don't know,' he said slowly. 'One minute I was fine, the next I felt so exhausted and confused that I had to lie down.'

'Did you have a lot to drink at the client dinner?'

Rob shook his head. 'I didn't go. I need to go now. Am I late?'

'It's after eleven,' Amy said. 'It will have finished.'

'What?' Rob looked confused.

'You didn't go? Where have you been?'

'I don't know.' He shook his head. 'I only remember going to the gym.'

Amy finally managed to flag down a taxi and she helped Rob get inside. He was asleep within a few minutes of the taxi setting off and didn't wake again until they were outside his block of flats. Amy watched him sleeping, overcome by affection and worry. Although he was groggy and confused, she couldn't smell alcohol on him. What if he'd had some kind of fit? Or if he'd been attacked and couldn't remember? The police hadn't really looked into it properly.

When they got back to Rob's home, Amy paid for the taxi with Rob's credit card. She longed to go upstairs with him and settle down in the master bedroom in the penthouse. But she couldn't. It wasn't her home.

Instead she helped him into the building and called Jen.

'Amy?' Jen said, surprised. 'Is everything OK?'

Amy took a deep breath and looked at Rob beside her. Now was the perfect time to tell Jen about her and Rob. But something made her hesitate. It was the middle of the night. It seemed cruel. And a part of her was scared of Jen's reaction, that she might never forgive Amy.

'Rob's with me,' Amy said. 'He's not that well, I saw him collapsed in the street and brought him back home.'

'Oh,' Jen said. There was a long pause as if she was thinking about what to say. Finally she just said, 'Thank you.'

'Shall I bring him up to the flat?'

'He can't get up here on his own?'

'No, not really. He still seems confused.'

Jen sighed. 'Well, I can't leave the children, so I guess you'll have to bring him up.'

THIRTY-NINE

Jen paced up and down the living room of the penthouse in her dressing gown, waiting for Rob and Amy to come up in the lift. Was this it? Was this how everything came to a head? With her, sleepy-eyed and drowsy, screaming at her husband and his mistress as they came back from some kind of date?

No. It couldn't end like that. As much as she wanted to lash out at them both, she had to remain in control, had to be the bigger person.

She heard the lift doors glide open in the corridor, the sound of muffled voices.

'Nearly there,' Amy was saying. 'Just a few more steps.'

Jen opened the door and saw Rob shuffling down the corridor, leaning heavily on Amy.

She wanted to kill him, but she put on a concerned face. 'Oh my goodness,' she said. 'Rob – are you alright?'

Rob mumbled something incomprehensible.

'I found him like this,' Amy said. 'He's in a bad way.'

'You just happened to be walking by?' Jen asked.

Amy blinked rapidly. 'I'd been out for a drink with some

friends. I was just heading back to the station and I saw him in an alleyway.'

Jen smiled tightly. 'Lucky you were there then.' She reached out and took Rob's arm. 'Leave him with me now,' she said. 'I'll look after him.'

Rob took a step inside.

'Let me know how he is in the morning,' Amy said quickly, as Jen began to shut the door.

When Jen woke up the next morning, Rob was still asleep on the sofa. It had been easiest for him to sleep there, rather than dragging him to the bedroom. He had hardly been able to keep his eyes open. And Jen couldn't bear to have him sleeping beside her in bed after Amy had brought him home.

Jen felt sickened by Rob's behaviour. Despite Jen going along with all his plans, he was still sleeping with Amy in their bed, and still going out for dates with her in the evening.

She thought of his texts to Amy. Were they really planning to start a life together after he disappeared? Could Jen bring herself to just ignore that, and take the life insurance money? Rob would be expecting her to share it. That was his whole plan. But she didn't have to. She could let them run away together and then leave them with nothing. Keep the money for herself and the kids.

She thought of the texts he and Amy had exchanged. How blasé they were about their plans. How casually they spoke about Jen, as if she was just an object in their way. *Leave my wife to me.* What did he mean?

She went to the sofa and gently shook Rob awake. 'Are you OK?' she asked.

'I don't know... what time is it? I need to get to work.'

'You came home last night with Amy. She said you'd blacked out.'

'Yeah. Amy? Oh, you mean Mia. Yeah, she found me in the street, and brought me home.'

'I didn't know you were friends,' Jen said curtly.

'We aren't really. She used to work with me. Before she worked on the reception here.' Rob looked anxious. 'I don't remember things very clearly. Did Amy say anything else about what happened?'

Jen stifled her irritation. He was worried she'd told Jen about their affair.

'Not much. What do you remember?' Jen asked. She wanted to understand when he'd blacked out and how long for.

He shook his head. 'Hardly anything... I know there was supposed to be a work dinner but I'm not sure I went... I remember going to the gym... but after that, nothing. Except... much later on... in Soho... I woke up on the street. The police came.'

Jen sighed. 'You need to see the doctor,' she said. 'It's the second time this has happened. There could be something seriously wrong with you.'

Two hours later, Jen was sitting opposite the doctor with Rob explaining his symptoms.

'I blacked out and can't remember anything,' Rob said. 'Nothing at all from about 7 p.m.'

'Are you under a lot of stress?' the doctor asked.

Rob shook his head. 'Not really.'

Jen frowned at him. Did lying come so easily to him that he would do it for no reason?

'He's been stressed at work,' she said.

'Things have been a bit difficult recently,' Rob admitted.

'And had you been drinking?'

'No, I don't think so.'

The doctor nodded. 'Well, stress can cause panic attacks

and other physical anomalies, but perhaps not symptoms as serious as blacking out. I'm just going to check you over.'

The doctor checked his pulse and his blood pressure. 'All looks fine,' she said, with a smile. 'I think it's probably nothing to worry about. Just a one-off episode.'

'He blacked out in the same way a couple of months ago,' Jen said.

Rob frowned at Jen. She knew he wanted to leave and get back to work.

'Hmmm... well, let me run some blood tests as well. I don't think it's anything serious, but just in case.'

Jen watched the doctor type something into her computer, and smiled. It had been the right thing to bring Rob to the doctor's. She was glad they'd have Rob's blackouts on record.

After he'd been to the doctor's, Rob insisted that he was fine to go straight to work and Jen went back home. She was still fuming at him and Amy, the way they had betrayed her and had the nerve to parade it in front of her with Amy bringing him home.

She needed to work out what she was going to do. There was no way she could rely on Rob or trust anything he said. She thought of his plan to disappear and remembered the burner phone he'd been keeping in the top of his wardrobe. She should check it again, see if there was any more information on it.

She went into the bedroom, and swept her hand over the top shelf of the wardrobe where she'd found it before.

It wasn't there. Rob had moved it. She climbed on a chair and peered into the back of the wardrobe. Moving aside Rob's spare gym kit, she saw a yellow folder at the back of the shelf. She pulled it out.

It contained everything she'd found before – the money, the phone and the passport, along with some additional documents.

She turned the phone on, but there were no new messages. The last message still said he would 'deal with' his wife.

She turned to the new documents. There were three envelopes, all from the bank. She opened the first one. It was for Lottie's child savings account.

Thank you for your request to withdraw all funds and close the account. A withdrawal of £5,000 has been made and the account has been closed.

Jen gasped. He had taken his daughter's money. Her university fund. To spend on his new life with Amy. How could he care so little about his kids?

The next two envelopes contained the same letter for Jack and Ruby's accounts. Rob had pocketed all their savings, transferring the money to his own account. Jen felt sick. He didn't care about his children at all.

She put the envelopes back and pulled out the next document. *The life insurance policy.* So this was it; their ticket to maintaining their lifestyle, keeping the kids happy and content, never wanting for anything. He must be planning to give her the policy so she could claim. She saw Rob's name in the middle of the paper, and a death benefit of £2m. He had taken out the policy six months ago.

Jen flicked through the terms, thinking of the money, the hole it would get them out of. Once Rob was gone she could replace all the money in the children's accounts. She'd go back to work and build her own life without Rob, and she and the kids would be happy. She was halfway through the sheets of paper when she suddenly stopped. There was a second life insurance policy. She saw her own name on the dotted line.

Rob had also taken out a policy on Jen.

If Jen were to die suddenly, Rob would pocket £2m.

She thought his plans to start a new life with Amy and the message he'd sent her.

Leave my wife to me. I'll deal with her.

FORTY

TWO WEEKS LATER

Jen put the final touches on the home-made hampers she'd prepared for the tombola at the school fete. All the parents had been asked to contribute something. Last year Rob had got his agency to provide a hamper from Harrods, but this year there'd been no mention of it, so Jen had got on with it and made some herself.

Jen was still pretending to be the perfect wife, but she wouldn't be for much longer. They would be in the Med soon, and then it would be game over for their marriage.

Once she'd found the life insurance certificates, it hadn't taken her long to work everything out. Rob's plan for disappearing had always seemed far-fetched because he'd never intended to go through with it. He had organised the vow renewal so it would look like they had the perfect marriage. But it was Jen he thought wouldn't be coming home from the holiday, not him. Suddenly the messages between him and Amy about getting rid of her and 'dealing with her' had taken on a new meaning. Rob would be the one claiming on Jen's life insurance, after he returned from the Med without her.

Jen shivered. She'd never realised how cold-hearted her husband really was, what he was truly capable of.

At first she'd told him she couldn't come on the trip anymore, said she'd stay at home with the children. She'd told him they needed some time apart. Rob had done everything he could to persuade her to come. He'd told her how essential it was that they go ahead with his plan, how he needed to disappear if they were to have any money at all.

In the end she'd agreed to come. But Rob didn't know what he was getting himself into, going to the Med with her. She'd made her own plans for him and Amy.

'Those look beautiful,' Rob said, as she tied a bow round the final hamper.

'Thank you.' She lifted her head to receive his kiss, trying not to flinch at his touch. 'They weren't too much work. I'm going over to see Mum soon, with Natasha, and then I'll join you at the fete later.'

'Yeah, sure,' Rob said. 'You know I'm always happy to look after Lottie and Jack. I'll take them to the fete and meet you there.'

Jen didn't respond. He made it sound like he was doing her a favour by looking after his own children.

When she arrived at her mother's care home with Natasha, Jen felt tense. They'd had a difficult conversation in the car, with Natasha still questioning why Jen hadn't left Rob. Jen hadn't been able to give her a good answer. As much as she'd wanted to confide in her about Rob and Amy and her plans for them both, she knew it was best to keep them to herself.

She'd wanted Natasha to come with her because she knew her mother would be difficult today. It was her last visit before she went on her holiday. But now there was tension between her and Natasha too.

Jen braced herself as she walked towards her mother's room.

'Don't worry,' Natasha said, placing her hand lightly on Jen's arm. 'It will be alright.'

'Oh, you're here,' her mother said, when they entered her room. 'On a Saturday.' She looked at Jen suspiciously.

'Hello, June,' Natasha said politely. 'Good to see you.'

'We can't stay long,' Jen said. 'Just wanted to see how you were. The kids have their school fete today and then we'll be on holiday next week, so I won't be able to visit.'

Her mother nodded. 'Don't worry about me,' she said bitterly. 'It's not like you'd think to invite me on your holiday.'

Ruby was toddling round the room, looking at a shelf full of unread books and magazines that Jen had brought on previous visits. Jen wasn't really sure why she'd brought Ruby along. Her mother never seemed interested in her, and the other children had started refusing to come with her as soon as they could talk.

She turned to Natasha. 'Do you mind just watching Ruby while I go to the toilet?' she said. 'I'm bursting.'

'Sure,' Natasha said. 'No trouble at all.'

Jen went into the bathroom and rifled through her mother's medicine cabinet. She found the pills she wanted and pocketed a bottle. She needed these now more than ever. Then she flushed the toilet, washed her hands and returned to the living room.

Natasha and Jen arrived at the school fete just in time to see the kids' races. Lottie was running the 100 metres and Matilda and Jack were in the sack race.

Jen spotted Rob over the other side of the running track and waved. He looked relieved to see her. Ruby was strapped into the buggy and he was rocking it back and forth to try and stop her from screaming, while he watched the races. Lottie's race started and Jen and Natasha cheered as all the kids crossed the line and were given a medal. Lottie came over to them, flushed with excitement.

'Did you see me, Mum?'

'I did. You did brilliantly,' Jen said.

After Jack and Matilda's race, Rob crossed the track and greeted Jen with a kiss.

'How's it been this morning?' she asked.

'Oh, all good,' he said. 'The kids have enjoyed looking at all the stalls and playing the lucky dip.'

'I've signed up to run a stall with Natasha,' Jen said.

'Yeah, I remember.' He smiled. 'What time do you need to go?'

Natasha looked at her watch pointedly. 'Now, really – we'd better go and set up,' she said. She took Jen's arm. 'Come on, Jen.'

Jen smiled apologetically at Rob. 'I'll see you later,' she said.

They went over to the cake stall and took over from the other volunteers, who were grateful to escape the queue of hungry customers. When there was a break in the steady stream of parents, Jen tried to spot Rob and the kids, but they were already lost in the crowd.

More people wandered over and Jen turned her attention back to the queue that was forming again and took a step back in shock. Amy was first in line.

'Amy!' Natasha said. 'What are you doing here?'

'I just wanted to come and support your kids in the races,' she said. 'They told me about them last time I saw them.' She looked at Jen. 'Lottie was so excited.'

Jen's blood ran cold, but she managed a smile. 'You've missed them, I'm afraid.'

'Oh, that's such a shame. I guess I'd better just enjoy the fete now I've paid my entry fee.'

'Did you want a cake?' Natasha asked.

'Yeah, a slice of the chocolate cake, please.'

Jen cut her a slice, her hand shaking as she held the knife. Why was Amy here, at her children's school fete?

'There you go,' she said.

'When will you be finished on the stall?' Amy asked.

'Not for another half an hour,' Natasha said. 'We can meet you after.'

'OK, then,' Amy said. 'I'll try and find the kids, say well done for their races.'

'They're with their dads.'

'Oh, right,' Amy said. 'I'll try and find Rob, then.'

Jen tried not to glare at her. She didn't want Amy alone with Rob and the kids. 'I think he might have already left,' she said.

'Oh no,' Amy said. 'I'm sure I caught sight of him a little while ago, by the bouncy castle. I'm certain he's still around.'

The customer behind Amy was shifting back and forth impatiently.

'We'll see you later, Amy,' Natasha said. 'What would you like?' she asked the next person in line.

As Jen cut the cake for the next customer, she watched Amy walk away. Suddenly she was aware of a stinging pain. She looked down and saw she had cut her thumb.

'Ouch!' she said, seeing the blood oozing out of the cut.

'I'll have a different piece, thanks,' the woman said, eyeing the blood with distaste.

Natasha glared at her, then grabbed some napkins and handed them to Jen. 'Are you alright?'

Jen put the napkins round her thumb. 'I think I'm going to need to get a plaster,' she said.

'Why don't you go and get one from the first aid tent? I can manage here.'

Jen looked at the big queue that had built up. 'Are you sure?'

'Yep. You can hardly serve cake when you're bleeding, can you?'

'Thanks, Natasha.'

Holding the napkins round her thumb, Jen hurried off. She'd get a plaster after she'd found Amy. She couldn't have her talking to Rob at her children's school fete. It was a complete intrusion on their family life. It felt like Amy and Rob were already muscling her out. Jen strode over to the bouncy castle but couldn't see her or Rob or the kids. There was an inflatable slide next to it and she spotted Lottie and Jack at the top.

'Look at me, Dad!' Jack was shouting out.

But Rob wasn't paying attention. He was deep in conversation with Amy.

Jen tried to control her fury as she came closer, and Amy smiled at her. 'Oh, hi, Jen,' she said. She leant forward and kissed her on the cheek. Jen looked at Rob, who was completely pale.

'Hi Amy, hi Rob,' Jen said. 'What's up?'

'Oh, nothing,' Rob said quickly, shoving his hands in his pockets.

'We were just watching Lottie and Jack on the slide,' Amy said.

'They look like they're having fun,' Jen said brightly.

'I thought you were working on the cake stall for another half an hour?' Amy said to Jen. Jen understood the undertone. She wanted Jen to leave her with Rob. But there was no way that was going to happen.

'I finished early,' Jen said. She held up her hand to show them the wad of napkins. 'I cut my thumb.'

'Oh, poor you, do you need a plaster?' Amy took one out of her bag. 'There you go.'

Rob looked at Amy. 'You said you were about to head off? That you had somewhere to be.'

Amy smiled. 'Do you want some family time, Rob?'

Well, it is the school fete,' Jen said. 'It's a time for families.'

'OK, then, I'll leave you both to it. Just think about what I said, Rob. And see you soon, Jen!'

Amy sashayed off, her skirt swaying.

'Everything OK?' Jen asked Rob. He was deathly pale.

FORTY-ONE

Amy took a deep breath as she walked away from Rob. She'd done it. She'd been brave and told him what he needed to know. The school fete hadn't been the best location, full of screaming children, but she knew she had to do it then. The sooner, the better. It wasn't the kind of news that could wait.

She put her hand to her stomach.

He hadn't believed her at first when she'd told him she was pregnant. He'd insisted that he'd always used a condom, that it was impossible. But then she'd reminded him of the time three weeks ago in his penthouse when Jen was away, and told him how she'd missed her period.

He'd been in shock at first, asking her question after question before he'd started to accept that it might be true.

'I'm keeping the baby,' she'd said, before he could suggest anything different.

'Oh,' he said. 'Perhaps you should take more time to think about it? There's no need to rush.'

'I've already thought about it. You're going to be a father again, Rob.'

Amy thought of her daughter. She remembered the agony

of giving birth, the joy of holding Gemma in her arms for the first time. And then the pain of leaving her with her father and his wife. She'd thought it had been the right thing to do, to pretend the baby was theirs. It had felt like she didn't have a choice. Now, she so desperately wanted to start again, to have a second chance, with Gemma, and with the new baby.

Jen had appeared then, apparently abandoning her do-gooder role on the school cake stall. If only she'd have some self-respect and leave her husband.

It was clear Rob loved Amy, that they were meant to be. And now she was offering him everything that Jen had. A little family of their own.

FORTY-TWO

On Friday night, Rob and Jen sat opposite each other, eating their dinner of takeaway pizza. Jen hadn't had time to cook today. It had been the last day of the school term, the kids had needed picking up at lunchtime, and then she'd had to pack for their flight tomorrow.

Rob was tearing into his pizza, and she could see he was nervous about their trip.

'Are you all ready for the holiday?' he asked. 'You're OK to go ahead with our plans?'

Jen nodded. 'I'm as ready as I'll ever be,' she said, softly.

'Good,' he said. 'I know you had doubts, but it's the right thing to do. For the children. Otherwise you and the kids will be left with nothing.'

Her stomach twisted. How could he pretend to care about his own children? He had stolen their money and was planning to leave them motherless.

'I've booked us in for the vow renewal ceremony on Sunday. Then I'm planning to disappear on Tuesday.'

'Let's run through everything once more,' Jen said. She

needed to fully understand his plans, to make sure hers tied in with them perfectly.

'Sure,' Rob said, clearing his throat. 'The police will think I disappeared during an evening swim in the sea. You should tell them I'd been drinking. They'll think I misjudged the tides and was washed out.'

Jen nodded. 'That makes sense.'

'There was a woman who went off the cliff into the sea a few years ago. Her body was never found.'

'OK,' Jen said. She'd researched the tides in detail. Most of the time the tides would wash a person out, but not every time.

'What will you do really?' she asked.

'I'll leave my clothes in a small pile at the bottom of the cliff, after it's got dark. Then you can drive me away. I've booked a motel in the name of my fake passport. It's about twenty miles away.'

'You're not even going to go into the water?' Jen said. This wasn't what he'd said before. He'd told her he was going to get into the sea and swim round the headland, picking up a bag of his clothes a bit further round the coast.

Rob shook his head. 'It's too much of a risk. The currents are strong.'

Jen thought of the two of them in the car. Was that when he planned to kill her? An accident on a clifftop road at night? Or getting her to drive him to an isolated spot and pushing her over? 'I can't drive you to a bed and breakfast,' she said. 'A camera somewhere will pick up the number plate of the hire car. And you can't just turn up at a bed and breakfast the night you're going missing. People will know it's you.'

'I'm going to shave my head,' Rob said, 'and when it grows back I'll bleach it. I'll look like a different person. Besides, if you don't report me missing until the morning, no one will be looking for me yet.'

Jen shook her head. 'We need to stick to the original plan. You get into the sea and swim round the headland. Once you've picked up your clothes and changed then you can shave your head, put on a baseball cap and hike to a nearby hostel with your new passport.'

'I'm not sure, Jen.'

'I think it's the only way for it to be convincing,' Jen said.

Rob frowned, reluctantly. 'You know I need you to be a hundred per cent committed to this, Jen,' he said. He reached out and squeezed her hand. 'We're a team, a partnership.'

'And that's why you need to listen to me. You need to get into the water. Otherwise I can't be involved in this.'

Rob nodded. 'OK, then,' he said. 'You win. I'll go for a real swim, round the headland.'

Jen squeezed his hand back. 'It's only about four hundred metres, Rob. And you've always been a strong swimmer. It should be easy for you.'

Jen smiled as she thought of the bottle of pills that she'd picked up from her mum and already packed in her handbag. If someone took enough and then went into the sea, they should be incapacitated enough to drown.

Really, it was a much better plan.

FORTY-THREE

The next afternoon, Jen got out of the hire car, stretched her legs and breathed in the sea air.

Finally they were here. In the Med.

As she unlocked the villa and went inside, she felt a sense of anticipation. She slipped off her sandals and made Lottie and Jack take off their shoes, too. Then she walked across the cold, terracotta tiles through to the living room, drew back the patio curtains and admired the view. Beyond the cliff edge, the sea stretched out endlessly to the horizon. From this distance it looked completely calm, but Jen knew that was a mirage. The sea was always rough around here, and only strong swimmers were advised to go in.

Lottie and Jack slumped onto the sofa and pulled the iPad out of the rucksack they'd taken with them on the plane. Rob was carrying Ruby round the villa, showing her everything. She'd only been a baby when she'd come here last, and she had no recollection of it. Jen's heart twisted as she thought of Ruby losing her father. She'd have no memory of him either.

Arriving at the villa felt like coming home. They'd come

here on their honeymoon and then every year since. They had photos of Lottie and Jack from every year, each year their faces slightly more mature, their smiles broader. They'd all been happy here.

She shivered. Everything was so different now. She didn't know exactly what Rob's plans for her were, how and where he was going to strike. She had to watch her back.

Rob came over with Ruby, and Jen's heart ached for her daughter. When all this was over, she was going to lose so much. But there was no other way.

'What's Mummy thinking?' Rob asked Jen.

'Only how much I'll miss you,' she whispered. 'We have such good memories here.'

He wrapped his arms around her tightly and kissed her ear. 'I'll miss you too,' he said. 'Desperately. But it has to be done.'

Jen nodded. 'Today is the last full day we have together. My friends are arriving tomorrow afternoon.' Jen had tried to persuade Amy and Natasha not to come, but she'd known it was pointless. Amy wasn't going to change her plans with Rob, and Natasha had insisted she come too, telling Jen she needed her friends beside her. Jen knew that once Amy arrived she would stake her claim on Rob. Jen was completely ready for it. She had a few home truths to tell her.

'Tomorrow morning will be spectacular,' Rob said. 'When we renew our vows. I've arranged a videographer to capture it all.'

'Evidence of our happy marriage?' Jen said, unable to suppress a bitter laugh.

'Don't be like that,' he said. 'We don't need evidence for us. We know we love each other. The video will be for other people, later. So they can see the depth of our relationship.'

Jen smiled tightly. When Rob went outside to uncover the pool, she took the knife rack off the side in the kitchen and hid it at the top of the cupboard in her bedroom. Then she went to the utility room, took the hammer out of the storage cupboard and hid it in the bottom of her bedside drawer. She thought of the life insurance Rob had taken out on her and shivered. She was sure if he tried anything, it would be after they'd renewed their vows, but she needed to be alert, just in case.

The next day the sun was shining and the water in the pool sparkled. Jen took the children out to play and they splashed around until they were exhausted.

'Come on,' Rob said, coming out from inside. 'We all need to get ready now. The vow renewal is at midday.'

'Sure,' Jen said. 'You shower the kids and get them changed, while I get ready.'

'What are the kids going to wear?' Rob asked. 'They need to be smart.'

'They should wear whatever you packed for them to wear,' Jen said.

'I didn't pack. You packed.'

'Then they need to wear whatever's in the suitcase.'

'I was thinking a suit for Jack and a formal dress for Lottie.'

Jen shook her head, as she towelled the children off by the pool.

'Lottie has some summer dresses,' she said. 'Jack will have to be in shorts.'

'Right,' Rob said, starting to pace up and down. 'It's a ceremony at an expensive hotel, Jen. I wanted everyone to look nice.'

Jen smiled sweetly, and handed Rob the towel so he could finish drying the kids. 'Oh, don't worry, Rob,' she said. 'The vow renewal is about celebrating our love for each other. That's all that matters, not anything else.'

He nodded. 'Of course. Sure.'

'You sort out the kids, and I'll get changed. I'll meet you by the door in an hour when the taxi's due.'

When they got into the taxi an hour later, Rob seemed stressed. Jen got into the front of the car, and let him sort out the car seats, before he sat in the back with the kids.

'Sit still while I do your seat belt up,' he said to Jack, irritated. 'Just stay still. We can't be late for our own vow renewal.'

Soon the taxi was off, along the winding coastal road, and Jen admired the view. The road was narrow and as they passed a caravan going the other way, she thought about how easy it would be to oversteer and for the car to tumble over the edge of the cliff.

After they arrived, they were taken outside to a green, grassy area, set back from the beach. There was an arch decorated in white flowers and four seats, three for the children and one for the videographer, who was already filming the outside of the hotel and the grounds.

The kids sat down and Rob promised them sweets after the ceremony, if they behaved themselves. Lottie sat up straight in her seat, staring fixedly at them. Jack slouched but was quiet, and Ruby was far too young to understand the instructions. Instead she toddled up to Jen and hid under her skirt.

The officiant, a suited hotel employee, laughed. 'It's always wonderful to have the children at these ceremonies,' she said. 'They really give them character.'

Rob smiled, and Jen stroked Ruby's hair.

'Are we ready to begin, or do you want a little longer?' the officiant asked.

'I think we're ready,' said Jen, smiling at Rob and glancing behind him towards the videographer, who was now standing with his camera pointed at them.

Rob put his arm around her and turned to face the officiant.

Ruby stayed by Jen, clutching her leg as they repeated their marriage vows to each other. Jen tried not to stumble over the words 'till death do us part'.

'You may now kiss your wife,' the officiant said, and they leant in towards each other, their bodies meeting as they kissed passionately. This would be the memory that her children held onto, Jen thought. This was the gift she was giving them. The belief that they were both happy when Rob disappeared, that their family life was perfect. She prayed that their vow renewal would mean that no one would think his disappearance was deliberate.

She thought of Amy, and for a moment she was tempted to shock Rob, tell him she knew all about his affair, let go of all the fury that had built up inside her. But she resisted the urge. She couldn't play all her cards now.

They ate lunch at the hotel's restaurant on the beach, and they shared a bottle of champagne to celebrate their marriage. Jen knew she only had a few more hours when it would be just their family of five. Amy and Natasha would arrive this afternoon.

When they got back to the villa, Rob disappeared off into a spare bedroom with his laptop.

'What are you doing?' she asked. She'd thought he would at least pretend to want to spend the evening with her after they'd renewed their wedding vows. But now he thought she was back on board with his fabricated plan to disappear, he wasn't even bothering to put in any effort with her.

'I just need to look a few things up before Tuesday,' he said. 'Double-check the tides. Just to be sure they'll believe I've disappeared.'

Jen tried to hold back a frown. 'Is it a good idea to do that on your computer?' she asked. 'What if the police look into your search history?'

'I'll delete the history,' he said. Jen swallowed. She

wondered if he was really checking if her body would wash out to sea. But if that was the case, then he really was stupid. The police would still be able to see everything he'd looked at even if he deleted the search history on his browser.

'Good idea,' she said, smiling. 'Do you want me to get you a drink?'

'Yes, please. I'll have a beer.'

'Coming right up,' she said.

In the kitchen she crushed up her mum's pills into the bottom of a beer glass and poured the cold beer on top of them. She wanted to incapacitate him. Amy would be here later, and then the two of them would outnumber Jen, put her on the back foot. It was better to have Rob out of the way.

And Jen wanted to monitor the effect the pills had on him. She'd given them to him twice now, but there was always room for error with the dosage. The first time he'd taken them had been a mistake. She hadn't realised until much later that Rob's first blackout was a result of her mixing her mother's anti-anxiety pills into the smoothie she made him for after the gym, instead of his vitamins. She'd been exhausted and groggy that day and must have reached for the wrong bottle of pills.

But the second time had been deliberate. After she'd found Amy's lingerie, she'd known she had to do something. She'd wanted to hurt him, make him confused and unsure. She'd wanted to stop him being able to see Amy. She'd mixed her mother's pills with his smoothie and he'd blacked out again. At that point, she hadn't thought of killing him, but the idea must have been somewhere in the back of her mind, starting to take shape. It was only later when she'd found the life insurance he'd taken out on her, that she'd known what she had to do.

The drugs were the easiest method. If Rob passed out in the sea and drowned, she could make it sound like an undiagnosed medical condition. The police had seen him in a confused state and he'd been to A&E and the GP after his blackouts, so there'd already be evidence of a problem on his medical records.

Jen made sure the pills had all dissolved in the beer, then took it through to Rob, passing it to him with a smile.

FORTY-FOUR

Amy heard the whirr of the plane's engine and felt the thrust as it took off into the sky.

'This is going to be an awesome holiday,' Natasha said, sitting beside her. 'Rob's place in the Med is out of this world. Jen's shown me photos before of their previous holidays there. I never thought I'd get to go!'

'It sounds amazing,' Amy agreed, smiling to herself. She thought of the last time she'd been there, how close she and Rob had been, how they'd had sex in every room in the villa. Now things had come full circle. She was going back.

She looked out of the window. She felt nervous this time. Everything was going to come to a head and she was going to have to hurt Jen. She'd never wanted that. She longed to be the kind of mother that she was, the kind who put their children first no matter what. In so many ways Amy wanted to be just like her, to occupy her world and live her life. But Jen just wouldn't take the hint and split up with her husband.

Amy didn't want to lose her friendship. Or Natasha's. But that might be the price of settling down with her soulmate, of living the life she was meant to live with Rob. She felt so torn.

Part of her wanted to become Jen, to have everything that she had, to take over her life. But another part of her longed to be her friend and confidante. She wasn't sure she could have it both ways.

She looked across at Natasha, who was studying the snack menu. Maybe she could get Natasha to understand things from her point of view.

'I have some news,' she said.

'Oh, really?' Natasha said. 'Good news or bad news?'

'Good news, actually.' Amy smiled.

'Go on then – spill!' Natasha said, closing the menu. 'Don't keep me in suspense.'

'I'm pregnant,' she said, unable to stop a smile spreading across her face.

'Oh my goodness – congratulations!' Natasha turned awkwardly in her seat to hug her. 'You and Jonathan must be so excited.'

'We are.'

'Wow. So I guess you won't be drinking on the holiday?'

'Nope. I'll be completely teetotal.'

'Well, Jen and I can make up for that!' Natasha said. 'You know, I've been quite worried about her. I thought she was going to leave Rob, but she's giving him a second chance. She's even agreed to renew her wedding vows. But he could really hurt her on this holiday.'

'I don't understand why she wants to stay with him.'

'Neither do I. The relationship's as good as over, but she just won't admit it.'

Amy felt a rush of relief. Rob had always said his marriage was dead and now Natasha was confirming it. Maybe everything would work out OK once Jen accepted the truth.

She had never wanted to be the other woman. Rob hadn't even told her he was married initially. Maybe Natasha would understand.

'There's something else I need to tell you,' she said to Natasha.

'What?'

'It's about Jonathan.'

'Oh – is he going to propose?' Natasha's eyes sparkled with excitement.

'No, it's not that.'

'What is it?'

Amy took a deep breath. 'It turns out he's married.'

Natasha's eyebrows shot up. 'Married?'

'Yeah. I didn't know at first. But then he confessed. They're separated but they still live together because he can't afford to move out.' It wasn't quite the truth, but it was close enough. And Rob had always said that he and Jen were separated.

'Oh, Amy. When did you find out?'

'A little while ago. I didn't want to tell you and Jen because I thought you might judge. I mean – because of everything that's gone on between Rob and Jen. I didn't think you'd see it from my point of view.'

'I'm sorry you thought you couldn't confide in us,' Natasha said. 'Finding out he was married must have been a real shock to you. You've always said he was your soulmate.'

'He is. He got married when he was young. It was a big mistake, but he tried to make it work for years. Then they separated and he met me.'

'It sounds difficult,' Natasha said. 'What's he said about the pregnancy?'

'Oh, he's really excited about it. Says he wants to get a place together. I'm hoping if we pool our money we might be able to afford to rent somewhere together.'

Natasha smiled at her. 'It sounds like a complicated situation,' she said. 'But don't worry. Jen and I will always support you. We're your friends.'

FORTY-FIVE

Jen sat in the living room, sipping her wine and waiting for Natasha and Amy to arrive from the airport. The kids were beside her, watching the television. In the spare room, Rob had collapsed onto the bed and fallen asleep about half an hour after he finished his beer. He was out cold. Jen had tried to wake him by shaking and prodding him, but to no avail. She thought she'd found the right dose of her mother's medication. He'd fallen asleep with his laptop open on an article about bodies swept out by the tides.

Jen heard a car on the driveway and got up. She took a deep breath. She was ready for whatever Amy had planned.

When she opened the door, Natasha and Amy were getting their bags out of the boot of their hire car.

'Jen!' Natasha cried, putting down her bag, running up to her and giving her a hug. 'This place is absolutely amazing... I've never seen anything like it.' She looked all around her, taking in the villa and the view to the cliffs.

Amy came over with her bag and stood beside her. 'It's really spectacular,' she said. 'Thanks for letting us stay, Jen.'

Jen smiled at them both. 'No problem at all, come on in.'

They left their bags and shoes in the hallway, and then Jen gave them a tour of the house, listening to Natasha exclaim over every tiny detail.

'Really, it's amazing, Jen. I could never normally afford a holiday somewhere like this.'

Jen took them outside and showed them the outdoor pool, hot tub and barbecue area. 'That's everything,' she said. 'You can see why Rob's parents named it Villa Paradise. I hope you have a wonderful time here.'

'Where *is* Rob?' Amy asked.

Jen tensed. 'Oh, he's fallen asleep,' she said. 'In one of the spare rooms. He was tired from such an emotional day. We renewed our marriage vows this morning.' Jen looked over at Amy with a serene smile and saw her face fall.

'You went ahead, then?' Natasha said.

'Of course,' Jen said, calmly. She could see Natasha biting her tongue, stopping herself from saying any more.

'Do you think he'll come and join us later?' Amy said.

'I doubt it, he's fast asleep.' Jen watched Amy's confusion. Clearly she and Rob had planned something for tonight. Perhaps they were going to tell Jen about their relationship. But their plans were scuppered now Rob was asleep. And Amy wasn't brave enough to tell Jen herself. She was just going to have to sit awkwardly through the evening.

'It gives us a chance to crack open the wine and have a good gossip,' Natasha said.

'Yes, let's go to the living room and I'll get the drinks out,' Jen said. 'You can both make a start while I put the kids to bed.'

'Oh, we'll help put the kids to bed, won't we, Amy? To thank you for hosting us.'

'Yeah, of course.'

Jen didn't want Amy anywhere near her children. She tried to think of something else she could do. The kitchen was still a mess from the kids' supper.

'I don't think it will take all three of us,' Jen said. 'Amy – would you mind going into the kitchen and cleaning it up? There shouldn't be too much to do. Then we'll be all ready as soon as the kids are in bed. Have you eaten? We've got lots of baguette and a variety of cheeses. Or else we could drive to the supermarket or order takeaway, although there isn't much nearby.'

'Bread and cheese sounds perfect,' Natasha said. 'French cheese and French wine... that's my idea of heaven.'

'Will Rob want something to eat?' Amy asked.

'If he wakes up hungry, he can come and get something out of the fridge,' Jen said. She hoped that if Amy drank a lot of alcohol on an empty stomach, her tongue might loosen and she'd reveal who she was and what she'd got planned. It would help if everything was out in the open before Rob woke up. Then Jen would have the upper hand.

'Right,' Amy said. 'I guess I'll get on with cleaning the kitchen.'

After they'd bathed the children and put them to bed, Natasha and Jen returned to the kitchen.

'Good job, Amy!' Jen said, patronisingly. 'The kitchen looks great.'

'No problem,' Amy said, pushing her blonde hair back behind her ears, nervously. Jen knew she was disconcerted by the fact that Rob was asleep.

'Let's reward ourselves with a drink,' Jen said, pulling a bottle of wine from the fridge. She wasn't planning to drink much herself, just nurse a glass of wine, but she wanted Amy to drink enough to let her guard down.

'What do you want, red or white?'

'I'll have white,' Natasha said.

'Amy?'

Amy flushed. 'I'll just have some water. I'm not drinking.'

'Oh, OK,' Jen said, her stomach knotting. Why wasn't Amy drinking?

Natasha was looking at Amy, whispering to her. 'Aren't you going to tell her?' she heard her say.

Jen clasped her hands together, bracing herself for what was coming.

'I'm pregnant,' Amy said quietly.

The world shifted beneath Jen's feet. 'Congratulations!' she said, so brightly she almost sounded manic. 'How far along are you?'

'Not far at all,' Amy said. 'It's very early days.'

'Oh,' Jen said. 'When I was pregnant I was told never to tell other people until I was three months in. Because of the risk of miscarriage.'

Natasha frowned at Jen.

'But that is such brilliant news, Amy,' Jen continued, her mind spinning. She was more certain than ever that Rob planned to start a new life with Amy and the baby. Could she really kill him if he had a child on the way? But it was only what he deserved. He planned to dispose of her, with no regard for their own children.

She clenched her hands together and tried not to think about it. She had accepted that her own children would have to cope with the loss of their father. This new baby was no different.

'Let me get you a glass of water, and we'll all sit down,' she said to Amy, trying to hide the shake in her voice.

They went to the living room and sat on the sofa, facing the patio doors that looked out on to the vast sea.

'So,' Natasha said. 'Things are going a bit better with you and Rob?'

Jen nodded, looking at Amy. 'Yes, the vow renewal was

really magical. It was by the sea, and it was so wonderful to have our kids there to witness it.'

Jen saw a flicker of emotion in Amy's eyes. She looked as if she might burst into tears.

'Well,' Natasha said, 'Amy and I were talking on the plane about a couple of day trips we could go on while we're here. The idea was to give you and Rob some space for family time. But if you get fed up with him, you're welcome to join us too.'

Suddenly, Amy got up. 'I'm just going to the toilet,' she said, as she left the room.

'Is she alright?' Jen asked Natasha innocently.

Natasha sighed. 'Her relationship with Jonathan is a bit more complicated than we thought. It turns out he's married. I think she's a bit worried about that, what with the pregnancy.'

Jen nodded. 'Maybe she's worried he won't leave his wife,' she said.

FORTY-SIX

Amy splashed water over her face in the bathroom. This was getting too much for her. Being caught in the middle of Rob and Jen and Natasha. Maybe she should never have come here, never put herself through this.

It had been a huge mistake. She and Rob were soulmates, but maybe that wasn't enough. He clearly didn't see it if he was renewing his wedding vows with Jen. Amy had thought he loved her, not Jen. She'd come to the Med so they could be together, spend the rest of their lives together. She remembered the last time they'd been here, in this villa, how in love they'd been.

Amy blinked back tears. If only Rob had been awake when she'd got here. Then they could have just told Jen the truth together, as soon as she'd arrived. But he'd gone and fallen asleep.

On the way to the bathroom, she'd stopped at the spare room and tried to wake him up, but he'd been out cold. It was so inconsiderate, so thoughtless. After everything she'd planned.

She frowned, confused. They were soulmates. But was this what soulmates did to each other?

She thought of Mr Beddow, the man she'd once thought she could trust more than anyone else in the world. She'd been wrong about him, too.

Amy took a deep breath and went out of the bathroom and back into the living room.

'Everything OK?' Natasha asked.

'Yeah, fine,' Amy said. 'Everything's fine.'

'Natasha was just telling me that you speak perfect French,' Jen said.

Amy blushed. 'I grew up in France. Actually, I went to school not far from here. It was an English-speaking boarding school, but I knew French too.'

'Oh wow,' Natasha said. 'Boarding must have been great. Those kind of schools have amazing facilities.'

Amy nodded. 'It's great for a lot of people,' she said. 'But I wasn't happy there. Luckily there was a couple on the teaching staff who kind of took me under their wing. Let me come back to their home to escape the bullies. They were like parents to me. My mum wasn't around much. And my dad left when I was young.' Amy wasn't quite sure why she was telling them all this. But just being near the school brought up a whole mix of emotions, and it felt like she needed an outlet for them.

'Do you ever visit them?' Natasha asked.

Amy shook her head. 'I haven't been back. I write to them though.' She didn't mention that they never replied anymore.

'We could visit them while we're here,' Natasha said. 'On one of our day trips.'

Amy nodded. 'I suppose so.' Before she'd come to the Med, she'd had a plan to go and see Gemma, to try and persuade the Beddows to share custody. But now it felt pointless. Not without Rob by her side.

'What's stopping you?' Jen said, curiously, sipping her wine.

Amy didn't know what to say. Everything was getting too much for her. Rob. Being close to her school again. The feeling of everything that was important in her life slipping away from her, out of her control. She burst into tears.

Natasha's arms were around her instantly. 'What's wrong?' she asked. 'Amy! What's up?'

Amy choked back tears. 'It's complicated,' she said. She felt the weight of the world on top of her. Suddenly she desperately wanted to tell someone what she'd been hiding all these years. And even if Natasha and Jen might hate her once they found out about her and Rob, they were her only real friends.

'It's my daughter,' she said. 'The one I told you about. She lives with them. Mr Beddow is her father. And they both looked after me in my pregnancy. I felt like they loved me and truly cared about me. They helped me hide the baby from the school, let me take a lot of time off ill when I got bigger. And when I gave birth, Mrs Beddow helped me in her own home.'

'Your teacher was the father?' Natasha said. 'That's illegal.'

'I know. He didn't want us to tell anyone, because he knew the police would come for us. We'd made a big mistake. It's just, our feelings were so strong.' Amy tried to explain. 'And we weren't hurting anyone. Mrs Beddow knew and approved. In fact, she welcomed me into their home. But the police would never understand the nature of our relationship. We had to keep it secret. We all did. The three of us. We were a family.'

'What happened?' Jen asked, softly.

'I had the baby. And then things changed. The school told me I couldn't stay on in the sixth form. Not because of the baby. The rest of the school didn't know about that. But because I'd missed so many lessons and because of my academic performance. Really, the school hadn't wanted me to do the sixth form at all, but Mr Beddow had fought for me to get a place, said that he'd tutor me to help me keep up. But as I hadn't kept up, I had to leave. Mr Beddow said he couldn't help me again. By this time I was so behind. And he was right. I didn't understand the work, and I'd had to miss months of school at the end of the pregnancy so that no one would guess. But really, I wasn't clever enough anyway. I should never have been there.'

'And when you left, they kept your baby?' Natasha asked, visibly shocked.

'They told me that was the best thing for her. They had this huge house on the school estate. And they were a loving family. Whereas I had nothing. No money. No partner. And a mother who was furious I'd been kicked out of school. I couldn't offer her the life they had. They told me that we'd keep in touch, that I could come and see her any time I wanted. But that turned out to be difficult. The school didn't want me back on the premises. And they had pretended the baby was theirs, that Mrs Beddow had given birth to her. I was shocked that anyone believed them, but they did. Mrs Beddow had taken a break from teaching around the time she would have been pregnant, so none of the staff had seen her for months. The Beddows registered her birth themselves. I had no claim on her.' Tears ran down Amy's face.

'And their house is close to here?' Natasha asked.

Amy nodded. 'About thirty minutes' drive. I just want to see her.' She felt a kind of pull towards her, a deep internal longing.

'We should go,' Natasha said. 'Tomorrow. I'll drive you.' She pulled out her phone and went into the maps app. 'Where is it?'

'I'm not sure it's a good idea,' Amy said. She longed to see Gemma, but she wasn't sure if she could face the past, face up to everything she'd lost. She thought of all the letters she'd sent to them over the years, how they'd stopped replying. They had told her they loved her, that she was part of their family. But they didn't want to see her.

'Why not?' Natasha asked.

'I don't think they'll want me there.' It all seemed too much.

'She's your daughter. It's important you see her, especially now you have another one on the way. They'll be siblings.'

Amy put her hand to her stomach and thought of her plan

to bring the baby up with Rob and Gemma in a happy family. She wasn't sure it was possible anymore.

Natasha put her arm round Amy and held her as she wiped the tears from her face. She felt a sense of relief from talking about Gemma. She'd kept the secret inside her for so long. And Jen and Natasha hadn't judged her like she feared. They'd supported her.

Half an hour later, Jen excused herself and went to bed, and Natasha and Amy stayed up talking deep into the night. Amy was grateful to have such a good friend. When Natasha called it a day and went to bed herself, Amy stayed sitting on the sofa, staring out into the dark night beyond the patio doors.

Then she got up to go to bed. She was supposed to be sharing a room with Natasha, but as she walked by the spare room, she peeked inside and saw Rob curled up, fast asleep on the double bed. Jen must have gone to bed separately, in the main bedroom.

Amy stood for a moment. She felt a deep longing to be held, to be loved. She wanted Rob's arms around her, to fall asleep against the warmth of his body.

She went to the bedroom she was sharing with Natasha and saw that she was already asleep. Amy took her suitcase and wheeled it into Rob's bedroom. Then she got ready for bed, and lay down beside him to sleep.

FORTY-SEVEN

Rob woke up feeling groggy, and rolled over in bed. He saw Jen's blonde hair on the pillow beside him, and reached for his phone on the bedside table. It was 8 a.m.

How was it 8 a.m.?

He couldn't remember the night before. The last thing he remembered was researching the tides on his laptop. But that had been mid-afternoon. He couldn't have fallen asleep and slept all this time, could he? Or had he blacked out again?

He felt uneasy, as if there was something he was missing, something he didn't understand.

He wasn't in the master bedroom. He was in the spare room. And Jen had come to sleep here beside him, instead of going back to the master bedroom by herself.

'Jen?' he said. Why wasn't she up either? Surely the kids would be up by now. They were sleeping right on the other side of the villa, near the master bedroom. Had he and Jen both slept through them waking up?

'Jen?' he said again, nudging her. Then he had a horrible sinking feeling.

The woman beside him turned over in the bed, and opened her eyes.

It wasn't Jen. It was Mia.

Rob couldn't quite compute what was going on. Why was she here, at his villa? Why was she in his bed?

'Rob,' Mia said, trying to snuggle up to him. He pulled away.

'Mia? What the hell? What are you doing here?' Rob's stomach knotted uncomfortably. He couldn't remember last night. What if he'd slept with her again and not remembered?

'I came to see you,' she said, 'so we could be together. And to help you leave Jen, once and for all.' She reached out and ran her hand through his hair.

Rob jumped out of bed. He felt a rush of relief when he realised he was still fully clothed. They couldn't have slept together.

'Mia, you know I'm not interested. I've told you so many times to stop following me. And now you're here. In my holiday home. How did you even get here?' He looked at her. She really was crazy, completely deluded. He wished he'd never set eyes on her.

'Jen invited me,' Mia said. 'Come on, Rob. Your relationship with Jen is so clearly over. We had such a good time together. We were meant to be. And now with the baby, we can be a family. This is our chance to be together. Don't deny it. Don't deny yourself.'

She grabbed Rob by the collar of his shirt and pulled him towards her.

Rob shrugged her off, pushing her away. 'Get off me!' he said, in an angry whisper. 'You're in my holiday villa, uninvited. You need to leave. Now. Leave, and get out of my life.'

FORTY-EIGHT

Rob watched as Mia ran out of the room, crying.

He couldn't believe that she'd turned up on his holiday. Was she one of the friends Jen had said was coming? She must have invited herself along. She was so deluded, so determined for them to be together.

He wasn't interested. He'd never been interested. She'd just been an office fling, the latest young temp in a long line. If she hadn't insisted on practically stalking him, he was sure he would have forgotten her name by now.

He'd realised she was going to be trouble when she'd kept asking questions about his wife and his marriage. He'd told her that he was separated, of course he had. It was always best to tell women what they wanted to hear. But Mia seemed to take it at face value, to believe him when he said he'd leave his wife for her. He'd said it without a second thought, it was what he always said. But she'd taken it seriously.

He'd slept with her a couple more times before he knew it was time to call it a day. He'd ensured her temp contract came to an end, told her he was very sorry about it but she had to leave the office. And that should have been that. They should never have seen each other again.

Except that she started to appear everywhere. She started working at his apartment block on reception and he couldn't do anything about it except avoid her. She went down to the seaside the same weekend he and Jen went on their romantic weekend away and phoned him to try and persuade him to meet. She sent him daily emails proclaiming her love, left several messages on his phone, and even booked reservations at expensive restaurants in his name, telling him to meet her there. He never turned up, but she just hadn't got the message, no matter what he did. When he told her to leave him alone, she'd threaten to tell Jen about their 'affair'. In Rob's mind it didn't even warrant that title. It had been completely meaningless to him.

Rob hadn't been able to block her completely, because he knew that the first thing she'd do was tell Jen about them. Not just about their relationship. Mia could tell her everything; about the dinners at expensive restaurants, the lunchtime escapes to hotels, she could even tell Jen how he'd taken her to the villa in the Med for a week. He didn't think his marriage could survive that. So he'd just had to ignore Mia and try to avoid her.

He'd been doing so well until that moment of weakness a few weeks ago. She'd turned up at his apartment. She'd just been there. Naked. Ready. Jen was away and he'd been out for lunchtime drinks with some old friends. And he'd come home to a naked woman, much younger than him, waiting in his bed. Who could resist that? He thought it would be one last time. He knew he was stupid even in that moment, but he was drunk and horny and she was just *there*.

And now she was pregnant and causing more problems than ever. She was determined to keep the baby, determined to trap him.

He hadn't realised she'd befriended Jen until she'd turned up at the school fete. And now it turned out that she'd gone to such lengths to befriend Jen that she was one of the two close friends who Jen had invited on their holiday. She was here, in *his* parents' villa, and she was going to ruin everything. If Jen found out all the details of their relationship, he was in huge trouble. She wouldn't trust him anymore. Mia had chosen the worst possible place to turn up, at the worst possible time. Because Rob was running scared. Everything was catching up with him. And Mia was only going to get in the way of his plan. He had to do something about her. He had to get rid of her once and for all.

FORTY-NINE

Jen splashed Lottie and Jack in the pool, and they erupted into peals of laughter. Natasha was with Ruby in the shallow end pouring water from one of Ruby's plastic cups to another. Jen felt a tug of gratitude for her friend. She'd always had enough energy to play with the kids, and everyone always had so much fun with her.

Jen hadn't seen Rob last night or this morning. She'd checked on him before she went to bed, just to make sure he was still breathing, and then returned to the master bedroom and enjoyed having the king-size bed to herself.

Today would be his last full day with the kids. She should probably wake him up soon, make sure he spent some time with them. She wondered how much the kids would miss him when he was gone. They didn't see so much of him at the moment, but it would be hard for them without a father. She'd always hated her own father for the way he treated her mother, but when he'd gone to prison she had still longed for him.

'Mummy, Mummy!' Jack shouted. 'Look at me!' Then he dived-bombed on top of her. Somehow he managed to kick her in the face.

'Jack, please, be more careful,' she said, when he resurfaced.

'Sorry!' he said.

'It looks like you need more sun cream on,' she said to him. His ears were bright red.

'Is it in your bag?' Natasha asked. She and Ruby had climbed out of the pool now and were sitting in the shade on a lounger playing a clapping game. Jen's bag was right beside Natasha.

'Yes,' Jen said.

'I'll get it,' Natasha said.

'No, it's OK,' Jen said quickly, swimming towards her. 'I can get it.'

Natasha was already rummaging around in the bag, but Ruby grabbed it from her and tipped the contents out over the paving stones.

Jen's heart raced. She'd put the pills in that bag. She hadn't wanted to leave them in the kitchen or a suitcase, or anywhere someone else might find them. It had seemed like the only safe place was the cavernous handbag she had with her all the time. But now its contents were spread all over the ground.

'I'll help you put that all that back,' she said, quickly, pulling herself out of the pool. She glanced back to check Lottie and Jack were all right, then started scooping everything up and throwing it back in the bag. She picked up wipes, hair clips, swim nappies, plasters, but she couldn't see the pills. She felt like she couldn't breathe. Her eyes met Natasha's, who was looking at her oddly.

Then she glanced at Ruby, who had the bottle of pills in her hands and was trying to open it.

'Ruby!' Jen said, just as Natasha took the pills from her.

'Little kids always pick the most dangerous thing,' Natasha said. She was studying the pill bottle. 'Hang on a minute.' She looked over at Jen, confused. 'These aren't yours. They're your mother's.'

Jen felt sick. Natasha couldn't work it out now. Not after all her planning.

'I... I've been having a lot of aches and pains,' Jen said, quickly thinking of the lie, 'and I didn't have time to go to the doctor, so...'

'How long have you been taking them?' Natasha asked quietly.

'Not that long. Life has just been so stressful lately. I need them to relax.'

'On our weekend away together, after our kiss... you took them then, didn't you? You were out like a light that night. I tossed and turned.'

'Yeah, I did,' Jen admitted. 'I take them every night.'

Jen held her breath, praying Natasha wouldn't ask any more questions, praying she wouldn't connect the pills to Rob being fast asleep when they arrived last night.

'They're addictive, you know,' Natasha said.

Jen smiled sadly. 'Yeah, I think I know. When life's less stressful, maybe I'll come off them.'

'If you're ever stressed you can talk to me,' Natasha said. 'I want to help.'

Jen longed to confide in Natasha, to tell her everything; about Amy and Rob, about her plans. But she couldn't risk telling her the truth and implicating her. Even so, she knew that if anything went wrong, Natasha would be the first person she'd call.

FIFTY

Amy couldn't stop shaking. She was curled up in a ball in the corner of the room she shared with Natasha, sobbing.

She couldn't believe what Rob had said to her, how heartlessly he'd pushed her away, shouting at her to leave. He didn't want her. He didn't want to be with her.

It just couldn't be true. He'd told her so many times he loved her, that he would leave Jen. He'd said that he wanted her.

And then he'd gone quiet after her temping job had finished. The link between them had been severed. At first she'd thought it was just because they didn't see each other at work anymore. There weren't the regular opportunities to sneak out of the office. But it hadn't only been that. She'd tried to reconnect. She'd tried so many times to make him see that they were soulmates. But he was always so distant.

She hadn't known what she'd done wrong. All she had to do was prove to him that they were meant to be. She'd booked dinners at expensive restaurants for them and got a job in his apartment block so it would be easy for him to see her. She'd even studied Jen to make sure that she wasn't lacking anything that Jen had, and changed her hair and image to match Jen's, because she thought that was what he liked.

She'd thought they were back on track when she'd let herself into his penthouse and they'd reconnected. But then he'd gone back to being cold. Even when she'd told him she was having his baby, he still wasn't interested. Amy just wanted to be in a loving family; it was all she had ever wanted. She didn't know what else she could do. It was like he was denying the existence of fate, denying the inevitability of them being together.

She'd made it so easy for him. Coming all the way to the Med. Joining him so they could tell Jen together.

But he'd pushed her away. Told her to go.

She didn't understand. Rob had started off so loving, so caring. But he'd changed. Just like Mr Beddow.

Amy swallowed. There was obviously something fundamentally wrong with her, something deep inside which was just unlovable. No one ever really loved her, they just used her.

'Amy?' Natasha was in the doorway, looking down at her. 'What's going on?' She came over and put her arm around her. 'I came to see if you were ready to go on our trip to your old school.'

Amy shook her head. 'I can't. I think I have to leave.'

'What? Why?'

'It's Rob,' she said.

Natasha looked confused. 'What about Rob?'

Amy sobbed harder. There was no point in lying anymore. She'd messed everything up. 'Rob's the married man I was seeing,' she said to Natasha.

'But what about Jonathan?' Natasha asked.

'There is no Jonathan. Only Rob.'

Natasha's mouth dropped open. 'What?' she said. 'You

mean you've been seeing Rob all this time? You were the person he was having an affair with?'

'I'm so sorry,' Amy said, through sobs. 'I thought he loved me. I really did. But he just used me.'

'But, what about Jen? How could you do this to her?'

'It started before I even met Jen,' Amy said.

'You didn't know she was his wife?'

Amy shook her head. 'I didn't know until we looked in Rob's emails and I saw his name. And then I just felt so guilty, I didn't know what to do. I tried to end it with Rob, but he said he still loved me.' The lies rolled off Amy's tongue easily. Jen and Natasha had always supported her. They were the only people who ever had. She'd been blind not to see that before. She needed to say whatever she had to to keep them as friends. They couldn't blame her for this. They were all she had left.

'You kept seeing him?'

'He said he loved me, that he was leaving Jen. And I thought she would want him to leave too. He'd fallen for me. It seemed like the best thing for everyone. But honestly, I felt so guilty. All the time. It was so hard.' Sometimes Amy felt like she wasn't real at all, like she was acting her way through life, playing a series of parts.

'Harder for Jen than for you,' Natasha said, bitterly.

'I know,' Amy said. 'I really messed up.' She felt sick now, at the thought of losing Natasha and Jen too. They felt like family. 'Do you think she might forgive me? Do you think we could all still be friends?' Amy knew it was a stupid question, that there was no chance, but she was desperate.

Natasha pulled away from her. 'We can't – Amy, I know you're upset. But you've completely betrayed Jen. You can't expect us to be friends now.'

'I'm so sorry,' Amy said. 'I know I was stupid. But Rob's used me too. He's lied and lied to me. He doesn't care about me at all.'

'Rob doesn't care about anyone but himself,' Natasha said.

Amy knew she was right. But now she was left all alone, with no one in the world who cared about her. She sobbed harder, as Natasha left the room.

FIFTY-ONE

Rob had been pacing up and down the spare bedroom, trying to get his thoughts straight. He needed to get Amy out of Jen's way, ensure that she didn't tell Jen the truth about them. He needed to get her to leave the villa. Right now. If Jen thought they were in any kind of relationship, there was no way he could trust her to help him with anything.

He still felt groggy, slightly unstable on his feet. He had a splitting headache and the pacing was making him feel weak and dizzy. He was starting to wonder if there was something seriously wrong with him, something more than stress. The blackout he'd had last night was his third. What if there was something physically wrong with his body? That couldn't happen to him. Not now.

Rob tried to put his worries out of his mind and focus on the present. He had to get Mia out of his villa. He tried to think of what would motivate her. Money, perhaps. He could bribe her to go away. Pay her off. He'd need to pay for a taxi to get her out of here and to the airport. Pay for a flight, too. It would be expensive, but it would be worth it. He just had to get her away from Jen.

Her suitcase was on the floor. He threw the hairbrush and phone charger she'd left by the bed inside and zipped it up.

Then he went to try and find her.

He heard the sound of laughter from outside, and as he stepped through the patio doors he saw Jen and the kids in the pool.

'About time you got up,' Jen said with a smile.

Rob breathed a sigh of relief. She couldn't have spoken to Mia yet. He walked over. 'I don't know what happened to me. I must have been exhausted. I just passed out while I was on my computer.'

'You've been stressed lately,' Jen said. 'But I'm sure life will be more peaceful soon.'

Rob nodded. 'Yeah, I think so,' he said, thinking of the new life he'd planned, away from everything.

'You should spend time with the kids today,' she said. He heard her unspoken words. *Before you leave tomorrow.* She was still planning to help him. She didn't know about Mia.

'Yes,' he said. 'I'm looking forward to it. I thought I'd take them down to the beach, a few miles up the road. There's a big sandy stretch up there. Very safe for paddling.'

'Sounds perfect,' Jen said.

'We should all go,' he said. 'Have a family day out together.' For a moment he felt a rush of emotion. It would be the last day they would spend as a family. Although he hadn't thought much about it before, there was something nice about all being together, something comforting and warm. He realised with a jolt that he would miss that, the feeling of togetherness.

'Sure,' Jen said. 'That would be nice.'

He needed to find Mia first, to get rid of her. 'I'll go inside and have a shower and get ready,' he said. 'Stay in the pool a bit longer. It looks like you're having fun.'

Rob gave them a casual wave and then went back inside. He saw Natasha in the kitchen, slicing an apple.

'Hello,' he said distractedly. 'I'm looking for Mia, have you seen her?'

'Mia...' Natasha looked confused for a second. 'Oh, Amelia. Amy. She doesn't want to see you.' Natasha glared at him and Rob realised she must already know about their relationship.

'You can't believe anything she says,' he said.

'You're a lying bastard, Rob,' Natasha said. 'I don't know how you can behave the way you do.'

Rob felt a surge of anger, which he pushed down. He couldn't get distracted by Natasha. He needed to find Mia.

'You don't even know me,' he said, as he rushed out of the kitchen.

He walked round the villa, looking in each of the rooms, until he saw her lying face down on the bed in the room she was sharing with Natasha.

'Mia,' he said, reaching out and grabbing her arm. 'You have to leave.' He pulled a wad of notes out of his wallet. 'I can give you some money for the flight back. Or you can go on a tour of France. Or have a holiday. Just somewhere else. Not here.'

Mia turned towards him. 'Get away from me!' she screamed.

Instinctively, Rob put his hand over her mouth and held her down on the bed. Jen mustn't hear this. 'Be quiet,' he hissed. He held up the cash again. 'Look, I have money for you. There's over €1,000.' He felt awful about parting with it. It was part of his escape fund. But it had to be done. If Mia told Jen about them, there wouldn't be any escape. 'You could have a brilliant holiday,' he said. 'Travel round France. Be completely free. Or I could pay for an early flight home, if you'd prefer.'

She pushed him hard, then rolled away, off the other side of the bed. She ran towards the door. He grabbed her arm. 'Mia!'

'I said get off me!' She ran out of the room and to the kitchen, Rob chasing after her.

'Mia! Wait! I'm trying to help you.'

'What's he doing to you?' Natasha said angrily. She was still standing at the kitchen counter, the knife in her hand.

'He held me down,' Mia said. 'He—'

Rob grabbed her again. 'Shut up – that's not true.' He put his hand over her mouth and she squirmed. 'I'm trying to help you, Mia.' He looked at Natasha, saw the shock in her eyes. 'I'm just trying to help her.'

'Get off her!' Natasha shouted.

But Rob didn't want to let her go, not until she'd agreed to leave. 'You need to go,' he said to her. 'Just take the money and go.'

Mia squirmed beneath him, and out of the corner of his eye he saw a glint of silver. Natasha had slid the knife across the countertop to Mia, and Mia reached out and grabbed it, her knuckles turning white as she gripped it tightly. Rob let go of her quickly and stepped back, just as Mia lashed out angrily and the knife sliced across his chest.

FIFTY-TWO

Jen walked into the kitchen with the kids in their towels, fresh out of the swimming pool. They were hungry and had come inside for a snack.

She saw Rob holding Amy at the kitchen counter, his hand over her mouth.

She took a step back, her mind spinning. What was going on? She'd thought they were planning to run away together. Had they had a fight?

'Lottie, Jack,' she whispered. 'Take Ruby into your bedroom, and start getting changed.' She pushed them towards the door to their bedroom, shielding Amy and Rob from their view. As they went inside, she closed the door behind them.

She turned back to the scene in the kitchen just in time to see Amy slash the knife across Rob's chest.

'What are you doing?' she shouted. She reached out and grabbed the knife from Amy, who was shaking and crying.

'He was holding her down. He had his hand over her mouth,' Natasha said. 'It was self-defence.' Jen tried to understand what was going on. Why would Rob be attacking Amy? Had they had an argument? What about the baby?

'She's crazy,' Rob said quickly. He was clutching his chest where the knife had slashed his skin. 'She's been stalking me. Following me for months. I haven't been able to get rid of her.'

Jen's mouth dropped open. She'd seen the messages between them. They'd been planning a life together. Why was he accusing her of stalking?

'It's not true,' Amy said. 'We were having an affair. I'm so sorry, Jen, but we were. And we were in love.'

Jen looked from Rob to Amy, shocked. He had dropped her, she realised. He had abandoned her so callously and thoughtlessly. Was it because of Jen? Had he thought she was going to tell Jen everything and ruin his plans? Maybe he had chosen Jen after all.

Jen saw the wad of cash still in Rob's hand and realised he had been planning to pay Amy off. Something must have changed between them. Now he was treating her like he'd treated Jen. Jen couldn't help feeling like she deserved it.

'How could you, Rob?' she said, turning to her husband. 'How could you have an affair with my friend? After everything I've done for you.'

'I'm so sorry, Jen,' he said, still clutching his chest. 'But it's not like she says. It was just a one-off, a mistake. Since then, she's become obsessed with me.'

'You told me you loved me!' Amy screamed at him. 'You told me you'd leave her, that we'd be together.'

Rob shook his head. 'You're a delusional bitch.' He spat the words out. 'It was a huge mistake sleeping with you.' He looked at Jen. 'Jen's the one I love.'

Jen felt like laughing. As if she'd believe him after everything he'd done.

'You managed to impregnate her,' Jen said calmly, enjoying seeing him squirm.

On the other side of the room, Rob's mobile phone started to ring. They all ignored it.

'Like I said, I made one mistake. One night. That was it.'

Natasha glared at him. 'We don't believe you, Rob.'

Jen saw that Rob had gone pale and that blood was dripping from his chest onto the terracotta tiles. She grabbed some kitchen roll and started mopping it up, but it had seeped into the grout and it wouldn't come off easily. *This is no good*, she thought. If Rob was going to drown in the sea, there couldn't be traces of his blood in the villa. If the police came to investigate, it would look suspicious.

'Where are the children?' Natasha suddenly asked.

'In their bedroom,' Jen said.

'I'll check on them,' Natasha said, as she left the kitchen, leaving Jen alone with Rob and Amy.

'How could you do this to me?' she asked Amy. 'I thought you were my friend.'

Amy burst into tears. 'I was, Jen. I mean, I *am* your friend. I was just in love.'

'I've asked her to leave,' Rob said, clutching his chest. 'She needs to get out of here.'

'I'll go,' Amy said quietly. 'I'll go and get my case.'

As Amy left, Jen turned to Rob. 'Why would you do this to me?' she said.

'I'm sorry,' he said. 'I really am.'

Jen turned away from him.

'Jen?' he said. 'Honestly, it's not how it seems. She stalked me. I was... almost afraid of her.'

Jen wanted to tell him just how much she despised him, that she wasn't even sure she could bear his company for even one more day. She wanted to tell him that she was far cleverer than him, that she would outwit him. But she couldn't. Tomorrow he'd be out of her life forever. She had to be patient.

'We need to sort out your injury,' she said. 'Bandage it up.'

Rob looked down at his chest. The blood was still flowing.

'You see!' he said. 'She slashed me with a knife. She's completely crazy.'

Rob's phone was ringing again, as Jen rooted around in the cupboard for bandages. She finally pulled some out from the back of the cupboard. She took a wet towel and started to clean Rob's wound.

'We're still going ahead with our plan tomorrow, aren't we?' Rob whispered urgently. 'We can have a nice family afternoon today first.'

Jen nodded. She was wondering how she could use Amy's impulsiveness to her advantage. Amy hated Rob now. Maybe she could do some of the dirtier work for her.

'Don't worry. We won't change the plan.'

She shivered, as she gently placed the bandages over Rob's wound. She thought of his hand over Amy's mouth as he held her down. She'd never thought of him as a violent man, but now it was clear what he was capable of when he was desperate.

Jen went to the kids' bedroom to check on them. The older two were colouring and Natasha was on the floor making a tower out of books with Ruby.

'Are they OK?' Jen asked.

'They're fine,' Natasha said. She stood up, and looked Jen in the eye. 'But are you OK? That must have been quite a shock.'

'Yeah, it was.' Jen didn't know what else to say.

'Rob showed his true colours.' Natasha squeezed her arm, and the physical sensation of her touch made Jen want to cry. No matter what, Natasha was always so kind to her.

'I need to make the kids' lunch,' Jen said. 'I'm taking them to the beach later.' She didn't want to cry in front of Natasha. She needed to keep her emotions in check.

'OK,' Natasha said. 'Well, I might go out for a drive in a bit, see some of the scenery around here. That is, if you'll be OK on your own?'

'I'll be fine,' Jen said, sounding more confident than she felt.

'Well, if you need anything, you know where I am. Just call me.'

Natasha left to go to her room, and Jen took the kids into the open-plan living room and turned the TV on. Then she started making the sandwiches in the kitchen, where she could still see them. Rob was nowhere to be seen. She wondered if he was getting ready to go to the beach with them, if he was still planning to go ahead with their family trip.

As she made the sandwiches, Jen's phone started ringing.

She looked at the caller display in surprise.

It was Rob's office.

'Hello?' she said.

'Hi, it's Grace. Sorry to call you, Jen. I can't get hold of Rob. Is he there with you?'

'No, he's not. And we're on holiday at the moment. He's not working.' Grace had no right to call them when they were away.

'Oh, right. Yeah, I know that. It's just, it's very urgent. I've been trying to call Rob but he's not answering.' The words rushed out of Grace's mouth as if she was running out of time.

'What's it about?' Jen asked, curious.

'It's serious,' Grace had said. 'It's the police. They're taking all the files from the office. The Riverview Apartments files. They're taking our computers too. As part of the investigation.'

'What?' Jen said, her stomach turning. 'The police? Is Rob in trouble?'

'I don't know. It's not looking good. Listen, you need to get Rob to call me. I can fill him in. But there's a big problem here. They say that the Riverview Apartments are unsafe. That someone forged the safety certificate. And – I don't know why – but everyone thinks it was Rob. They think he committed the fraud.'

'I'll get him to call you,' Jen said.

She thought of them returning in a week's time to the pent-house, the kids back home, fast asleep in their bedrooms. 'Are the apartments safe, Grace?' she asked.

'I don't know. I don't think so.' Grace stumbled over her words. 'They failed the safety checks. But someone covered it up.'

FIFTY-THREE

Amy had packed her bag, tears sliding down her face. She couldn't believe how much she had messed everything up. Rob wasn't her soulmate. He couldn't be. He wasn't even a nice person. All these months she'd obsessed over him, spent every waking moment thinking about him. It had all been a waste of her time.

Now she had nothing. No boyfriend. No friends. And she had to get out of here. She didn't even know where she wanted to go. Or where she could afford to go. She hadn't taken Rob's money. And she couldn't afford a flight home. She'd have to find a cheap hostel somewhere, settle down for the night, put it on her credit card. Or maybe she could stay at her old school. They'd have spare rooms in the summer holidays. Maybe Mr and Mrs Beddow would take her in, like they used to. They had been like a family to her when she was younger. But then they'd started ignoring her letters and emails. They'd cut her off entirely. Just like Rob.

But wasn't that where she should be? With her daughter? Her own flesh and blood. She'd always felt like she belonged with them, and she felt a huge longing for her daughter. She'd be five now. She wanted to find out what kind of child she'd grown into. She needed to be with her.

Amy didn't want to see Rob or Jen again. She felt too humiliated and ashamed. She couldn't believe she'd slashed Rob with the knife. But she'd been terrified with him holding her like that.

Amy sneaked out through the side door, and made her way round the villa to the driveway. She thought of the time she and Rob had spent in the villa together, the week in heaven they'd had, just the two of them. It had meant everything to her, but nothing to him. It was time to let it go.

On the driveway, she saw the hire car Natasha had driven here. She put her suitcase beside it and tried the door. It was locked.

Natasha had the key.

The last thing Amy wanted was to go back inside the house. But she needed the hire car to get away. There was no way she could afford a taxi.

Amy went up to the kitchen window and peered inside. Jen was there, facing away from her, making sandwiches. She could see the kids behind her in the open-plan living room, watching the television. As she was looking through the window, the front door opened and Natasha came out.

'What are you doing?'

Amy jumped back from the window. 'I was just... I need the car keys. I'm going to leave. Just like they want.'

'You can't drive the hire car. I'm the only named driver.'

Amy stared at her. 'But I need to leave.'

'If Rob wants you to leave, he should be paying for your taxi and accommodation.'

'He offered me money, but I turned him down. I can't go back in and ask him now. I just can't. Just let me leave. I need to get away from all this.'

Natasha sighed. 'I was going to take the car and go on a trip out. I think Rob and Jen need some time to talk. I don't want to be in their way.'

'Could you drop me off?'

'Where are you going?'

Amy swallowed. 'To my old school.'

'To see your daughter?'

Amy nodded.

'Are you sure now's the right time? You've had an emotional morning.'

'I was thinking that I could stay there. Spend some time with Gemma.'

Natasha looked worried. 'What if they say no?' she said.

Amy tried not to cry. 'How could they?' she asked. 'They can't deny me the chance to see my daughter.'

Natasha squeezed her arm. 'I'll come with you,' she said.

As Amy watched the rolling fields pass by the car window, she remembered when her mother had first dropped her off at the boarding school. She'd been so excited. But almost as soon as she'd arrived she'd realised that she didn't fit in and she'd quickly grown to hate it.

It had been ten years ago, and the start of the feeling of emptiness that had always been inside her. Her father had already left when she was tiny, and her mother had little interest in visiting her in the holidays. She had always longed for a family and a place where she felt safe. Mr and Mrs Beddow's house had provided that.

They were the only people who had ever taken an interest in her. They didn't have their own children so they would 'adopt' the children who were struggling socially, having them round to their huge house on the school premises for dinner.

And then Mr Beddow had fallen in love with her, and they'd started their relationship. His wife had known all about it, inviting Amy to stay in their home overnight. They had both loved her, they always used to say.

It had been the only time she'd felt part of a family. She'd thought she could have that again with Rob, but it had proved impossible.

They got to the school and pressed the buzzer on the gates. The person on the other end of the intercom let them in without asking who they were. She supposed the security was more lax in the school holidays. As Natasha drove up the winding drive, Amy felt overcome with nerves. She wondered what her daughter would look like now. She wondered if she'd recognise her, if she'd instantly know she was her mother, immediately feel connected to her.

Amy directed Natasha down the driveway and then right to the staff houses. The house was at the end of the lane, one of the bigger properties with its own garden.

'It's just there,' Amy said. 'I can get out here. I'll get my bag from the boot.'

'I'm not leaving you,' Natasha said firmly. 'I'm coming in with you. We need to knock and introduce ourselves. They aren't expecting us.'

Amy frowned in annoyance. She should have come back years ago to see her daughter. They should have been expecting her for years. She deserved to see her child.

'OK,' she said.

As she walked up the pathway to the door, vomit rose unexpectedly in her throat and she swallowed it back down. She'd come up this path so many times to see Mr Beddow. She'd always been so excited, had always felt so lucky to be the one they had chosen. But now she was older, it struck her that there was something a bit sordid and dirty about it. The couple had been in their forties. She'd been sixteen when the relationship started, seventeen by the time she'd had Gemma.

She stared at the brass lion door knocker, the same one

they'd had all those years ago. Suddenly she wanted to be anywhere but here. She felt like the world was closing in on her and it was all a big mistake.

Natasha lifted the door knocker and rapped on the door.

Amy took a step back, and then the door opened.

A woman in her thirties with short dark hair stood in front of them. 'Hello!' she said, cheerfully, with an Irish accent. 'I saw the car pull up. What can I do for you?'

'Are Mr and Mrs Beddow in?' Amy said, peering round her.

'Mr and Mrs Beddow? Oh, they don't live here anymore. They left a couple of years ago. My husband is one of the house-masters now, so we took over this house.'

'Oh, right,' Natasha said. 'Well, we're sorry to bother you.'

'No problem at all. It can get a bit boring here sometimes in the school holidays. It's very quiet... I'm grateful for the disturbance.'

'Did Mr and Mrs Beddow move to another school?' Amy asked, trying to understand how it was possible that they didn't live here anymore. How could they have left without telling her where they'd gone? They'd taken her daughter.

'Oh, no,' the woman said. 'They both left teaching. There was a bit of a scandal with one of the teenage students here. Rumours about Mr Beddow. It was all hush-hush, but I don't think he could get another job.'

Amy swallowed. He'd met someone else. Another student after her. She hadn't been special at all. Not even to him.

'Do you have an address for them?' Natasha asked.

'Yeah, of course. I'll write it down for you.'

When they got back to the car, Amy squeezed her eyes shut, trying not to cry. The family had moved on, and they'd taken her daughter with them. She needed to find her.

FIFTY-FOUR

Jen stood on the sandy beach, the wind in her hair, watching her children build sandcastles with Rob. She was still trying to digest everything that had happened that morning. Rob's run-in with Amy, his complete denial of his affair. And then the call from Grace. The call that had opened her eyes to just how little her husband cared about his family.

As she'd made the kids' sandwiches, she'd realised the truth. Rob was running away from more than just financial problems. He'd committed fraud. He was in trouble with the police. And he'd sold unsafe flats to his clients. He'd let families with kids live in their apartment building when he knew he'd forged the safety certificate. He'd let his own wife and family live at the very top of an unsafe building. How could he? Ruby had nearly fallen off the balcony and he'd still said nothing, letting them continue to live there. He didn't care about them at all. He'd put his kids in danger without a second thought.

Feelings of anger and disgust had overwhelmed her as she cut the sandwiches into squares. She'd wanted to confront Rob, to take the hammer and smash his head in. She'd wanted to let all her rage out. He didn't deserve her and the kids.

Jen had tried to calm down, her head pounding. She just had to wait until tomorrow. She had to stick to her plan, and get rid of Rob calmly and sensibly, so that there would be no trace of what she'd done. Now, more than ever, she needed him out of her life for good.

Pretending to be a happy family at the beach felt almost painful. She was repulsed by her husband and wanted to be as far away from him as was physically possible, and yet she still had to pretend. For the children. This was their last day as a family, the last memories of their dad. She had to make it special. Tomorrow she would send them to their usual holiday club to keep them out of the way. They would stay overnight as they sometimes did to give Rob and Jen a night off from child-care. In the morning, they would have lost their father.

Tears pricked Jen's eyes, and she wiped them with the back of her hand. She hated to think of doing something so awful to her kids. But it was the only way. His behaviour had taken everything from them and put them in danger.

In front of her, Jack was filling up the bucket with sand to make a castle and Lottie was finding shells to decorate it, while Ruby sat beside them digging up the sand with her hands and letting it fall back through her fingers. Jen pulled out her phone, stepped back and took some pictures of the kids with Rob. She imagined the photos taking pride of place on their bedside tables as they grew older. Their final memories of their father. She'd post some of them on Instagram later, evidence of their happy life together.

She put down her phone and looked around, then approached a passing couple. 'Would you mind taking a photo of our whole family?' she asked.

'Of course,' the woman said, smiling and taking the phone.

Jen sat down in the sand and put Ruby on her lap and got the kids to gather round her. Rob knelt down beside her. His phone started ringing in his pocket and he pulled it out and looked at it. Jen saw the name on the caller display. *Grace*. Rob quickly put the phone back in his pocket then looked up at the woman taking the photo. Jen hadn't told Rob what Grace had said to her earlier, but she could tell from the way Rob was ignoring her calls that he knew why she was calling. He had a guilty conscience.

'There you go,' the woman said, handing the phone back after she'd taken the photos. 'I've taken a few. I hope they're OK.'

'Thank you.' Jen looked through the photos. There was one with them all smiling straight at the camera. She wondered how the kids would remember this day, whether they'd think back to it fondly.

Earlier they'd stopped at a playground, and while the children had played on the swings and slides, they'd finalised their plans for Rob's disappearance tomorrow. Jen knew now that Rob's plan to disappear had always been real. He wasn't secretly planning to run away with Amy or dispose of Jen. He needed to disappear to escape the police and the fraud charges.

Rob would leave his pile of clothes by the sea, and then swim out round the rock face to the beach on the other side. He'd pick up the rucksack he'd left there earlier, dry himself and change, then hike to a hostel, using his new name to check in. Before Jen reported him missing the next morning, he'd shave his head and keep moving from hostel to hostel, across Europe.

Jen had the pills ready. If she crushed them into a drink just before he went down to the beach, then he would be incapacitated, and once he started his swim he would surely drown. But it would be hard to get the timing right. He needed to feel weak and woozy once he was in the water, not before.

If her plan worked, then his body should wash out to sea. If it didn't, then the drowning would still look accidental: death by misadventure. According to Jen's research on the public computers in the local library, the medication should have already disappeared from his system by the time they did a post-mortem.

Everything felt risky, but it was Jen's best chance to start again, to have a new life with her children.

As Jen looked out to sea, her phone rang.

Natasha.

'Hi,' she said, 'what's up?' It was hard to hear over the roar of the waves.

'I'm with Amy,' Natasha said. 'We're looking for flights to get back to the UK. There aren't any in the next few days.'

'Oh,' Jen said. 'Can she travel back another way?'

'The Eurostar's fully booked too.'

Jen frowned. 'Has she got somewhere to stay?'

'No, not yet. It's the height of the season. We're struggling to find anywhere with a free room.'

Jen glanced over at Rob, who was playing with the kids. She could see the bandages she'd placed over the knife wound on his chest. She thought of how Amy hadn't hesitated once she'd had the knife in her hand. Rob had really screwed her over. She was right to be furious with him. Amy was the only person who hated Rob as much as Jen did. Maybe she could be an ally. Or a suspect if the police ever got suspicious. Either way she could be useful.

'Why doesn't she come back to the villa?' Jen asked.

'Are you sure?' Natasha said, surprised.

'Yeah,' Jen said. 'She can stay in your room. Just tell her to keep out of my way.'

FIFTY-FIVE

'Jen says you can stay in the villa until your flight home,'
Natasha said to Amy. They had stopped at a café while they
looked up accommodation and flights for Amy and phoned Jen.

'What?' Amy asked, through her tears. 'Why?'

Natasha shrugged. 'I don't know. It's very kind of her, given
the circumstances.'

Amy's body shook with sobs. She was taken aback by Jen's
actions. 'She's always been kind to me,' she said, quietly. 'A part
of me wished Rob had had a different wife, someone easier to
hate. I really valued our friendship.'

Natasha sighed. 'What you did was unforgivable.'

'I know,' Amy said shakily. 'I'm sorry. I regret everything.
Now I know what he's like...'

'Didn't you always know?' Natasha asked. 'Even when I
worked with Rob briefly, it was obvious he was a womaniser. I
always thought Jen was too good for him.'

'I believed what he told me about wanting to be with me,'
Amy said. 'I trusted him when he said he'd leave his wife. How
could I have been so stupid?' She put her head in her hands.
'I've always been like this, I don't know why. I trusted Mr and

Mrs Beddow too. I thought they had my best interests at heart. But he's taken my daughter and not even told me where they've moved to.'

'We have the address now,' Natasha said, gently. 'We can pay them a visit. Make sure you see Gemma.'

Amy put her hand to her belly and thought of the life growing inside her. The baby would be tiny at this stage, so small and fragile. But soon Amy would have two children. She needed them to know each other, to be a family. She needed to get Gemma back.

But without Rob, what could she really offer her?

'I wish I could have kept Gemma,' Amy said. 'Maybe they'll be willing to share custody. Then my two children can be proper siblings.' Her heart ached as she thought of her daughter, imagining the feel of her small body in her arms.

'Maybe,' Natasha said, but Amy could hear the hesitation in her voice. No doubt she thought Amy was completely crazy to think she stood a chance of getting access to her daughter.

'What's the address?' Amy said. 'Can we go there now?'

Natasha looked at the piece of paper in her hand, then typed the address into Google Maps. 'It's about an hour away,' she said. 'Maybe it's best if we get some sleep and go tomorrow. It's been a stressful day.'

Amy felt a wave of disappointment wash through her. 'OK,' she said reluctantly. 'Do you promise you'll take me?'

'Of course,' Natasha said.

They drove back to the villa in silence, thoughts of Gemma and Mr and Mrs Beddow swirling around Amy's head.

When she got back she went straight to the bedroom, walking quickly past the living room where she could hear Jen and Rob playing a board game with the older children. It wasn't right, Amy thought, that Jen had all of that love, and she had nothing. It wasn't fair. But perhaps she deserved to be alone.

She had never been good enough. Not for Mr Beddow, not for Rob, not even good enough to have real friends.

She sat on the bed for a moment, not sure what to do with herself. Her stomach suddenly cramped, and she bent over in pain. A feeling of complete hopelessness washed over her as she made her way to the toilet. As she sat down, her underwear revealed what she had feared. Her period had started.

FIFTY-SIX

That evening, Jen and Natasha sat together on the sofa, sipping their wine. The kids were in bed and Rob had gone out to the driving range. He'd told Jen he needed to go and hit some golf balls to calm down and de-stress before the big day tomorrow. She was glad to have him out of the way. It was taking all her mental resources to behave like she still liked him, when really she despised him.

'It's been a long day,' Jen said to Natasha.

'Yeah, I know. Thanks for letting Amy come back and sleep here. She had quite a rough time earlier. We went to see her daughter, but she'd moved.'

'Oh,' Jen said. 'So she didn't see her?'

'No. We have their new address. We'll try again tomorrow.'

'Is she alright?' Jen asked.

'Not really. I think Rob's rejection has hit her really hard, but what did she expect?'

'Hmm...' It was Amy's own fault. But now Jen knew Amy a bit better, she could see how naive and vulnerable she was. Rob shouldn't have got involved with her in the first place. He'd taken advantage of her.

'He's a bastard,' Natasha said, moving closer to her on the sofa.

'Yeah,' Jen said. 'He is.' There was no point hiding her feelings about Rob from Natasha anymore. She rested her head lightly on Natasha's shoulder, grateful to have her friend beside her.

'I'm surprised you've been so kind to Amy,' Natasha said, running her fingers through Jen's hair. 'After what she did.'

Jen frowned. 'She betrayed me,' she said. 'But she's so young. And I understand why she was taken in by Rob. He probably told her whatever she wanted to hear to get her into bed.'

'You're being much nicer than I'd be,' Natasha said.

Jen smiled. 'I don't have the energy to be angry,' she said. The truth was, now that she had seen how much Amy despised Rob, how much he'd humiliated her, she realised that Amy would be a good person to have on her side.

'What's she doing now?' Jen asked Natasha.

'She's just reading in her room, I think.'

'Why don't you see if she wants to come and sit with us?'

Natasha looked confused. 'Are you sure?'

'Yeah, why not? We women need to stick together.'

'OK, then.' Natasha gave her an odd look, but disappeared and then returned with Amy a few minutes later.

'Amy,' Jen said, her voice syrupy-sweet, 'why don't you join us? I'm afraid we don't have many soft drinks. Do you want some water? I heard you had a stressful day.'

'Thanks,' Amy said, staring at the floor. 'Are you having wine? I could do with a glass.'

Jen raised her eyebrows. 'I thought you were pregnant?' she said.

Amy's face fell. 'Yeah,' she said. 'I thought I was. My period was late. But I got it today.'

Natasha reached for the wine bottle, poured Amy a glass, and handed it to her.

'Really?' Jen said. 'That's a bit of a coincidence, isn't it?'

'What is?'

'Well, it's just convenient. Now you and Rob have split up, you're not pregnant anymore. Almost like you were lying about it in the first place. So you could keep him.'

Amy took a gulp of wine. 'It wasn't like that. When my period didn't come, I was so sure I was pregnant. I felt it in my bones.'

'Didn't you take a test?'

'I didn't think I needed to.'

'I'm sorry,' Natasha said, putting her arm round Amy. 'It must be difficult to take it in.'

Amy nodded, wiping a tear away. 'Maybe it's fate,' she said. 'Rob never wanted the baby.'

A tiny part of Jen felt sorry for Amy. She seemed so unhappy.

'He said he'd leave you,' Amy said quietly. 'And I believed him.'

'He can be charming,' Jen said. 'But he's lied to us both. He said he loved me, that I was the only one for him.'

'I can't believe all the lies he told,' Natasha said.

'I hate him,' Jen said, finally being honest with her friends and giving voice to the rage that had built up inside her.

'You can do so much better than him,' Natasha said, moving closer to her. 'So can you, Amy.'

'I can't believe he held his hand over your mouth like that,' Jen said. 'It was an assault.' Jen had never seen Rob do anything even slightly violent before. But then again Rob had always been in control of everything, always got his own way. There was another side to him.

'I was terrified,' Amy said. 'That's why I took the knife – I'm so sorry...'

'Don't be sorry,' Jen said. 'I understand. We need to look out for each other.'

Amy smiled tentatively. 'I know I've messed up,' she said. 'But I was hoping that after this holiday, the three of us could still be friends.'

Jen tried not to laugh. Amy was so deluded. Instead she nodded sagely. 'We'll have to see each other at the cat shelter and in the apartment block. I think we can try and put this behind us and start again.' Jen knew she needed Amy and Natasha onside. Whatever happened to Rob tomorrow, she needed them to be telling the same story as her. She needed their loyalty.

Amy smiled. 'Thanks, Jen.'

Natasha looked from Amy to Jen, confused. 'I think you're both drunk,' she said. 'I never thought you could be friends again after this.' She smiled. 'But I'm not complaining.'

'So what happened with going to see your daughter? Natasha told me she wasn't there,' Jen said, wanting to change the subject from Rob before she gave too much away.

'They'd moved away because of some kind of scandal with another young girl at the school,' Natasha said. Tears started to fall down Amy's cheeks and Jen passed her a tissue.

Amy wiped her tears away. 'I don't think they want to see me. Mr Beddow – Gemma's father – I don't think he ever really loved me. Him and his wife pretended my daughter was theirs. They don't want me in their lives.'

'That's horrific,' Jen said, genuinely shocked. She couldn't imagine the pain if someone took her babies from her. 'They can't steal your daughter from you.'

'I let them,' Amy said, tearfully. 'I said she was better off with them than with me.'

'You were young,' Jen said. 'They took advantage of you. They groomed you. And then they stole your baby.'

Amy tipped her wine glass back, and Jen could see that the

reality of her relationship with her teachers was only just sinking in. 'It wasn't quite like that,' Amy said. 'I loved him. I loved them both. They looked after me.'

Jen looked at Amy and saw how young and vulnerable she had been.

'Do you want your daughter back?' she asked her.

'Yeah,' Amy said. 'Of course I do.'

Jen nodded. 'They can't stop you seeing your own daughter. Tomorrow, Natasha and I will come with you to see them and we won't take no for an answer. We'll make sure you get to see her.'

FIFTY-SEVEN

Rob got up from the bed and started to get dressed. He went over to the window of the hotel room and looked out as he pulled on his trousers.

'Come back,' Lizzy said. 'It's the last time I'll see you for two weeks. We have to make the most of it.'

Rob looked at his watch. He'd told Jen he was at the driving range. He couldn't be too long.

He looked back at Lizzy. He had wanted her ever since he first laid eyes on her in the office. They'd become closer and closer, until finally she'd given in to his advances. Mia had still been on the scene then, but he'd been tiring of her. Lizzy was more effortless, cooler. She kept him on his toes. There was no mystery with Mia, and soon her whiny desperation only drove him further towards Lizzy.

She'd played hard to get at first, but he'd eventually succeeded in getting her into bed. They'd been together for three months. He could see it lasting for a few years, perhaps more.

'I have to go,' he said. 'I've left some stuff here, in the grey duffel bag. Just some shoes and clothes. And some special cufflinks my father bought me for my twenty-first. It's not a huge amount. I can buy the rest later.'

'I'll put them in my suitcase for Italy,' Lizzy said. She grinned. 'I can't wait to see you there. It will be such an adventure.'

He leant in and kissed her. She was so young and naive. He hadn't explained why he was running away. She didn't know about the problems with the flats or how much trouble he was really in. But he'd had to tell her he was going to fake his own death, and that she couldn't tell anyone she was meeting him in Italy.

She had thought it was all a joke at first. Until he'd explained about the life insurance. Her eyes had lit up at the thought of the one million pounds Jen would hand over. He hoped she wouldn't find out the real reason. She'd moved on to a better job at another estate agency a few weeks before, so he didn't think she'd heard yet about the investigation into the fraud at his office.

Thinking of the police at his office made him feel physically sick. He'd had so many messages from Grace telling him to call her, but he couldn't face returning her calls. He had made a huge mistake. The builders of the flats had lied to him. They'd told him they were just waiting for the safety certificate for the apartment block to come through. They'd said it had been signed off but there was an administrative delay. In the meantime Rob had so many buyers lined up for the flats, and he wanted his commission. So he'd forged the safety certificate for the building, planning to replace it with the real one once it came through. Except the real one didn't come through in time and the flat purchases had gone ahead using his forgery.

When it became clear that the safety certificate was never going to materialise and the building hadn't passed the checks, he was in far too deep. He had already bought the penthouse at a huge discount. It was in no one's interest for anyone to find out about the building's problems.

He'd bought the life insurance just in case he was discovered. Taking out a single policy in his name would have looked suspicious, so he'd taken one out in Jen's name too. And then he'd started planning how to disappear and convince everyone he'd died. It was the only way out of the hole he was in, the only way he could avoid prison and have some money from the life insurance to live on.

Luckily he'd managed to convince Jen, but then Mia had turned up, threatening to ruin everything. He thought Jen was back on his side now, but there was no way she could find out about Lizzy.

'Do you really have to go back to the villa right now?' Lizzy asked, wrapping her arms around him.

'I have to spend my final night with Jen,' he said. It was his duty to at least do that.

She took his hand. 'Can you show me first?' she asked.

'Show you what?'

'The place you're going to disappear.'

He smiled. 'Why do you want to see that?'

'Just so I can imagine it,' she said.

He hesitated for a moment, then nodded. 'OK.'

Rob drove back towards the villa and Lizzy drove behind him. They parked at the end of the driveway, out of view of the house. He got out of his car, shutting the door quietly, and Lizzy did the same.

'This way,' he said, taking her hand.

Without the headlights on they struggled to see in the dark, and Lizzy tripped over a small rock. He caught her and she laughed nervously.

'Careful,' he said, his eyes adjusting to the moonlight. He

took her through a small gate to the clifftop path that led round to the end of the garden of their villa.

The wind lifted her hair, as she looked back towards the villa. 'Is that your place?' she said. 'It looks spectacular.'

'Yeah,' Rob said, smiling. He wished he'd had the chance to take Lizzy there like he'd taken Mia. He'd miss the villa once he was gone. But it was just one of many things he had to leave behind to start afresh.

'I wish I could see inside.'

Rob could see the light was on in the living room. He couldn't risk it. 'I'm afraid not,' he said. 'Jen's inside.'

'Can I see the place where you'll disappear?' Lizzy asked.

'It's just up here.' Rob led her along the clifftop path to the point where the cliff jutted out into the sea.

'Down there,' he said, pointing down. 'Can you see the path carved into the cliff? I'll go down there for a swim and leave my clothes on the rocks. I'll swim round to the next beach, pick up my bag and hike away.'

'I can't see the path,' Lizzy said, as she stepped closer.

'Be careful,' he said. 'Don't go too close to the edge.' In the dark, it was difficult to see where the cliff ended and the midnight air began.

She shivered and he took her hand and enveloped her in a hug. With the wind blowing through their hair, he kissed her.

'I'm going to miss you,' he said.

'It's only two weeks,' Lizzy said, smiling. 'We'll be together again soon.'

FIFTY-EIGHT

After Amy had gone to bed, Jen and Natasha sat up chatting. Rob still wasn't back, and it was gone 11 p.m. Jen wondered if he was really at the driving range or if he was doing something else he didn't want her to know about. But she was past caring. As long as he came home tonight, in time for his 'disappearance' tomorrow, then there wasn't a problem.

For a moment, she considered that he might have changed his plans. Perhaps he was on to Jen, aware she wasn't on his side anymore, worried what she might do. She frowned, as Natasha topped up her wine glass. She was nervous about tomorrow and it was making her paranoid.

'It's so nice you've been so forgiving of Amy,' Natasha said.

'Thanks,' Jen said. Natasha had sat back down closer to her, their shoulders now touching.

'You've been so calm about the whole thing. It's almost like... you already knew about Amy and Rob.'

Jen looked at Natasha, longing to confide all her plans, all the secrets she'd kept for so long.

'I'd guessed something was going on,' she said.

Natasha looked at her. 'You're such an enigma, Jen. I never

know what you're really thinking. Sometimes you seem so closed off.'

'Things have been difficult lately.'

'You know you can trust me, don't you?' Natasha said, quietly.

'Yeah, of course.'

'You know I've always been attracted to you.'

'I didn't know until that kiss the other week,' Jen said truthfully. She felt a fluttering of possibility in her chest, the briefest idea of a different future after Rob had gone.

'I thought you weren't interested because you were still in love with Rob. But you haven't been in love with Rob for a long time, have you?'

Jen shook her head. 'I think I started to fall out of love when I found out he was cheating,' she said. 'He didn't seem like the man I married anymore.' The tension in the air was palpable, and she could feel Natasha's breath on her neck.

'Were you ever interested in me?' she asked.

Jen swallowed and finally turned to face her, allowing Natasha's lips to meet hers. For a moment, Jen's thoughts stopped as she lost herself completely in the kiss.

When Jen pulled away, Natasha was breathless. 'You've been hiding things,' she said, stroking Jen's hair. 'You've been pretending to be happily married for appearance's sake.'

Jen nodded. 'And for the kids,' she said. 'I live for the kids.'

She wondered what Natasha knew, what she'd figured out.

'I've been thinking, since I saw your mother's pills in your bag,' Natasha said. Jen held her breath. 'You said you were going to leave Rob, but then you changed your mind. No matter what he did you seemed unwilling to split up with him. I didn't understand.'

'It was for the kids,' Jen said. 'That's all.'

'Rob keeps blacking out, doesn't he?' Natasha said. 'The first time he went to A&E, the second time Amy found him, and when we arrived in the Med, he'd just fallen asleep early for no reason. But you didn't seem to worry about his health.'

'Of course I was worried,' Jen said. 'Even after everything that's happened, he's still my husband.'

'I know you, Jen. I've... admired you for a long time. I know you're not telling me the full truth.'

Jen stayed quiet, unsure what to say. Could she really trust Natasha?

Natasha took a deep breath. 'You've been using the pills to drug Rob, haven't you? That's why he was fast asleep on the first night of the holiday.'

Jen ran her hand through Natasha's hair. There was no denying it now. 'You know me too well,' she said.

'I'm right,' Natasha said, incredulous. 'You were drugging him! Oh, Jen.'

Jen snuggled up into Natasha's embrace. She was going to have to tell her everything now. Otherwise, as soon as Rob disappeared into the sea, Natasha would know Jen had drugged him.

'Natasha,' she said. 'Can I trust you with a secret?'

FIFTY-NINE

The next day, Natasha drove Amy and Jen to the Beddows' house, while the kids were at their holiday club. It took them a long time to find the track to their farmhouse. The entrance was unmarked and overgrown, and the track itself was muddy and uneven. Natasha cursed as the hire car bounced over the potholes.

Natasha pulled up outside and Amy looked up at the farmhouse from the back window of the car. This was where Mr and Mrs Beddow lived now. With Gemma. Her daughter. The place looked run-down, with tall weeds growing outside the front wall. This wasn't what Amy had expected. When they'd lived at the school, they'd had a perfectly kept garden full of roses, lovingly maintained by the school's gardener.

Amy studied the house, looking up at the bedrooms and wondering which room was Gemma's. She imagined Gemma looking out of the small window over the farmland. It must be wonderful to grow up in the peace and quiet of the countryside. Amy imagined her room was full of toys and games. Mr and Mrs Beddow had always wanted a child of their own, and she was sure they would have spoilt her daughter, given her every-thing she wanted.

Amy thought about what Jen had said last night, about how she and Natasha would make sure Amy saw Gemma. She deserved to see her. She had let the Beddows take Gemma as she knew they could give her a better life than she could, but now she wasn't so sure that had been the right decision.

'Are you ready to go in?' Jen asked gently, from the front of the car.

'I don't know,' Amy said. She wasn't sure she could face them after all these years. It had been so good to speak to Jen and Natasha last night about them, to tell the truth about exactly what had happened. They were the only people in the world who knew. Her mother hadn't visited her at boarding school in the last months of her pregnancy and so had never even known Amy had had a child. If the other staff at the school had worked out she was pregnant, then they'd never said anything. Besides, she'd been taken in by the Beddows by then, looked after by them in their house, barely allowed to leave. When Gemma was born they might have asked questions, but the Beddows had told everyone she was theirs.

'We'll be beside you,' Natasha said, turning round and squeezing her knee. 'You won't have to do this on your own.'

'Thanks,' Amy said. She was so glad to have their friend-ship. Last night it had felt like Natasha and Jen were the family she'd never had, the only people she could confide in. She was pleased they could both come with her today.

Amy eased herself out of the back of the car and Natasha and Jen got out of the front. The noise of the car doors shutting echoed around the empty landscape, but there was no response from inside the house.

'Are you sure this is the right address?' Jen asked. 'No one seems to be home.'

'I'm certain,' Amy said.

'Do you want to knock, or shall we look around first?' Natasha asked.

'Let's look around,' Amy said. She wasn't ready to knock yet; she wasn't ready to face the couple who had once meant so much to her.

They walked round the outside of the house, taking in the dilapidated outbuildings. There was a former cowshed, the metal gate hanging loose on its hinges. In the corner of the shed were bottles of chemicals, rope and some jerrycans of petrol. The back of the farmhouse looked in a worse state than the front, loose roof tiles hanging precariously over the edge of the guttering.

In the overgrown back garden, Amy looked around for children's toys. She'd expected to see a swing, a slide, maybe a children's wheelbarrow or spade. But there was nothing. Among the weeds she could see a rusty rake and a pair of gardening shears. This wasn't a place for children to play.

Amy felt nauseous. This couldn't be the place where Gemma was growing up. She couldn't have given her up to this life.

'Let's go and knock,' Jen said decisively. 'See if they're in.'

She went round the front of the house, followed by Amy and Natasha.

Jen marched up to the door and knocked. There was no answer.

'Maybe we should just go home,' Amy said. 'They're not in.'

'No,' Natasha said. 'You're not leaving. You need to resolve this while you're in France. You need to see your daughter.'

Jen knocked again, harder this time.

The door was suddenly flung open. 'What do you want?' the woman asked angrily.

Amy recognised her immediately. Mrs Beddow had aged rapidly in the five years since she'd seen her. She'd lost about three stone of weight, her unruly dark hair was flecked with grey and her eyes were sunken.

'Mrs Beddow?' she said tentatively. 'It's me, Amy.'

'Amy?' She looked at her suspiciously. 'Oh, Amy. You've dyed your hair blonde. You look different. But why are you here?'

She wasn't pleased to see her. 'To see my daughter. Gemma.'

'Gemma isn't here.'

'Just let us come in,' Natasha said, putting her foot in the door to stop it closing.

'Leo!' Mrs Beddow screamed. 'Leo! Come downstairs! There are people at the door bothering us again.'

They heard quick footsteps on the stairs, and then Mr Beddow appeared, looking the same as always. His blond hair was sun-bleached and his face was tanned.

'What do you want?' he said to Amy.

'Don't you recognise her?' Mrs Beddow said. 'It's Amy. The girl before Jessica.'

'Oh!' he said. 'Oh, I see. Oh yes, I do recognise her now.' He peered at Amy, looking her up and down. 'What does she want?'

'She wants to see her daughter,' Jen said firmly.

'Her daughter?'

'Gemma...' Mrs Beddow whispered. 'She's here to see Gemma.'

'Well, she can't see her, can she?'

'We're not leaving until we see her,' Natasha said. 'You abused Amy and then you stole her baby from her. You should be in prison.'

'Haven't we been punished enough?' Mrs Beddow asked. 'Leo's lost his job. And Gemma, well, she's gone.'

'Gone where?' Amy asked, swallowing the bile that had risen up in her throat.

'She was an ignorant, naughty child,' Leo said. 'From the beginning she cried so much. She was difficult. We had to give her away.'

'They took her away,' Mrs Beddow said, tears running down her cheeks. 'After what you did to Jessica.'

'I didn't do anything to Jessica.'

'She was underage,' Mrs Beddow said. 'She was too much of a risk.' She turned to Amy. 'We lost Gemma,' she said. 'We lost our daughter when Leo was accused. She's been sent to foster care. She'll probably be adopted.'

'It's none of their business,' Leo said as he kicked Natasha's shin hard. Reflexively she withdrew her foot from the door.

Mrs Beddow shut the door in Amy's face.

Amy rapped on the door again. 'You need to tell me where she is!' she shouted. She banged her fist on the wooden door again and again until her hand was red raw. 'Just tell me where she is!' she screamed again and again.

'They can't get away with this,' Natasha said. 'They stole her from you and then neglected her.'

Amy thought of her poor baby daughter, trapped with the Beddows. No toys to play with. The couple bringing teenage girls back to the house to 'entertain'. Not caring for her or playing with her or loving her.

She thought of the way Mr Beddow had spoken about Gemma, calling her naughty and ignorant. She was his own flesh and blood but he hadn't loved her. And all that time, Amy had been trying to forget about her daughter, trying to leave her alone, so she could have a good life with them. She'd been so sure that Mr and Mrs Beddow would love her and care for her. But they hadn't.

Natasha started shouting up at the house. 'Come back out!' she said. 'You need to face us.'

'They can't get away with this,' Jen said. 'It's not right. There needs to be some kind of justice.'

Jen was right. They did need to be punished, but Amy knew no one would care. No one had cared about her at the time. The school had turned a blind eye. And the police would never believe that they'd abused her. If she wanted any justice she had to get it herself.

Amy was overcome by a sense of hopelessness. She'd lost everything. She had nothing left to live for. All she wanted was for them to pay for what they'd done. Suddenly she remembered the jerrycans of petrol in the cowshed. She ran over to the shed and picked one up, along with a rag that lay next to it. She covered the rag in petrol, and then went to the front door.

'Amy!' Natasha shouted. 'What are you doing?'

But Amy had already taken a cigarette lighter out of her bag, lit the rag and shoved it through the letterbox.

SIXTY

'Oh my god!' Jen said, as she saw Amy drop the flaming rag through the letterbox.

Natasha banged on the front door. 'We have to let them know there's a fire,' she said urgently.

There was no response from inside the house.

Already the flames were taking hold behind the door. Jen could feel the heat of them.

Natasha went round the back of the house. 'Fire!' she screamed. 'There's a fire!'

'We need to call the emergency services,' Jen said, looking at her phone. 'But I don't have any reception.'

Amy was staring at the closed door, as if in a trance.

'Right, let's get in the car and drive until I have reception.' Jen grabbed Amy's arm and dragged her towards the car.

'We can't leave them in that house,' Natasha said. 'They'll die.'

'We can,' Jen said. 'We have to. We can't go inside to help them. We'd be risking our own lives.'

Natasha looked at her phone. 'I don't have reception either.'

Then she climbed into the driver's seat. Jen pushed Amy into the back of the car and sat down beside her.

'Let's go!' she said.

Natasha drove quickly down the track and then stopped and indicated to turn onto the main road.

Jen looked at her phone. Still no reception.

Amy was twisted round in her seat, staring back at the house. When Jen turned round she could see that smoke was already billowing from its roof.

Her phone had one bar of reception now and she tried to phone the fire brigade, but the call wouldn't connect.

'Oh my god,' Natasha said, looking in her rear-view mirror. 'We can see the smoke from here.'

She turned onto the main road. They hadn't gone far when two fire engines raced past them, their sirens on.

'They're going to them now,' Jen said.

Amy was still looking out the back window. 'What will they do to me?' she whispered softly.

When they got back to the house, Rob was in the pool, swimming laps. The kids were going to stay overnight at the holiday club, like they did every year.

Jen, Natasha and Amy sat on the sofas in the lounge. Jen poured them each a glass of wine.

'That was intense,' she said.

'I keep checking to see if it's made the news,' Natasha said. 'But there's nothing online except a couple of photos on social media.'

'Let me see,' Jen said, taking the phone from her. The photos were from fifteen minutes ago, and all they showed was a plume of smoke on the horizon.

'Maybe they've put the fire out already,' Jen said hopefully. 'We saw the fire engine go by. They'd have got there quickly.'

'I can't believe I did that,' Amy said, her breathing shallow. 'I didn't mean to, I just hate them so much. They gave my daughter away. I wasn't thinking of the consequences.'

'It was stupid,' Natasha said. 'You could go to prison.'

'They deserved it,' Jen said, indignantly. 'After what they did to her.'

A tear ran down Amy's cheek. 'Should I ring the police?' she asked. 'Confess?'

'Maybe,' Natasha said, getting up and pacing up and down. 'You might as well. You're bound to be caught.' She paled. 'And our hire car is probably on some camera somewhere. We hired it in *my* name. Surely they'll find us.'

'Hang on a minute,' Jen said, thinking of her own plans. She couldn't have the police here, at the villa. Not now. 'Let's not get ahead of ourselves. We don't need to call the police. They'll come to us if they have any questions.'

'I don't want them to have to come and find us,' Natasha said. 'Won't they think we're all responsible, if Amy doesn't confess?'

'What if the Beddows died in that fire?' Amy said quietly. 'It would be because of me.'

Natasha looked at her phone again. 'They haven't died,' she said, her voice full of relief. 'Someone's commented that two people escaped from the house before the fire properly took hold. Unharmed. There's a picture of the Beddows with the firemen. They're both fine.'

The colour drained from Amy's face. 'They'll know it was me,' she said quietly. 'They'll know I was the one who set fire to the house.'

'But will they tell the police that?' Jen asked. 'Because if they do, you can explain that they abused you and then took your baby. That's a crime. I think they'd prefer to stay quiet.'

'Are you sure?' Amy asked, uncertainly.

'Honestly, Amy,' Jen said. 'You have nothing to gain from

speaking to the police. The Beddows aren't going to want any
more trouble.'

After Jen had calmed Natasha and Amy down, she went to see
Rob at the swimming pool.

'Everything OK?' he asked, looking up at her.

'Yeah, fine,' she said. He didn't need to know about the fire.
It was best no one knew they'd been there. These days, it felt
more natural to keep secrets from him than to share parts of her
life.

'Why are you letting Amy stay in the house?' he asked.

'There were no seats on the plane back. And it seemed
sensible to keep her here. She's a loose cannon. We can't afford
to let her out of our sight. Not at this crucial stage. If we treat
her poorly, she could start prying and ruin our plans.'

Rob nodded. 'She's crazy,' he said. 'You have no idea what
I've had to put up with.' He looked at Jen as if expecting sympathy. He didn't get any. 'Just keep her away from me.'

'OK,' Jen said. Jen thought of the baby Amy had told Rob
she was carrying. He didn't even seem interested in it, or
concerned about what would happen to it when he
disappeared.

'Are you all ready for tonight?' Jen asked.

'As ready as I'll ever be,' he said. 'I've put my bag in the
undergrowth on the next beach along. I'm going to go down
around 9 p.m., when it's pitch-black. You can say you discovered I was missing in the morning.'

'Sure,' Jen said. She looked at him for a moment and tried to
see the man she'd once loved. It was like looking at a stranger. 'I
want to come down and see you off,' she said. 'It will be the last
time we see each other for a long time.'

He pulled himself out of the pool and his lips met hers as he kissed her. It would be one of their last kisses and it took all Jen's mental strength not to push him away. 'It will be hard without you,' he said. 'I love you.'

'I love you too,' Jen replied, the lie rolling easily off her tongue.

SIXTY-ONE

Rob and Jen walked hand in hand to the clifftop and the start of the path which zigzagged down the side of the cliff. It had felt like forever as they'd waited for it to get dark so they could carry out their plan. Now Rob felt full of nerves, as if he might be making a huge mistake. It would be a long time until he saw his children again. But it would have been the same if he'd been locked away in prison. He doubted Jen would have brought them to visit. She never used to visit her own father. He thought of Lizzy in Italy. It would all be OK. A new life would be waiting for him.

Jen had brought a couple of bottles of beer with her, and now she passed one to him. 'Dutch courage,' she said as he accepted it gratefully, needing to calm his nerves and still his shaking hands. Jen clinked her bottle against his and then brought hers to her lips and took a gulp.

'Let's walk down the footpath together,' she said. 'We can drink these on the way.'

They walked down towards the sea in silence, as if everything they had to say to each other had already been said. Jen stuck close to the solid wall of the cliff, as if she was afraid of the drop on the other side. She'd never been afraid on this path before, but then everything felt different in the dark. It was hard to see where they were going.

'What did you say to Natasha and Amy?' Rob asked. 'Where did you say you were going?'

'I told them it was a beautiful evening to go for a walk,' Jen said. 'They said they might join me later. I told them I wanted to spend a bit of time on my own first.'

'Let's get on with it then,' he said.

As he navigated the uneven path down to the little beach, he felt uneasy. His hand shook as he gripped the handrail on the steps down. He took another glug of beer to calm his nerves. The bottle was almost finished.

He made it to the bottom of the path, Jen beside him.

She reached out and took his empty bottle from him and put it in a plastic bag. Rob smiled to himself. It was typical Jen, making sure she took away her rubbish.

Rob changed out of his clothes and into his swimming trunks, folding his clothes and leaving them in a neat pile. Then he turned to Jen. 'So this is goodbye,' he said. 'For now.' He started to shiver. Although it was a warm night, he was cold in just his trunks.

Jen wrapped her arms round him and lifted up her face for a final kiss. As his lips met hers he thought of all the years he'd loved her, what a good wife she'd been. He supposed that he hadn't always been the perfect husband, if faithfulness was one of the criteria, but he had always provided her with everything she could have ever wanted.

'You're freezing,' she said, as she pulled away. She rubbed his arms vigorously. 'You'd better get swimming. The exercise will warm you up.'

He nodded, gave her one final kiss and then strode into the water. He let his body submerge but found the shivering got worse. He had to get going. He looked ahead of him at the small bay. He needed to swim round the cliff that jutted out, to the next beach. The distance to the end of the cliff looked further than he remembered. A wave barrelled into him and for a moment he was underwater. He came back to the surface and started a steady crawl.

But his arms weren't cooperating with his brain. Suddenly everything felt foggy and he was overcome by exhaustion. He tried to swim but he couldn't. He felt himself sinking under. He recognised the feeling, suddenly remembering. This is how he'd felt before he'd blacked out. So tired he could hardly move, barely even lift his hand.

He needed to get back to the shore. Now. Something was terribly wrong. He fought the exhaustion and tried to pump his arms through the water, but he was being carried further out.

This couldn't be it; this couldn't be how it ended. No. He was going to meet Lizzy in Italy. He was going to have another life, away from all his troubles. A fun, exciting life.

He had to get back to the shore. He focused on the beach and kicked harder and harder. He put all his energy, all his concentration into just getting back there.

He saw Jen on the beach watching him struggle. Why didn't she get into the water? Why didn't she come and help him? She didn't understand that he was drowning. He tried to shout out for help, but when he did his mouth filled with water and he sank back underneath the surface again. He fought his way back up.

He could see Jen still. She was looking directly at him. And then suddenly it hit him. He understood. The beer. It had been drugged. She'd wanted him to drown out here.

SIXTY-TWO

Jen watched Rob step into the sea. She could see he was a bit unsteady on his feet, but he hadn't seemed to notice. All her efforts were paying off. It had been difficult to get the pills into his beer bottle. She'd had to crush them up first and then stir the beer with a straw. But it was worth it so he could drink the beer on the way down to the beach. She must have timed it just right. It was starting to work just as he entered the sea. She hoped she'd got the dose right. Enough for him to drown.

Rob ducked down into the water, and Jen expected him to start swimming out. But as a wave hit him, he was forced under. He came back to the surface and started to move his arms but seemed to be struggling to swim. She could feel his confusion. He sunk under the water once more and she held her breath. The drugs were working a bit too quickly. It would have been better if they'd kicked in when he was out at sea.

He fought his way back up, and she watched him use all his energy to claw himself forward, towards the shore. He was on his feet now, unsteady in the waves. But he was coming out of the water.

This wasn't going to work, she realised. She looked at the

pile of clothes Rob had left on the shore. It could still look like he'd drowned when he'd gone for a misguided late night swim. She could still get his life insurance and make a happy, peaceful life with her children. But he needed to be in deeper water to drown and be carried out to sea.

She picked up her phone and quickly messaged Natasha. Jen had told her everything about her plan the other night, and she'd said if Jen needed anything at all, she could be there to help.

There's trouble with Rob. I need you at the beach.

Jen watched Rob clamber out of the sea, crawling up the shore on his hands and knees. The bandage covering the wound to his chest was sodden. Jen felt ill. If his body was ever found the knife wound could give them away, prompt the police to investigate. She had to make sure his body was never found, that the strong tides carried it out.

'What happened?' she asked, quizzically. 'Are you OK?'

'No,' he gasped, as he got to his feet. 'I'm not OK. I feel awful.' He started stumbling towards the path that led up the cliff. 'I need to get back,' he said, shakily. 'I need to lie down.'

'Do you need a hand?' Jen said.

'No, I'm fine,' he said, pulling away from her. He was still in his swimming shorts, and he slipped on the concrete steps that led up to the path, banging his knee.

'Let me help you,' Jen said, holding out her arm.

He refused to take it.

Jen climbed up easily and stood a few steps above him. She saw the fear in his eyes. It would be so easy to just push him back down, watch his body bounce down the stone steps. He would most likely die. But his body would still be here. And she could be tried for murder.

He climbed slowly up the steps until he was standing

unsteadily beside her. A small wooden fence was the only thing between them and the fall to the rocks below.

When he turned to Jen, she saw his eyes were full of rage. 'What did you do to me, Jen?' he asked quietly.

'What do you mean?'

'You drugged me, didn't you? That beer... you've been causing my blackouts.'

Jen smiled. He finally understood. 'Did you really think you could take me for a fool, Rob?' she asked calmly, the light wind blowing through her hair. She pushed down her emotions, her rage. She wanted to remain in control.

'No, of course not. Amy was lying. You know that. We never had a proper affair.'

'You slept with her though. And others, too, I'm sure of it.'

'But Jen – I chose you. You know I did. I always wanted to be with you.' He stumbled over the words. 'The others meant nothing to me.'

'You think I should be grateful you chose me?' Jen shot back, her anger finally showing. 'Is that what this is? You think you've got lots of women fighting over you?'

'We're married. We just renewed our vows. Of course I thought you wanted me.'

'You've got such a big ego, Rob,' Jen said. 'You still think you're some kind of catch, when you're just a lowlife criminal who's about to disappear and abandon his kids. Whose greed put his kids' lives in danger in an unsafe building, and who stole his kids' savings. What on earth makes you think anyone would want you?'

'You wanted me, Jen. I know you did. We were good together. A team.'

Jen laughed. 'I believed that, once. I truly did. I did everything at home, every bit of housework, looked after the kids, cooked all the meals and kept everything running smoothly. I was doing it for us, for our kids. Because I believed that if we worked together, then we could build a better life for them. But then I realised I was the only person on our family's team. You only cared about yourself. You never shared your money with me, not properly. You saw me as some kind of cheap help.'

'What are you complaining about? You got to sit at home all day, going to the gym and getting your nails done while I did all the real work. So what if I had a bit of fun while you got to spend my money?'

Jen laughed. 'You have no idea, do you?'

Rob put his hand to his head. 'What have you done to me? Am I going to black out again?'

Jen nodded. 'You were supposed to black out in the sea,' she said coldly.

Rob seemed to rally then, suddenly lunging at her, despite his fading strength. Now her back was against the small wooden fence, and she could feel it bending under her weight. She tried to push him off, but her feet started to slip on the wet stone, and she was sure they were going to slide out from under her. Rob was pushing her shoulders, as if determined to force her over the edge. She was sure the fence was about to break beneath her, throwing them both over the cliff and into the sea. Jen pushed back, praying that the drugs would kick in properly soon and knock him out.

'Jen!' A voice shouted from further up the cliffside path and Jen saw Amy running down the slippery path two steps at a time. She leapt at Rob, grabbing his shoulders and pulling him away from Jen. Rob lost his balance and slipped, falling and hitting his head with a sickening crack.

'Are you OK, Jen?' Amy asked. 'I was walking on the cliffs and I heard voices. I knew it was Rob. Has he hurt you?'

Jen's breathing was fast and shallow and it was a moment before she could catch her breath. 'I'm fine,' she said, shivering.

They both looked down at Rob. Jen could see his eyes were losing focus, zoning out.

Amy kicked his limp body. 'You deserved that!' she screamed. 'How could you treat us like this?'

Jen put her finger to her lips. This situation was rapidly getting out of her control. Amy was unpredictable. Where was Natasha? She'd said she would come. Rob looked like he was fading away.

But he couldn't die here. They'd be blamed. He needed to drown. He needed to be washed out to sea. It would be OK if he was found months from now, but he couldn't be found immediately. The police might work out what had happened. Her mind whirred, and she thought of the other people who'd drowned here: a man, ten years ago, whose body hadn't washed up until three years later; a woman four years ago whose body had never been found. As long as the tide was right and the water was deep enough Rob would be washed out. She just needed to get him into deep water.

Jen watched Rob's eyes flutter closed and he passed out.

'Oh my god!' Amy said. 'Is he OK?'

Jen prodded him with her foot. He didn't stir. He was out cold. They were a third of the way up the path. Below them the sea was shallow and rocky. If they just went up one more flight of steps they'd be by the rest bench. That was where the best views were, and where she knew the cliff overhung deep water. It was her best chance of Rob's body being washed away.

'Hello?' Jen heard another voice call out. *Natasha.* She glanced up at the clifftop and saw a light, which must be from her phone.

'We're down here,' Jen shouted. Her voice echoed round the cliffs, and she realised she'd been far too loud. What if someone else had heard her?

But they couldn't have. The neighbouring properties were far away.

She heard a noise at the top of the steps, saw Natasha making her way down the path.

Jen came up a few steps to meet her.

'What happened?' Natasha asked.

'Rob tried to go for a swim,' Jen said. 'But he felt woozy in the water. He came out and attacked me, and Amy rescued me from him. He's hit his head and passed out.'

Natasha looked from Jen to Amy, and Jen saw her realise that Jen was lying for Amy's sake.

'We need to get him to hospital,' Amy said.

'Can you help me carry him up the steps?' Jen asked.

Natasha was staring at the plastic bag beside Jen that contained the two empty beer bottles. She had carried it up the steps and then dropped it when Rob attacked her. Luckily the bottles hadn't smashed. She couldn't leave them behind for the police to find.

Natasha knew what Jen had planned, but now seeing Rob in this state, she looked worried.

Jen grabbed Natasha's arm and pulled her close. 'Remember what he did to me,' she said. 'Remember you said you'd help. If Rob's gone, then we can be together.'

'I didn't actually think you'd go through with it,' Natasha whispered.

Jen glanced at Amy who was staring at Rob's still body. 'We need to move him,' she said.

Natasha swallowed. 'OK,' she said, then lifted Rob's legs. 'You two take the arms.'

Amy and Jen took an arm each, and Natasha began to climb up the steps backwards. Rob was heavy and the steps were slippery so it was awkward carrying him, but they made steady progress.

Soon they got to the platform over the cliff edge, with the bench.

'Let's stop here,' Jen said, panting. They lowered him onto the ground.

'Is he OK?' Amy said, looking down at him. 'He's not... dead?'

It would have been better if he was already dead; easier to persuade the others to drop him into the sea.

'Oh my god,' Jen said as she reached down and felt for his pulse. It was still there, beating steadily. 'I think you're right,' she said. She put her hand over his mouth as if to feel for his breath. He was still breathing.

'He's gone,' Jen said. 'He's dead.' She put her hands over her face, as if in shock.

'Oh no!' Amy said, her hands flying to her face in terror. 'I killed him. I *killed* him! What are we going to do? Should we call an ambulance? Is it too late for first aid?' She looked at Jen for guidance. 'I learnt it at school, but I can't really remember...' She knelt over Rob.

'It's too late, Amy,' Jen said. 'I wish it wasn't.'

Amy's eyes darted from side to side. 'If he's already dead... who should we call?'

Jen looked down at Rob on the ground, saw the bandages over his knife wound and had a flash of inspiration.

'If we call the authorities, they'll think you killed him,' she said to Amy. 'Your DNA is all over him. And you knifed him before. You'll go to jail.'

'Can't we say it was self-defence? I was trying to help you!'

'You set fire to a house earlier today. And you slashed Rob with a knife. They'll never believe you.'

Tears started to run down Amy's face.

'It will be OK,' Jen said. 'It will be OK if we stick together. We can throw him in the sea.'

Amy looked shell-shocked. 'But what will happen to him?'

'His body will wash away. Out to sea. It won't be found. The tides here are strong.'

Jen looked at Natasha, praying she was thinking of their

future together, praying she wouldn't tell Amy that Jen had drugged Rob.

'It's a good idea,' Natasha said. 'No one but us even knows he has a knife wound. We have to stick together.'

Jen could see Amy's brain whirring. They were offering her a get-out clause, a way to escape her mistakes.

'We'll always stand by you, Amy,' Jen said. 'But we don't know what the police will think. And Rob's already dead. We can't help him now. The best thing for everyone is to dispose of the body.'

Amy nodded through her tears.

Jen went over to the bench and stood in front of it, looking at the sheer drop below. The waves crashed against the cliff face. If she had understood the tides correctly, in an hour or two the tide would start to retreat and Rob's body would be taken out with the waves, out to sea.

Jen looked at Natasha. 'Let's carry him to the edge,' she said.

'Hang on a moment,' Amy said quietly. 'I need to say good-bye.' She bent over Rob's body and kissed him lightly on the cheek. Jen prayed she wouldn't notice his shallow breathing. But Amy was too distraught to be paying proper attention. 'I'm so sorry,' she said softly into his ear. 'It wasn't meant to be like this.'

'Come on, Amy,' Jen said. 'We don't have much time.'

Amy stood up and wiped the tears from her face with the back of her hand. Then the three of them picked up the body, Natasha the legs, Jen and Amy the arms. Tears were running down Amy's face.

When they got to the edge, they stopped. Jen looked up above them, scanning the clifftop path, checking no one was out there watching. There wasn't a single artificial light. Only the light of the moon and the stars. In a different life it would have been magical, even romantic.

Her life with Rob flashed before her eyes: meeting him at school, going to the wonderful house his parents owned, their wedding day, getting pregnant. It had all seemed so full of the promise of a family life so much better than the one she'd had as a child. That had all ended when he'd sacrificed their family for his own greed. The whole life they'd built together had ended. And now it was the end of Rob's life too.

'Bye, Rob,' she whispered. Then she spoke calmly to the others. 'We need to launch him into the sea as far away from the edge as possible. We should swing him out.'

They nodded, speechless.

'On the count of three,' Jen said.

'One, two, three...' In unison, the three of them swung the body out towards the sea, letting go at almost the same time.

They watched Rob fall like a rag doll through the air, his loose limbs flailing, before he flopped into the water with a splash.

He disappeared under the surface, and Jen almost expected the submersion in the water to wake him up, for something instinctive inside him to realise how close he was to death, somehow overcome the effects of the drugs and force him to fight his way to the surface.

But he didn't come up. Jen watched the place where he'd entered the water as the minutes ticked by. He didn't reappear. She looked out over the expanse of sea for the white skin of his body, but there was nothing. He hadn't resurfaced. He was gone.

THREE DAYS LATER

The London Times

02.08.2024

Family man who disappeared in France thought to have drowned

Police in France are looking into the disappearance of a West London man, Rob Peterson. He and his wife were on holiday with their three children and two friends at the time of his disappearance earlier this week. His clothes were discovered on a nearby beach and it is thought that he went for a swim late at night and got into trouble in the sea.

The coastguard has now called off the search at sea, and Peterson is thought to have drowned. His wife, Jen Peterson, is distraught. 'Rob was a strong swimmer,' she told us. 'I don't believe he can be dead. We renewed our wedding vows on Sunday, in front of our three children. I haven't told them yet what's happened to their father. They're expecting him back. He can't have drowned.'

Rob's parents, Hugh and Penny, have flown to France to help look for their son, and also to care for their grandchildren. 'We'll do whatever it takes to find him,' Penny said. 'I know he's out there. A mother always knows. We need to find him for the sake of the children. He's a wonderful father and husband.'

However, medical reports show that Rob had a history of blackouts and may have had an undiagnosed heart condition, which may have contributed to him getting into trouble in the water.

THREE WEEKS LATER

Lizzy sat at a beach bar on the Italian coast, sipping a cocktail. She was bored of the small beach town now. There wasn't much to do or see, and she didn't speak the language. Each day passed in exactly the same way: a swim in the sea, lunch by the beach, some sunbathing, then drinks at a local bar.

She'd been here over a week and although she'd spoken to some other tourists and been on a couple of day trips, she hadn't made any meaningful connections or had many conversations.

Rob should have turned up a week ago. She knew he'd carried out his plan to go missing. It had been reported in the newspapers. His clothes had been found on the shore, exactly like he'd said they would be. He was supposed to make his way across France and come and meet her here. He was meant to bring cash so she could move out of the run-down hostel she was staying in and into one of the nice hotels. But he hadn't bothered to turn up. He'd dumped her, just like he'd dumped all the others. She should never have given in to his charms, never dared to believe he saw her differently to any of the other women he'd slept with from the office. He'd told her how much he loved her, how she was different from the others. She had really believed he thought she was special. She had even quit her job for him.

So much for their adventure travelling around Europe together. Perhaps he'd met someone else on his journey over, she thought bitterly. Or perhaps he'd decided he didn't want to share the insurance money.

Lizzy sighed. She supposed she'd have to go back to her job at the estate agents. Luckily she wasn't at Rob's company anymore. She'd heard on the grapevine that there had been some problems, something to do with fraud. Several of the staff were suspended while an investigation took place. She had another sip of her cocktail, and decided that she'd leave the next day. She'd see a bit more of Europe and then travel home. She wasn't going to wait around for Rob a day longer.

SIX MONTHS LATER

Jen finished unpacking the final box, placing the vases and family photos on the living room mantelpiece. It had taken nearly a week, but now every single box was unpacked.

Her children were staying with her parents-in-law the week before Christmas, while she moved into her cottage in the countryside and got everything ready for them. She had been Christmas shopping, put up the tree and decorated their new home. Everything looked magical, each room twinkling with fairy lights. Their stockings hung above the original Victorian fireplace. She couldn't wait for them to see the house, imagining the delight in their eyes. She knew the first Christmas without their dad would be hard, and she wanted to make it special.

It had felt strange moving out of London, but she knew it was time to move on, and start afresh. It hadn't been easy to get the life insurance money. The police had concluded that Rob was responsible for the forged safety certificates, and questions were raised about whether he had taken his own life. After many phone calls, and a lot of paperwork, the insurance company had finally paid out. Jen had found a small cottage in the countryside, and had been able to buy it outright with the insurance money. She still owned the penthouse, but it couldn't be sold until the problems with the building had been rectified. The legal wrangling over who should pay for fixing it was likely to go on and on.

She'd moved her mum into a care home nearby, so she could visit her easily, and had found a job locally as an estate agent. The pay and commission wouldn't quite cover her childcare and her mum's care home fees, but she'd make up the shortfall with the insurance money until her salary increased. She was looking forward to working again, and getting stuck in to selling local properties.

Jen looked at the photos she'd put on the mantelpiece. They were mainly of her and the children. But there was one with Rob – the one that had been taken on the final day they'd all had together on the beach. Everyone was smiling. A bittersweet memory.

Jen folded up the final cardboard packing box and put it in the back room. Natasha and Amy were coming round tonight to celebrate her new home, and she needed to get ready.

At 7 p.m. the doorbell rang, and there they were.

She embraced Natasha in an awkward hug. 'Hi,' Natasha said softly. It had been two weeks since she'd seen her. Jen and Natasha's relationship had petered out soon after Rob's death. Natasha had been anxious after he died, worried they'd be discovered and haunted by feelings of guilt. Any spark between them quickly faded. It was hard to be together when they reminded each other of the awful thing they'd done. Jen had thought she could live with it, but some days she'd still have nightmares and wake up in a cold sweat.

'Your house is amazing,' Amy said, as she stepped inside. There was no hint of envy anymore. Amy was a different person now. At first when she'd returned to England, she'd been scared of being blamed for the fire at the Beddows and for Rob's disappearance. Like Natasha, she'd been racked with guilt. But no one had linked Rob's disappearance or the fire to Amy. The Beddows had told the police that Mrs Beddow had accidentally started the fire herself, and they had never investigated further.

As the months went by Amy had become more confident. She'd managed to secure a job as a personal assistant in an investment bank and was renting a studio flat by herself in a cheaper part of London. She was much happier since the French authorities had agreed to a DNA test on Gemma and confirmed that she was her mother. She had been to visit her for the first time last month, and now she wouldn't stop talking about her. Gemma was a gorgeous wide-eyed five-year-old full of energy and fun, who loved playing outside in the mud. Amy was planning to bring her back to England as soon as the French authorities approved it. Gemma was already clamouring for a pet cat when she made it to the UK.

Jen felt happy for Amy, in spite of everything. She understood the drive to do anything for your children, and was glad Amy was letting go of the past.

'Come in,' Jen said. 'Let me show you around.'

She gave them the grand tour, showing them the children's bedrooms and the little garden with the swings and the slide.

'You seem happy, Jen,' Natasha said.

'I am,' Jen said. It had never been Rob that made her happy, just the security he'd provided. And now she had that for herself. She'd was due to start her new job next week, and she had enough money in the bank to feel comfortable. She'd secured the future for her and her children, the life she'd always wanted. It was everything she'd dreamed of since she was a child. And now she had it all.

Her life was carefree, except for the nightmares. In spite of everything, Jen feared that one day Rob would show up again at her door, demanding his share of the money. She'd done a double-take when she saw a toned man with Rob's build and curly dark hair at her gym in London. She saw his face in every mid-thirties man in a suit making his way to work, thought she saw him in crowds at train stations and in the background of local news reports. He'd always be there, in her mind, haunting her.

But the nightmares were a price worth paying to be free. Free to be herself, free to start again. She was finally back in control, and she'd never give that up for anyone ever again.

A LETTER FROM RUTH

Dear reader,

I want to say a huge thank you for choosing to read *My Husband's Affair*. This book has been a lot of fun to write, and I've enjoyed putting the characters in all sorts of crazy situations. I really hope you enjoyed the ride! If you did, and want to keep up to date with all my latest releases, just sign up at the following link. Your email address will never be shared and you can unsubscribe at any time.

www.bookouture.com/ruth-heald

If you enjoyed *My Husband's Affair*, I'd be very grateful if you would write a review. I can't wait to hear what you think, and reviews make such a difference in helping new readers discover one of my books for the first time.

I love hearing from my readers – you can get in touch on my Facebook page, through X, Goodreads or my website.

With best wishes,

Ruth Heald

www.ruthheald.com

ACKNOWLEDGEMENTS

My Husband's Affair, like all my books, has been a team effort. Thanks firstly to my husband and children who are always there, and unfailingly supportive.

I can hardly believe that this is my eighth psychological thriller. That would never be the case without the brilliant team at Bookouture, who have supported and encouraged me throughout my writing career. They are such a lovely team, always willing to fit my schedules around school holidays and other life commitments.

This book began with an idea that I shared with my editor, Laura Deacon, and we worked on fleshing it out together. I'm very grateful for her help in articulating the hook and themes of the book, and germinating the seed of the idea into a workable synopsis. Thanks to Ruth Tross, who, in Laura's absence, helped me develop the idea further during the first drafting phase.

I owe huge thanks to Ruth Jones, my current editor, who has helped me to beat this book into the shape it's now in. She's been very supportive throughout the process, helpful and full of ideas to improve the book and make the crazy plot just that bit more believable. I'm also thankful to my copy editor, Laura Gerrard, proofreader, Jenny Page, and cover designer, Lisa Horton. I'm looking forward to hearing Tamsin Kennard bring the audiobook to life.

As with every book, I've come to depend on my beta readers, Charity Davies and Ruth Jones (another Ruth Jones!) for their insightful feedback early on in the process.

I'm also grateful to the wonderful publicity team at Bookouture, who are forever cheerleading for all of us, and the broader team at Bookouture who do everything they can to support every author's book.

Once again, thank you to my writer friends who know the ups and downs of this journey all too well, and who are always there for me.

Finally, thank you to my readers. It's wonderful to think of my work being read and enjoyed all over the world.

PUBLISHING TEAM

Turning a manuscript into a book requires the efforts of many people. The publishing team at Bookouture would like to acknowledge everyone who contributed to this publication.

Audio
Alba Proko
Sinead O'Connor
Melissa Tran

Commercial
Lauren Morrissette
Jil Thielen
Imogen Allport

Data and analysis
Mark Alder
Mohamed Bussuri

Editorial
Ruth Jones
Melissa Tran

Copyeditor
Laura Gerrard

Proofreader
Jenny Page

Marketing
Alex Crow
Melanie Price
Occy Carr
Ciara Rosney

Operations and distribution
Marina Valles
Stephanie Straub

Production
Hannah Snetsinger
Mandy Kullar
Jen Shannon

Publicity
Kim Nash
Noelle Holten
Myrto Kalavrezou
Jess Readett
Sarah Hardy

Rights and contracts
Peta Nightingale
Richard King
Saidah Graham

Milton Keynes UK
Ingram Content Group UK Ltd.
UKHW010100030424
440481UK00004B/189